The Master of Hawthorn Manor

by

Rhonda Hanson

The Master of Hawthorn Manor

by

Rhonda Hanson

ISBN 978-0-9703817-1-2

Copyright 2024

by

Grace Under Pressure Publishing
P.O. Box 337
Bell Buckle, TN 37020

graceunderpressure.com

Certain image components designed by Freepik.com

Dedication

THE MASTER OF HAWTHORN MANOR is dedicated to those who have been so kind to read my books over the years, provide me with much needed, and appreciated feedback, point out the dreaded typo, and who have expressed a desire for me to continue writing.

You all know who you are, and I can't convey enough gratitude for your encouragement, and enthusiasm.

Although this book is quite a departure from my previous works, I hope it still manages to engage every booklover, and gives him or her a pleasurable reading experience.

Rhonda Hanson

The Master of Hawthorn Manor

Audra Campbell looked around the grounds of her Aunt Celeste's home, taking in the neatness of the flower beds, and waving at curious, old Miss Hepplewhite across the street, while waiting for her knock to be answered.

A large collie had come around from the back yard, and wagged his tail in greeting. She smiled down at him, and scratched his ear with a light touch, before reaching to try the doorbell.

The dog decided he liked Audra, and looked up at her to determine if she liked him as well.

"I'm sorry, buddy," Audra laughed. "I don't come bearing treats, I'm afraid."

The door opened, and Aunt Celeste clapped her fingertips together in happy delight, before reaching to gather Audra into her arms.

"You're here!" she cried, giving her niece an extra squeeze, her eyes crinkling with her big smile. "I was afraid you might have changed your mind, but I kept watching for you."

"Why did you think I'd change my mind, Aunt C?" Audra returned the squeeze, and added a peck on the cheek.

"I was just afraid to get my hopes up, I guess." Aunt Celeste searched around for her luggage, and a crestfallen look swept over her face. "Are you not staying?"

Audra looked behind herself, before realizing what was upsetting her aunt.

"I am, I just left everything in the car. I can get it later after I've rested up. Long drive," she added, grinning at her aunt's rapid change of expression, back to joy.

She looked beyond Audra, and shook her head with a grin.

"It won't be long before Myra Hepplewhite will be coming over to borrow a cup of sugar."

Audra turned to wave again at the curious neighbor.

"She never seems to remember that she's diabetic."

"Well, come on in, honey, before she goes blind from staring, and let's see if we can get a cup of tea going," Aunt Celeste suggested. "Or coffee. Whichever you prefer."

Audra followed her in, and looked down as the handsome collie stealthily joined them. "Is he allowed inside?" she asked, before closing the door.

"Oh, my, yes," her aunt declared. "Dexter's as much a part of this house as the furniture is. He has the run of the place, but if he gets in your way just scold him, dear, and he'll behave."

Dexter rested his soulful eyes on Audra, as if to ask her not to believe he could ever get in anyone's way, and she had to laugh at him.

"I'm watching you," she warned, opening her fingers into a vee, and pointing them to her eyes, and then at him.

She stood looking around her aunt's lovely home, noting that very little, if anything, had changed since she last saw it over four years ago.

"I'm glad it's still like I remember it," she said softly, reaching out a hand to touch the old grandfather clock. "It's all the same. Except for Dexter," she added. "He's new."

"He's a rescue," Aunt Celeste informed her, leading the way into the large kitchen. "But it's still unclear as to who rescued whom!"

She reached into the cabinet that Dexter was standing next to, and pulled out the treat he knew she kept there.

"Off with you, Dexter! Audra and I want to get caught up. Go kill your biscuit."

He took the biscuit in his mouth, and trotted out through the open sliding doors to the patio while Aunt Celeste held up a teapot in one hand, and a coffeepot in the other with a question in her eyes.

"Coffee, please." Audra chose easily.

"Still black and strong?" her aunt laughed.

"Yes, ma'am!"

Aunt Celeste smiled placidly, and went about brewing a fresh pot of coffee.

Audra reached up for a long stretch, then smiled at her aunt's quick, light movements. She had always reminded Audra of a little bird, dainty and petite, with her blonde hair still youthful, and pixie short. Aunt Celeste had bold, brown eyes that could never hide whatever she was feeling, so she usually just went ahead and said it.

She was in her element now, getting the coffee ready for her niece, and checking the cookie jar for a snack. She was still wearing her excitement like a robe.

Audra watched Dexter lolling around on the patio, apparently "killing" his biscuit before eating it.

She let her eyes roam around the comfortable kitchen, and reflected on what it had been like for her to live here from the time she was a freshman in high school until after she graduated.

Her Aunt Celeste was her father's twin sister, and took Audra in after her parents left the country to be missionaries.

Leaving Audra with her Aunt Celeste was only supposed to be a temporary arrangement, but once she settled in, and began to do so well in school her parents agreed to allow her to stay during their time away.

Aunt Celeste had never married, having devoted herself to her career as a very successful real estate broker, and eagerly welcomed her only niece into her home, going out of her way to create a loving environment for her.

Audra's mother had succumbed to a bacterial infection that failed to respond to antibiotics, and her father had come home briefly for the memorial service, and to spend some time with his daughter.

He returned to the mission field soon after, feeling that it was what his late wife would have wanted.

After graduating, Audra eventually joined her father on the mission field, not because she was called to that ministry, and not because he asked her to, but because she thought that having his daughter with him in the wake of his wife's passing would help him adjust to the loss, and not feel so alone.

When the time came that he was able to convince her that he really was able to carry on, and that she should focus her aim on whatever direction she wanted to pursue, she agreed to return to the states with both reluctance and excitement, still concerned about her father, but looking forward to being with her aunt again.

Aunt Celeste brought two cups of coffee over to the kitchen island, where Audra sat perched on a barstool. She pulled one out for herself, joining her with a smile, and sliding the cookie jar within reach.

"Everyone at church is going to be so excited to know you're back!" she announced with a pleased expression. "And look at you! You're absolutely beautiful, Audra. I'll have to beat the young men off you with a stick."

Audra laughed at the image that conjured up: her Aunt Celeste ferociously waving a stick in the air, and yelling for any potential suitor to get back.

"I think you're playing fast and loose with the word *beautiful* there, Aunt C," she observed.

Aunt Celeste tilted her head back, and lowered her lids to view her niece critically, taking in her long, dark, russet hair, her stunning green eyes with naturally thick lashes, and olive skin that clearly showed the amount of time she had spent outdoors while on the mission field with her father, and decided that she was judging without bias.

"I think you need to look in a mirror," she retorted. "My goodness, your hair has grown longer than I've ever seen it! It's almost to your waist. I hope you're not planning on cutting it any time soon."

"I've thought about it," Audra admitted, lifting a strand of her silky straight hair, and glancing at it critically. "It just sort of hangs there."

"What do you want it to do, stick straight up in the air?" Her aunt laughed happily, just glad to have her niece back at home, and having fun kidding her. "You leave that gorgeous hair alone, Miss Thing!"

4

"For now," she agreed, laying her hands against her warm coffee cup, and continuing to let her eyes roam around, reacclimating herself to a room she had spent many hours in, watching her aunt make dinner, hearing about what pending deal she was working on, and learning this and that about the community in the form of a little harmless gossip.

"So, what's new?" she asked casually, picking up right where they'd left off.

Aunt Celeste widened her eyes. "In over four years, what's new? Everything, honey!"

"That's my informal opener," Audra grinned. "But I do know, good and well, that if there's anything going on in this town worth mentioning, you know all about it."

"Are you calling me a gossip?" Aunt Celeste demanded, pretending to be offended. She relaxed her shoulders, and smiled cryptically.

"Actually, you haven't been back long enough to hear the latest buzz, but sooner or later you will, so I guess I'll be the first in line to fill you in."

Audra raised her brows, and gave her aunt a quizzing look.

"Martin Satterfield's wife just died."

Audra's expression soured. "That's that guy who scowls at everybody. He and his wife used to come sit in church, and she was dressed to kill, and smiled at everyone as if she were on a parade float, but he just looked out the window and frowned. It's a wonder the glass didn't break! Wasn't that his name?"

"It still is," Aunt Celeste commented lightly. "And his wife just died. This month, in fact."

Audra pictured the tall, blonde woman who was always dressed in expensive designer clothes, carefully coiffed and manicured, and who always seemed to be posing. She seemed to consistently maintain a cool, condescending air toward the entire congregation, with the exception of a few men, and Audra had always wondered why she and her dark, brooding husband even bothered to come to church.

"Funny you should use the expression 'dressed to kill', though." Her aunt interrupted her thoughts. "Because how she died is a bit of a mystery."

Audra sat up straight, and waited for more.

"Supposedly, she fell down the stairs," Aunt Celeste informed her.

"You don't believe that?"

She shrugged. "I guess it's possible."

Audra studied her aunt for a moment, conflicted. She actually knew more about Darlene Satterfield than she'd ever admitted, but had decided long ago not to say anything to anyone about it.

After some disturbing facts about the woman became clear to Audra, she remembered taking special note of Martin Satterfield the next time she saw them at church, to determine if what she knew might have something to do with his stern, irritated demeanor.

Audra felt certain that he had to have known what she knew about his wife's activities, and the fact that he apparently did nothing about it, and continued to make these silly, meaningless, public appearances with her, which he obviously resented, made Audra decide that she could never have any respect at all for him.

She realized that her aunt was becoming curious about her long silence.

"I remember that she was attractive," she finally offered quietly.

"Yes," Aunt Celeste agreed. "Her looks were important to her." She sighed, and glanced down at Dexter as he wandered back in, and made himself comfortable on a rug.

"Of course, it's too soon to have any sort of autopsy results, if there even was one. I expect there must have been, but if she fell down the stairs, I'm sure it'll just be the typical blunt force trauma."

"Typical?" Audra grinned playfully at her. "Aunt C, you missed your calling. If you consider blunt force trauma to be typical, you should be working in forensics."

"I could, I bet!" She looked delighted at the prospect of that, before changing her expression to one that was harmlessly benign.

"The old housekeeper that always worked for the Satterfields is still there, but her health is beginning to deteriorate pretty quickly, so the church is asking women to take food over to the house, and see if Martin needs anything."

"Why just women?" Audra folded her arms and frowned. "Why can't men do that?"

"Oh, honey, you know good and well, men don't do that sort of thing. It always falls on the ladies."

"I don't see why it should," her niece grumbled. "Besides, what woman would want to go into that big, old, creepy house? It sounds like a man's job, to me."

"Don't forget, his wife *lived* in that big, old, creepy house," Aunt Celeste pointed out. "But Hawthorn Manor is not creepy. It's actually listed on the historical registry, and that mansion has been in the Satterfield family for generations. The woodwork alone is unbelievable, and the grounds are quite extensive."

"That's real estate broker talk," Audra teased. "But that's okay, you can't help yourself."

"The senior Martin Satterfield used to open the house up during the Christmas season way back when," Aunt Celeste said. "Of course, I used to visit with his wife, Maureen, there on occasion, but at Christmas, it was like seeing it for the first time. The place became breathtaking.

"But after he passed, and his namesake inherited it along with the rest of the estate, he stopped that tradition, and the public hasn't been allowed in since."

"I'm surprised his wife didn't insist on allowing the public in," Audra replied dryly. "Martin Satterfield is not exactly a 'people' person, but she always seemed to thrive on being surrounded by as many people as possible, especially if all eyes were on her.

"I figured she just came to church to be seen as a Satterfield, but I never could figure out how she managed to get him to come with her. It was always obvious that he wanted to be anywhere but there. In fact, he always seems as if he'd rather be anywhere at all other than where he is, at any given moment."

"That's true," Aunt Celeste conceded. "But no one is completely who they seem to be. Everyone has a story."

"What's *his* story?" Audra asked, not necessarily because she wanted to know, but because she wondered if Aunt Celeste also knew more about Darlene Satterfield than she was admitting.

Aunt Celeste thought about her question with a bit of sadness in her expression. "Well, you know that Martin's mother, Maureen, was my good friend."

"I remember you had a friend named Maureen, but I guess I never knew her last name."

"She and Martin's father were both killed, along with their driver, in an accident. I guess it's been quite a few years ago now, but you never get over something like that.

"Martin received word while he was in Europe, and came back immediately. It was a great shock, not just because they were his parents, but because he was especially close to them."

Audra allowed herself to feel a decent amount of sympathy at hearing this, although she didn't see how it excused his behavior, particularly when he'd look her way in church, and appear to be taunting her. She glanced over at her aunt with a question in her eyes.

"I remember when I used to live here, that you got a phone call about friends of yours who had died suddenly. Was that call about the Satterfields, then?"

"Yes, but if you didn't make that connection back then, it's probably because, like you said, you didn't know Maureen's last name. Anyway, Martin married Darlene very soon after that, although I'd have to agree with you. He always looked miserable whenever they were seen together. I couldn't tell if that was because of her, or if he was still just grieving."

Aunt Celeste sighed and shrugged, abandoning that particular mystery.

"We may never know. Anyway," she added, getting up to carry their cups over to the sink, "don't be surprised if you and I get tapped to be on the church's hospitality committee. Clarice Bishop is drafting people, right and left, and Clarice doesn't accept excuses."

Audra twisted her mouth into a grimace. "That man wouldn't know hospitality, if it bit him in the butt, and I, for one, do not volunteer."

"Oh, you're so sweet," Aunt Celeste laughed. "Imagine believing that we have a choice! Aren't you just the cutest?" She leaned over the counter, and tweaked her niece's cheek.

"But, don't worry," she comforted. "Neither of us may ever be called upon to provide the obligatory casserole. There's an entire group of eager mothers, all wanting their single daughters to be the next mistress of the Satterfield estate."

Audra laughed, and then stared in disbelief when her aunt didn't laugh with her. "Are you serious?"

"You better believe it," she replied. "In fact, Dee Sanders has already made a couple of visits to Hawthorn. I expect she wants to establish herself early in the running, especially since that daughter of Lynette Jordan has also begun her campaign."

Audra shook her head in wonder. "You'd think they'd at least wait until after the funeral," she observed. "But you said this month, not this week, so I guess that's already happened."

"Nope," Aunt Celeste answered, coming back around to her barstool roost. "I've been watching for the obituary every day, but there's been nothing about it, so I asked Marcia Fife, who's the editor. You remember Marcia?"

She waited for Audra's nod. "She said she's been given nothing to print, and when she reached out to the funeral home, the director told her that arrangements have been put on hold, and asked her not to put anything in the paper until he contacted her with the details."

Audra narrowed her eyes and thought about that.

"That's pretty odd, Aunt C. Martin Satterfield seems like the kind of man who would just want to get it all over with."

"Oh, I doubt seriously that it's Martin Satterfield who's causing the delay," Aunt Celeste speculated. "Things are about to get pretty interesting around here."

Chapter Two

Martin Satterfield sat nursing his pipe alone in his bedroom, staring bleakly into the embers of a fire that needed to be stoked, if it was to continue to provide any comfort at all.

When Mrs. Isabelle Draper, or Izzy, as the family had always called her, came to see if he needed anything before she retired to her quarters, and offered to add some wood, knowing of course, that he wouldn't allow her to even attempt lifting a single stick of firewood, but willing to at least ask, he thanked her softly, but declined as she knew he would.

She had hoped her offer would prompt him to add more wood himself, but he continued to sit motionless with no further remark. The old housekeeper looked at him with concern, silently noting that the room was certainly growing chilly, but decided to say nothing more.

This particular part of the old house had never been vented to allow electric heating and cooling, and the young master had never seemed to mind, so no renovations had been made, even after he and the late Mrs. Satterfield were married.

Darlene Satterfield had insisted on her own suite of rooms in another wing, citing the lack of modern conveniences as something she couldn't possibly tolerate, but excuses for her doing so were hardly necessary.

Her husband had seemed to find it amusing that the woman acted as if this would be a disappointment to him, and acquiesced without complaint, but remained where he was.

Izzy resisted the urge to try one more appeal for his comfort's sake, and gently closed the door behind her, leaving the heir of Hawthorn Manor, as the house had been christened by one of his whimsical ancestors, to his grim solitude.

He noted her departure with little more than a glance, and returned to his sober contemplation.

Any hopes for a peaceful evening had been in vain, as he was paid yet another visit by one of the police department's detectives.

Martin had seemed to instinctively know that it was the detective who had arrived at his door, even before he began knocking on the glass sidelights, and calling out that he had more questions, and had told Izzy to remain in her quarters until the man had gone.

Detective Vance seemed to be disgruntled over the fact that he had been unable to unravel Martin Satterfield's claim to have not been home when his wife died, and was resolutely committed to discovering a hole somewhere in his story that he could exploit.

Unfortunately for the detective, Martin was in the company of several friends who had secured a lodge for a week of hunting, and each man's story dovetailed with the other's, not to mention his old housekeeper's insistence that she had personally delivered the message that contained the invitation for the hunting trip, and had packed Mr. Satterfield's things, and watched him leave, herself.

In spite of this, Greg Vance had returned unannounced, and had gone over his same questions, obviously hoping to annoy the late woman's husband into slipping up in his account, but he had coolly and quietly repeated everything he'd said before, all the while eyeing the detective with an icy calm that was unnerving.

Detective Vance had intended to rouse a more animated response when he asked Martin Satterfield if his late wife had any medical issues that might have contributed to her fall down the stairs. "Other than the pregnancy, I mean," he had casually added, watching his potential prey's face carefully.

Martin had remained silent, and when he finally lifted his eyes to meet the detective's, they were unreadable.

"She hadn't complained of any issues," he offered, the timbre of his voice giving no evidence of emotion.

Detective Vance had finally taken his leave, but not without fairly promising that he would be back, and Martin had locked the door after him, and climbed the many stairs to his room where he sat now, letting the detective's words echo in his head, which was beginning to ache with a dull throb.

He wondered to himself if Darlene had really been pregnant, or if this was just some police tactic designed to incite him. The autopsy results had not yet been provided to him, but a police detective might very well have already been made privy to them, and he suspected that this was the case.

In any event, Martin was confident that the incompetent detective, who appeared to be a bit agitated, was posing questions that he already knew the answers to.

Martin was well acquainted with the coroner who had arranged for the autopsy, and had reached for the phone to ask him about the detective's claim that his late wife had been pregnant, but hesitated, then hung the phone up.

He wasn't sure he was ready for it to become common knowledge that he had been completely unaware of his late wife's pregnancy, or for it to be revealed that it would not have been his child, if the police had requested that any testing be done to determine paternity.

He rested his head back, and looked up vacantly at the ceiling, absently running his hand through his mane of dark hair, and allowing the detective's intentional revelation to add a severity to his already stern features.

Martin Satterfield was a handsome man, but his stoic, somber nature never softened his countenance, nor calmed his stormy blue eyes. A suppressed hint of anger seemed to continually burn in those eyes, and only the elderly Mrs. Draper was not made to feel uncomfortable by it.

She had been in the Satterfield's employ since Martin was an infant, and had doted on the child, and now maintained a respectful affection for the man.

Martin cradled his neglected pipe in one hand, noting that it had gone out as it often did, but not bothering to relight it. It was his one vice, if it could be considered as such, but he usually let it die without coaxing it to burn. It served its purpose to soothe him, whether he actually smoked it or simply held onto it.

He looked at it now with a grimace, feeling that it had failed him, and rose up out of his chair to retire for the evening.

He climbed wearily into bed after his shower, and lay with one arm up, resting the back of his hand on his forehead. The moon filtered through the trees, and made patterns on the wall, and across the covers. Martin closed his eyes, and returned to the thoughts he'd been having while standing in the shower, letting the water beat down on his back and bowed head.

He had been patient enough, he'd decided. He'd had no objection to delaying the funeral as long as the coroner's office had needed more time, but that was no longer the case. He didn't owe anything to the police, and resolved to contact the funeral home the next morning, and arrange to go ahead with the service.

The pastor of the church that he and Darlene had both attended had assured him that he would adjust his calendar when the need arose, in order to accommodate him, so he felt reasonably sure that he would be able to handle short notice.

Martin found Pastor Reynolds to be a decent sort, as pastors go, but although he had only attended church because Darlene placed a high value on social interactions as the mistress of Hawthorn, and enjoyed the attention of the congregation, he personally hadn't any use for churches.

It would have suited him if she'd just attended without him, but of course, she insisted on the two of them being seen together. It was easier to just go, and be done with it, than to have to deal with her hysterical rants about his not allowing her to be linked with him in public as a Satterfield.

He knew his mother and father wouldn't be pleased to have discovered his lack of enthusiasm for spiritual matters, as they were devout in their faith, so he had dutifully attended with them whenever he was home, but it had made no meaningful impression on him.

He did, however, admire the strength and peace that his parents had seemed to derive from going to church.

14

His mother had once told him that it wasn't going to church that gave her that strength and peace, but having a relationship with God. That had been beyond his grasp. He simply didn't understand what she could have meant.

He let out a sigh as the sweet memory of both his mother and father settled into his thoughts, and held onto it for a moment, before a layer of loneliness insisted on covering it. He had loved his parents dearly, and he felt that when they died, love and kindness died with them.

Martin drew in a deep breath, and willed his rampant thoughts to recede, and after a while, sleep finally brought him a few hours of relief.

The master of Hawthorn Manor kept a light hold on Izzy's arm, having discovered to his alarm, upon his return from abroad, that she was becoming increasingly feeble.

He stood with her now, among the assembled group of people who attended Darlene Satterfield's unremarkable funeral.

He wouldn't have minded if it had rained, because it might have discouraged some from attending or made them leave early, but the weather took no notice of the occasion, and was pleasantly mild, almost vexingly so.

Martin was aware of the many whispers and innuendos, regarding the fact that his late wife was being laid to rest in the church's cemetery, rather than in the Satterfield family burial ground at the estate, but he resolutely paid no attention, and the good pastor asked no questions, but took pains to ensure that a nice plot was made available for Darlene Satterfield.

He stood gazing down at the grass, as Pastor Reynolds conducted the simple graveside service. He knew that Martin wished for brevity, and did his best to keep his remarks concise while still managing to touch on the importance of being prepared for eternity.

Martin let that thought settle in his mind for a moment, then dismissed it impatiently when it began to challenge him. He wasn't sure he wanted eternity to exist.

He let his eyes travel around the gathering, marking the presence of not only the irritating Detective Vance, but of Phillip March, who refused to meet his gaze.

The sight of both men caused a slow-burning anger to begin to cast its shadow across Martin's face, and he clenched his jaw and inadvertently tightened his hold on Izzy's arm, before realizing it, and giving her a quick glance of apology.

Izzy appeared especially pale and shaky, and seemed to be trying to partially conceal herself behind Martin in a way that helped to shelter her from the observations of others she hadn't expected to see.

Martin continued to glower at the evasive Phillip March, then allowed his stare to settle elsewhere, acknowledging Celeste Campbell's presence with a slight nod, and noting the young woman with her, who seemed curiously familiar to him.

His attention returned to the pastor, as he heard him request that heads bow for prayer. Martin knew this would conclude the service, and a sense of relief settled on him.

Several people attempted to engage him after he had thanked the pastor, and moved to lead Izzy away from gravesite, and he mumbled terse, quiet responses, while continuing to steer her gently toward the waiting car, where his driver stood by to open the door.

An enormous release of pent-up tension washed over Martin, as he firmly put the service and his dead wife out of his mind, concerned only with leaving this day behind him.

When they arrived at Hawthorn, Martin escorted Izzy into the house, and she asked his pardon so that she could lie down for a short rest.

He had moved all of Izzy's things from her upstairs quarters to one of the main floor suites a few weeks before, so that she wouldn't have to climb the stairs anymore.

Normally, she would have protested the special treatment, but she had begun to feel breathless, and tired much more easily, and accepted that it was for the best.

Martin let her get settled into bed, then tapped lightly on her door before entering. He came over to rest on the side of the bed, and favored her with a rare, soft smile.

"Are you worn out, Izzy?" he asked, taking her hand in a little caress.

"I've been worn out all my life," she said with a little laugh that he shared with her.

She gave his hand a weak squeeze.

"Don't you be worrying about me, young Martin," she said with a hint of displeasure. "You've got enough to worry about."

"Can I do anything for you?" he asked, with a slight catch in his voice. "Would you like something from the kitchen?"

"You stay out of my kitchen," she returned, patting his hand with hers. She made him smile, and was glad.

He reached over to indicate the intercom phone with a touch. "If you need me, Izzy, I'll just be in the den."

She nodded and closed her eyes, a faint smile flitting across her face. "Thank you, young Martin," she whispered.

He stood and reached a finger down to brush a light stroke across her forehead, more little boy than grown man in that moment, and watched her with concern for a bit longer, before leaving her to rest.

Chapter Three

Audra pulled a few things from the trunk, or as she jokingly called it, the "frunk" of her prized possession, a chrome blue, 1969 Karmann Ghia Coupe. She could feel the eyes of their neighbor, Myra Hepplewhite, and wondered if she was using her binoculars.

The thought made her giggle to herself, as she lifted a large, leather portfolio case, and rested it on the driveway beside her laptop, then checked for anything else before closing the car's front trunk, and loading herself up.

Apparently, Myra Hepplewhite had decided that the Campbell girl wasn't keeping drugs in her hippie car after all, and had ended her surveillance from behind the living room drapes, probably, Audra suspected, with disappointment.

She brought her things into the house, and Dexter hopped out of his bed, looking up at her as if he would have carried her stuff in, if she'd just told him what she was up to.

"You're a big help," she praised him insincerely, and he followed her to her room to help some more.

She laid everything on the foot of her bed and shooed Dexter out, in front of her, then headed for the back patio to see if Aunt Celeste was off the phone, yet.

She smiled up at her from her lounge chair, and lifted one hand over her eyes to be able to see her niece, in spite of the bright sunlight. "You didn't have to run off, honey. That was just a call from the office, it wasn't personal."

"Oh, I know," she said, landing in an Adirondack chair, and pushing her hair out of her eyes. "I was looking for some things, and remembered they were still in the car, and I thought it would be a good time to go bring them in.

"Dexter was no help," she complained with a grin, reaching over and roughing up his beautiful coat.

He wagged his tail happily, as if she'd just lavished more praise on him.

Aunt Celeste looked at her niece with blatant curiosity.

"That reminds me, Audra Campbell, where, in the world, did you get that beautiful car you showed up here driving? You certainly didn't bring it from across the ocean!"

She laughed at that, then her face softened. "Well, you remember that Mom had taken out a life insurance policy when she and Dad were leaving to go overseas, and named me the beneficiary."

Her aunt nodded, and did remember, since she had actually handled things when the insurance company was ready to remit the death benefit to Audra.

"It wasn't huge or anything, but I did use some of the money to buy the car. I had been looking online right before I was about to return here, and was hoping to find something in the area I was flying into, and just drive it here, instead of renting a car, because I knew I needed one of my own.

"But I didn't dare hope for anything like that one. I'd been wanting one of those all my life, but it always eluded me so I'd stopped even thinking about having one someday.

"I was just looking for any little thing that I could get around in, but when I pulled up the classifieds for that town, it was one of the first things I saw. So I called the seller, who had completely restored it, and told him I was returning to the states, and asked him if he would hold it for me if I paid him a deposit."

Aunt Celeste drew in her breath. "Without even seeing it, first? Honey, I wouldn't have pegged you for a gambler!"

She grinned and gave her a helpless shrug. "I know, but I lost all my reason and logic the minute I saw the ad. He wanted a couple of thousand just to hold it.

"I had to trust him, and he had to trust me, I guess. But he turned out to be a really nice man, who had several classic cars that he had been working on. I guess it's his hobby.

"He ended up coming down on the price when he found out I was coming back from mission work. I explained to him that Dad is the missionary, and that I was only helping him, but that didn't seem to matter. It's pretty much in mint condition."

"I'll be the judge of that," Aunt Celeste declared. "You need to take me for a drive."

Audra was more than ready, since she hadn't owned the car long enough to stop thinking of it as fun.

She hopped up, and reached out a hand to tug her aunt up from her chair.

"Let me get my keys," she practically sang out.

She walked her aunt around the car, pointing out the odd trunk location, and explaining to Aunt Celeste that some models were convertibles, but that she'd been glad to learn that this one wasn't. She'd always believed that the novelty of having a convertible top wasn't worth the trouble of maintaining it.

When they finally got into Audra's car, Aunt Celeste was suitably impressed.

"What year is this?" she wondered.

"It's a sixty-nine," Audra told her, and she looked over at her niece with amazement.

"Honey, without even stopping to do any math, this car is at least fifty years old, and it looks like this? It doesn't even smell old!"

She reached over to touch the walnut steering wheel, and then found something else that surprised her. "It has air condition?"

"Not all of them did, but this one does, and it works!"

Audra grinned, and prepared to back out of the drive, when her aunt let out another shocked exclamation.

"When did you learn how to drive a standard shift?"

"That's pretty much all they drive where Dad is," she replied. "But this is an autostick. You do shift, but no clutch, which, believe it or not, was hard for me to get used to. I've had to learn not to rest my hand on the top of the shift knob, or I might just end up in neutral, right in the middle of the freeway. It doesn't take much!"

Aunt Celeste just shook her head in amazement. "Well, let's take this baby into town, and show it off!"

Audra was happy to oblige her. She drove them downtown, and completed the square a couple of times, before pulling into a parking space in front of a coffee shop that Aunt Celeste suggested stopping at.

She ordered their coffee, and Audra grabbed a table for them by the window so that she could keep an eye on her car.

There was a bit of a line, but Aunt Celeste never minded waiting since she knew practically everyone in town, and she would simply turn every queue into an opportunity to visit and get caught up.

Audra smiled as she heard her aunt laughing at something, and let her gaze wander around, realizing that she had missed living in this town and going to school here. Some things had changed, but not enough for it not to feel like home.

She drew her mouth into a scowl as she saw Phillip March, an investment banker, coming out of the courthouse, and her beautiful, green eyes darkened with contempt.

She hadn't been able to believe that he would have the nerve to attend Darlene Satterfield's funeral, and had silently fumed about it the rest of the day. His very appearance now was enough to ruin Audra's previous reflections about this town, and her fondness for it, and she added that to the list of reasons that she disliked the man.

By the time Aunt Celeste made it to the table with their coffee, however, the object of Audra's scorn had gotten into his car and driven away, and she had managed to focus her attention on more pleasant aspects of the square, and was able to forget all about Phillip March.

"Well," Aunt Celeste began, leaning close in a confidential manner, "the word on the streets is that now that Darlene Satterfield's funeral is over and done, apparently, it's no holds barred."

"What do you mean?" Audra gave her a blank look.

"Martin Satterfield," she replied. "Well, not actually Martin himself, but those women who are vying to be the one he turns to for comfort."

Audra wrinkled her brow and frowned. "Aunt C, you are flat out kidding me!"

"I most certainly am not," she denied.

A look of distaste washed over Audra's face. "Can't that man wait until his late wife is cold, before he starts auditioning replacements?"

"Oh, honey, it's not Martin!" Aunt Celeste said, laying a hand on Audra's arm. "I'm sure he's as annoyed by all this as you seem to be. But when he married Darlene Parks, you'd have thought the world ended around here. Girls were actually crying! You'd have thought he was Paul McCartney!"

"Why?" Audra said the word with the same intonation as if she'd said "yuk".

Aunt Celeste sat back, and gave her a look of disbelief. "Are you seriously trying to convince me that when you lived here, and saw him at church, you didn't actually notice what that man looks like? Honey, God was especially good to Martin Satterfield!"

Audra laughed at her aunt's comical declaration. "All I saw was a sullen, brooding guy who, I expect, would have snarled like a junk yard dog if anyone had greeted him."

"Oh, people greeted him, or at least they tried," Aunt Celeste returned. "Married or not, those girls at church went out of their way to try to get a response from him, although I will admit that it was always less than genteel."

"Genteel!" Audra scoffed, and rolled her pretty eyes. "Well, if he was mean to them, they had it coming, since they were silly enough to ever expect anything civil from him."

"Now, I may have to start keeping a tally of how many times you make disparaging remarks about Martin Satterfield, and try to determine what the catalyst is." Aunt Celeste leaned back to fold her arms and examine her niece closely. "Was that man mean to you or something?"

"To me?" Audra laughed. "Hardly! Believe me, I have never put myself in a position for him to be mean to me, but if he had been, he would have regretted it."

"Oh, I've no doubt that's true." Aunt Celeste smiled, but continued to look at her as if in deep thought.

"You really seem to have an unusual resentment toward Martin Satterfield, honey, and that is just not like you. I'd like to know why."

Audra began to feel uncomfortable, and looked away just in time to see Dee Sanders getting out of her car. She grinned and pointed a finger in her general direction, and Aunt Celeste looked over at her, watching her tidy her hair, and straighten her blouse, then shook her head.

"Oh, good grief, who is that girl primping for? Does she think that Martin Satterfield would ever walk into this shop? To begin with, he wouldn't sit still long enough in a public place for anyone to be tempted to try to speak to him, and besides that, he wouldn't come in, and order coffee to go, and have to drink it from a foul, paper cup!"

Audra grinned at her aunt's unintentional suggestion that the heir of Hawthorn Manor wouldn't lower himself to drink from anything but the finest china.

"Well, my money is on her walking in, and scanning the room just long enough to realize her efforts were in vain, and turning around and stomping out. It's a good thing her competition isn't in here. That could get interesting."

Aunt Celeste laughed at the thought. "When Dee Sanders and Torey Jordan both end up at Hawthorn at the same time, and probably with the same casserole, it'll most likely end up in the police blotter, because the fur is gonna fly!"

When Martin Satterfield looked through the sidelights of Hawthorn Manor's front door, and once again saw Detective Greg Vance, he frowned and muttered an oath under his breath before opening the door, and stepping out onto the veranda.

His stance clearly established the fact that the detective was not going to gain entry into his home.

"Afternoon, Satterfield!"

"Yes," Martin acknowledged stiffly. "It would appear to be afternoon."

Greg Vance pulled his notepad out of his pocket, and felt around for his pen. "I have a few more questions for you!"

"Do you?" Martin asked dryly. "And you drove all this way, when you could have simply picked up a telephone?"

"I was in the neighborhood," he replied.

"Original," Martin commented, leaning back against the doorframe, and crossing his arms.

The detective made a move forward, as if he assumed it would cause the homeowner to stand aside and allow him to pass, but he was confronted by a tall, quietly seething man who was more than capable of refusing to grant him access.

"Look, Satterfield, we can do this the easy way, or we can do this the hard way," the detective began, before Martin lifted up a silencing hand.

"I choose the hard way," he answered impassively. "You are not to return uninvited to this property again."

"Are you gonna make me get a warrant?"

"You may employ whatever methods you feel will serve your purposes. That does not alter the fact that if you continue to come onto this estate without first acquiring permission, I will take appropriate action."

"And what would that action be?" he demanded.

"Appropriate," Martin stressed, his voice coated with ice. "You are currently considered to be trespassing on private property. You may leave now."

Martin stood riveting Greg Vance with something in his eyes that was unlike anything the man had encountered before. He seemed to be not only sending him an ominous message, but slowly inching closer.

The brash detective began to have an uneasy sense that he was about to spring, and he hurriedly put his notepad away and took a few steps back.

"Of course, you realize that assaulting an officer is a felony," he warned the master of Hawthorn Manor, whose only reaction was a slow, daunting smile that seemed to indicate his willingness to risk it.

Greg Vance finally returned to his vehicle and left, and Martin stood looking in his direction with the heat of anger still smoldering.

He finally went back inside the house, locking the door, and meeting the worried eyes of his old housekeeper, as he turned around. She seemed anxious, and was clasping the hem of her apron with tight fingers."

"You are not to concern yourself, Izzy," he said softly. "I'd like for you to get some rest, and not fret over this anymore. I'll take care of it."

She lingered, blinking back tears, and he came over to put his arm around her and lead her to her room.

"Have a lie down, Izzy," he said in hushed tones, and she sat down on the side of her bed and raised her eyes to his.

"Alright, young Martin," she agreed feebly. "Just for a little while."

He smiled down at her, and brushed his hand against her cheek before leaving her to sleep.

As he closed her door and made his way to his library, his countenance once again frosted over, dark and determined.

"I'll take care of it."

Chapter Four

Audra laid the newspaper down, then slid it across the kitchen island counter to her aunt, tapping the photo of Darlene Satterfield for emphasis.

"They don't usually run a post-funeral piece," Aunt Celeste mused, reaching for her reading glasses.

"That's not what it is," Audra replied, resting her arms on the counter, and waiting for her aunt to read the article.

"I don't recognize the writer," Aunt Celeste said slowly, removing her glasses and wearing a look of indignation. "But I find it hard to believe that Marcia Fife would have let this run. She's usually more responsible than this."

Audra pulled the paper back around to study the image of the late Darlene Satterfield.

"I guess it's a nice photo," she observed. "But I don't understand the point of this article. It certainly didn't answer any questions. I can't imagine why someone felt the need to write this story, if all he was going to do was create suspicion without providing any facts. Unless creating suspicion *is* the point of it."

Aunt Celeste frowned, and leaned over to see the name of the writer again, wrinkling her brow, trying to place it.

"I know everyone at that paper, Audra," she claimed. "The local newspaper and the real estate business always maintain a close relationship. This Greg Vance is not on staff there, not unless he was hired in the last few days, and this is hardly the way to make his debut."

Audra agreed with that. "Anytime an article begins with the words 'speculation remains' you can safely assume that's all it is. Speculation."

Her aunt nodded. "Well, this is certainly the last thing Martin needs right now. I'm going to call Marcia and ask her what this is all about, and who this Greg Vance is."

She hopped up to go find her phone, and Audra gleaned through the article again, feeling a bit of sympathy for its target, Martin Satterfield, regardless of how she felt about him.

Even though she had formed a dislike for the man several years ago, and felt no need to change that, she wasn't convinced that he deserved this kind of flagrant and unwarranted hit piece.

She shook her head, and glanced down at Dexter, who had come into the kitchen for a treat, and found his owner to be elsewhere. He managed to look disappointed, and Audra took pity on him.

"Well now, let me see if I can guess, Dexter," she laughed, as he followed her over to the treat cabinet, with his happy tail wagging. She handed him his biscuit, and opened the sliding doors to let him go "kill" it on the patio, then settled back down, as Aunt Celeste came in with a thoughtful look on her face.

"Well, there's a reason I didn't recognize the writer," she began, pulling her stool around to rest on it. "He doesn't work for the paper."

"Then why was he able to write the article?" Audra asked in confusion.

Aunt Celeste put her glasses back on to glance at the article again, but looked over the rims of them at her niece.

"He's a police detective," she stated flatly, making it clear that she disapproved.

"Can they just do that?" Audra demanded in surprise.

"I suspect this Greg Vance wrote the article, intending to draw Martin Satterfield out," she said tightly, frowning at the newspaper.

"I fussed at Marcia for allowing it, and she said she didn't blame me, but that she did insist that no direct accusations could be made, and that the detective had to put his name on the article. She said he was quite willing to do that."

"Oh, I bet!" Audra twisted her mouth into a grimace.

"Marcia said he was at the funeral," Aunt Celeste added. "He was the one with the overcoat, although there was hardly a need for one on such a nice day."

Audra laughed, remembering him. "Maybe he saw that detective on television wearing one, and fancies himself to be that caliber of an investigator."

Her aunt laughed with her. "Oh, *that* guy!"

Aunt Celeste's eyes twinkled with humor. "I loved him, I never got enough of watching him. Trust me, Greg Vance will never be that guy; I don't care how many overcoats he owns. Not if he employs tactics like this."

She pushed the paper aside and shook her head. "I hate it for Martin, though. It's very well established that he was out of town when his wife died, but even if he wasn't, I'd never believe he could be responsible for her death or anyone else's.

"Of course, I knew his parents much better than I know him. He was away for several years abroad. But the Satterfields were a good, upstanding family. Martin displays a lot of his father's qualities.

"Well, other than his reticence," she added, "which makes him appear to be aloof, I guess. His father was much more talkative, and had a great sense of humor."

Audra gave a little shrug. "He must take after his mother, apparently."

"Oh, Maureen Satterfield was just lovely!" Aunt Celeste declared. "She was such a beautiful woman, and very gracious, and welcoming."

"So he is his *own* person, then," her niece decided, with a roll of her eyes, and her aunt reached over and gave her hair a little tug.

"Be nice," she chided.

Audra grinned disarmingly, and continued to flip through the newspaper until she found the classifieds.

"I'm in the valley of decision," she confided to her aunt. "The money is there if I want to go to college, but I can't seem to work up any enthusiasm for it.

"Besides, all colleges seem good for in this day and age, is to challenge everything you believe about God, and tell you that you're wrong."

She continued to let her eyes travel through the classifieds, while her aunt considered her thoughtfully. "Well," she replied, "college isn't for everyone. I didn't go, and neither did your dad, but we're both doing what we love to do."

She studied her niece closely. "What happened to your plans to work in interior design?"

Audra let out a sigh. "I guess they just sort of drifted away when I went to be with Dad, after Mom died. I mean, I took those early classes, and some online courses. I did pretty well, but..."

She let her words trail off, and her aunt reached over to touch her hand.

"Not every interior design job requires a college degree. Besides, there's no reason why you can't resume taking online courses, if you feel you'll benefit from them, and do something else in the meantime. Your old aunt might actually have a good idea brewing in her head."

Audra folded the paper, and gave Aunt Celeste her full attention.

"You could use your skills as a designer to stage the houses I list," she suggested happily. "I'd pay you, of course. I have to pay stagers anyway, so why not pay a stager that I love?"

Audra felt a sense of excitement, but hesitated. "Aunt C, I couldn't take money from you. You let me live here."

"You're not exactly a freeloader, Audra," she protested, with a frown. "You're family!"

"I know, but still." Audra was conflicted. She loved the idea of staging homes, but couldn't bring herself to accept money from her aunt.

"Just listen." Aunt Celeste wasn't done with the campaign to persuade her.

"I don't sell houses so rapidly that staging for me would be a full-time job for you anyway, so you could augment your income by other means.

"You could stage for some of my agents, as well. Besides, I'm always being asked if I know anyone who does design, and I could direct them to you."

"I don't have a lot of experience," Audra pointed out sadly. "And my portfolio is pretty much just the designs I turned in for my courses. I did manage to keep those."

"That's all you need," Aunt Celeste assured her. "That, and my recommendation which, if I say so myself, carries a bit of weight in this town."

Audra sat mulling it over, before glancing up to find her aunt silently entreating her.

"Well, I guess we can move in that direction," she conceded, and Aunt Celeste clapped excitedly.

"The Pennington home is going on the market next week," she informed Audra. "You are going to have such a good time staging it! It's a beautiful home, and they've already moved, so it's sitting empty. It's a blank canvas."

"Is that the stone house with all the willows in the front of the property, and the pond?"

Audra's pretty green eyes flickered with excitement, and she drew in her breath when Aunt Celeste nodded. "Oh, I've always wanted to see the inside of that house!"

"You're gonna love it," Aunt Celeste promised. "And we can run over there this afternoon so you can take a good look at it and get some ideas. I've already taken pictures, but you may want to take a few as well for your own purposes."

Audra reached over, and gave her aunt's hand a little squeeze. "Honestly, Aunt C, if this works out, I may never leave here again."

"If that's the case, then we'll just make sure that it works out," her aunt replied.

Martin Satterfield glanced up, as Izzy made her way slowly into the kitchen, and he could easily hear that she was struggling, and out of breath.

He quickly put away the newspaper he had been glaring at, stowing it beneath the table, and stood to his feet, coming around to pull out a chair for her to sit down.

She waved a hand of protest, and made her way over to the stove, inspecting the signs of his having made his own lunch, which had consisted of a can of soup and some crackers.

"Young Martin, what have you been up to?" she demanded, turning to look back at him accusingly.

"I'll clean that up, Izzy. Come sit down," he urged, trying again to convince her.

"That's all I've been doing," she declared, looking back at the stove, unable to hide the faint wheezing that accompanied her words. "I could have done this for you. I wish you had called me."

"I need to talk to you," he said, still gesturing at the chair. "Come, Izzy. Please," he added, when she hesitated.

She looked at him curiously, but did as he asked, and lowered herself slowly into the chair he was resting his hands on.

Martin sat down and rested his expressive blue eyes on the old housekeeper that he had loved all his life, and although those eyes were normally clouded with more restless emotions, they reflected his affection for her, now.

Isabelle Draper had been almost as much a mother to him as his own mother had been, and certainly the grandmother he had never had in his life. She had always maintained a devotion to Martin, and an unswerving faith in him that he knew he didn't deserve, although he had tried to.

He looked at her bleakly, a small and frail woman, her hair now white, and her eyes dim, and felt a pang of regret at how she had fallen into steady decline, following the unexpected, and shocking deaths of both his parents.

She was the only family Martin had left, and he longed to do whatever he could to not only restore her to health, but to make amends for the vindictive, and abusive treatment that his late wife had inflicted on her.

He leaned closer, to persuade her to listen to him.

"Doctor Wilhite is coming this afternoon to see you," he stated simply.

She returned his direct gaze, but her old eyes faltered as she sadly realized that she wasn't being asked to agree. She glanced down at her trembling, wrinkled hands and studied them quietly, before looking back up at him with the hint of tears.

"He's going to say that I can't continue to work for you," she said in a broken voice.

"I expect so," Martin agreed soberly, lowering his head.

She let her eyes travel back down to her hands, and finally asked in a faint whisper, "When would I have to leave?"

Martin looked up quickly, his brows drawn in confusion, and stared at her. "What do you mean? You're not leaving!"

She didn't seem to hear him, and he reached to take her hands in his.

"Izzy, you're not leaving," he repeated, more softly this time. When she kept her head bowed, he pressed her hands lightly to get her to look at him.

"You're a member of the Satterfield family," he assured her, with more emotion than he had felt in many years. "I want you here with me for a long time. But, you have to stop trying to do things that you can no longer do, and just take care of yourself."

Martin watched her carefully to make sure she was listening to him.

"For me, Izzy. Don't leave me," he whispered, a single tear surprising them both, as it made its way down his cheek.

The gentle, delicate old woman reached her hand to his face to wipe the tear away, and looked at him with tenderness.

"Young Martin," she said, smiling sweetly, but sadly, "we both know that I can't live forever."

"Don't say that, Izzy," he begged. "Doctor Wilhite is one of the best doctors in the area, and he'll see to it that you regain your strength."

She shook her head, and he silently pleaded with his eyes for her to agree with him.

"Your family has given me the best life I could ever have hoped to live."

Her words were spoken between shallow breaths, but she said them with a full heart. "And I know I'll be seeing Master Martin and Mrs. Maureen soon.

"I'm not afraid," she added, watching the handsome man's distressed face closely. "I asked Jesus to save me when I was just a young girl. I know where I'm going, and I'm not afraid."

Martin leaned back in his chair, and crossed his arms, looking away and blinking rapidly, in an angry attempt to gather himself.

"It's not time for that!" he snapped in an abrupt, irritated manner, refusing to let her surrender to what she knew was inevitable.

Izzy considered him with a pang of sorrow, seeing him in this moment, not as the furious, stern master of Hawthorn Manor, but as the little boy she had cared for and cherished, all of his life.

It grieved her to realize that he had made no place for God in that life, and to think that when she left this world, she very well might never see him in the one to come.

"I suppose," she began, in an attempt to pull him out of his hopeless state, "that I'd better fix myself up a bit before the good doctor arrives. I must look a fright!"

She reached up a hand to touch her snowy hair, and laughed softly.

Martin gave her a cheerless smile, and rose when she did in case she wanted his help, back to her room.

She patted the arm he offered, then reached up to also touch his face with her fingertips.

"I can manage, young Martin," she chided, with another light caress.

He watched her make her way back through the house to her suite of rooms, as a sense of foreboding, and the all too familiar weight of loneliness once again settled on him.

Chapter Five

Pastor Reynolds rested a hand on Martin Satterfield's shoulder, and gave him a compassionate clasp. "I can't tell you how sorry I am," he offered quietly.

Martin nodded, but continued to stare down with empty eyes at Mrs. Isabelle Draper's final resting place. Other than the funeral home director and the interment staff, Pastor Reynolds was the only other person allowed to witness the graveside service.

Martin's grief was too keenly felt, too bitter for him to permit any onlookers, and their robotic sympathies.

Pastor Reynolds looked over at the double, black granite stone that memorialized the senior Martin Satterfield and Maureen Satterfield, and a faint trace of fondness flitted across his face.

"When you were abroad," he said quietly, "and your parents attended church, they always brought Izzy with them."

He glanced up and allowed Martin to see the smile that this memory gave him.

"Izzy would always try to encourage me, and I needed it back then. I'd never pastored before, and I was fairly wet behind the ears.

"Unfortunately, my sermons were not the best, even though I tried, and Izzy, being the honest woman that she was, would always try to find something to compliment me about. I soon learned that if she praised the beauty of my tie, that meant the sermon was terrible."

Martin allowed a faint smile, in spite of himself.

"I began applying myself," Pastor Reynolds admitted, looking away, across the grounds, as the memory of those earlier days were reflected in his eyes.

"I worked so hard at my sermons, to get that coveted endorsement from Isabelle Draper."

He laughed, and gave Martin another light touch on his shoulder. "But those were few and far between. I did find some comfort though, in the knowledge that I owned some pretty magnificent ties."

Martin made no response, other than to reluctantly allow a second soft smile to hurry across his face.

Pastor Reynolds had both eulogized Izzy, and prayed with a sincere sense of compassion and loss, and as the gravediggers now prepared to complete their task, he wordlessly compelled Martin to stroll back with him, across the grounds toward the Satterfield home, believing that this part of a funeral was best unobserved by family.

Martin paused, as they neared the house, and crossed his arms tightly, looking around at nothing in particular, his eyes bright with unshed tears. His bearing indicated that he wished to enter his home alone, but he didn't say so. He simply stood waiting.

"If anyone is familiar with the phrase 'suffering in silence', it's you, Martin," Pastor Reynolds ventured with empathy. "I've come to understand that it's simply your way. It's how you choose to cope, so I won't encroach.

"As long as you know that it doesn't have to be that way," he added, giving him a knowing looking. "And as long as you know that I'm immediately available, and a phone call away."

Martin nodded in appreciation, his only acknowledgement a clasp of Pastor Reynolds' hand, and the briefest eye contact.

He watched the kind minister drive away, then allowed the funeral director to inform him of last minute details that he didn't care about.

He stood in place until the gravediggers finished, and everyone had left the Satterfield property, then turned to look back at the new mound of earth that blanketed the remains of his dear Izzy.

Martin slowly retraced his steps back to her graveside, and remained motionless, until grief insisted on expression, and a wounded, painful moan escaped him. Hot tears found their way down his face, and he stood running his hands through his hair with quiet, wild desperation.

He looked around frantically, with the stark realization that he was truly alone in this world, with no one left who cared anything about him.

He'd tried so hard to keep Izzy with him. After her doctor had explained to Martin that her heart was failing her, and that it was too weak to sustain life much longer, he sat with her day and night, longing to talk with her, but knowing that the effort was too great for her.

Instead, he clung to her hand until it became evident that there was no more life in it and even then, it was Doctor Wilhite who removed Izzy's hand from Martin's grasp, and who quietly made him realize that she had left him.

Her last words had been used to tell him that she wanted him to ask Jesus to save him, so that she could see him again. He had smiled, and told her not to worry about him, and in vain, entreated her not to leave him.

Martin stood now, looking at Izzy's grave, the graves of his parents, and the graves of generations of Satterfields who had lived and died before him, and felt suddenly overwhelmed at how futile and meaningless life had revealed itself to be.

He found himself wishing he had never cared for any of them, and angrily wiped the tears from his face, and walked away to return to Hawthorn Manor, and shut the door on all of it.

Doctor Paul Amos had known Martin Satterfield for much of his life, and had a fondness for the man despite his air of detachment, and his taciturn nature. It was because of his regard for him, that he regretted the mission that brought him to Hawthorn Manor, but he knew that he was expected to do his duty as coroner.

He sat across from Martin now, and pressed the tips of his fingers together, eyeing him with some concern.

"I'm so sorry to learn of Izzy's passing," he began, but Martin sat rigidly in his chair with no response, waiting for him to get on with it.

Doctor Amos accepted his friend's desire to have his grief left untouched, and proceeded with his task of informing him of the autopsy reports he had been expecting.

"As to your late wife's autopsy findings, I suppose the first thing to speak about is cause of death."

He leaned forward, and looked at Martin in a manner that compelled him to meet his gaze. "Your wife did not die because of falling down the stairs," he said bluntly.

Martin allowed only the slightest flicker of reaction to alter his otherwise stoic demeanor, and continued to wait without comment.

"Of course, initial observations seemed to lend credence to the assumption that she met with an unfortunate accident. At first glance, there was nothing to contradict that, without the benefit of an autopsy.

"The initial report stated that she was found on the stairs, with her head positioned on the bottom landing against the newel post, indicating that she had fallen, striking her head on the corner," he commented, peering through the bottoms of his glasses at his notes before continuing.

"It was Izzy who found her."

A wince of pain slightly contorted Martin's face, but only fleetingly.

"Izzy stated that she called 911 immediately, but did not touch Mrs. Satterfield's body, and of course, there is no reason to doubt that."

Doctor Amos continued to work through the job at hand in spite of his misgivings, not seeing the slight twitch of Martin's facial muscles as he heard this.

"Martin, your wife's death was caused by strangulation. The ligature marks around her neck, and broken hyoid clearly indicate that she was dead before her head encountered the newel post.

"This is also supported by the fact that the wound associated with her head striking the post was not enough to cause death, and by all appearances, seems to have certainly been a post-mortem event."

"Staged."

Martin Satterfield's one whispered word brought a nod of confirmation from Doctor Amos.

"From all indications, yes. Staged."

Martin raised his eyes to meet those of the coroner, and a flash of anger was in them although when he spoke, it was with a considerable amount of restraint.

"Doctor, you can't possibly be implicating Izzy, and I'm growing weary of expecting the police to make the effort to verify where I was. If you're implicating me, then just say so, and if you're not, then tell me your conclusion."

Doctor Amos leaned back in his chair, and considered the man's resentful response, then prepared to offer the rest of his findings.

"Your wife was pregnant," he said simply.

"Vance said that," he acknowledged, but added nothing more, and Doctor Amos exhibited surprise.

"You want to ask me if I knew, but you seem to be reluctant to do so," Martin observed quietly.

"Did you?" He waited.

"I did not."

The doctor returned his glasses to his pocket and nodded, as if his suspicions had been confirmed.

"It wasn't yours," he stated simply, and Martin looked at him with no emotion at all.

"Is that a question?"

"It's a finding from the sample you provided," the coroner replied. "But did you know it wasn't yours, Martin?"

"I just told you that I didn't know she was pregnant, Paul. Did you forget already, or is this the same sort of tactic that Detective Vance employs?"

Martin left off with concealing his growing irritation, and shifted in his chair impatiently.

"I didn't forget," his friend replied. "You know who the father was." He appeared confident of that fact.

"Are you asking me?"

Doctor Amos sighed in defeat.

"I know what you're going to say, and yes, that's a question for the police, and not for the coroner, but Martin, you consistently make it so difficult for anyone to help you!"

Martin raised one brow in surprise. "Are you trying to help me, Doctor Amos?"

"Yes, Martin, I am! Don't you realize the importance of the identity of the father of your late wife's baby? It takes the spotlight off of you, and places it on someone else with motive!"

"Someone *else*," Martin repeated slowly. "Not someone *instead* of."

The coroner threw up his hands in aggravation, and Martin decided to spare him anything further.

"Is that the extent of your findings, then? Darlene did not fall down the stairs, she was pregnant, and with someone else's baby? Is that all?"

"Isn't that enough?" Doctor Amos snapped.

"Who ordered the DNA test?"

Martin's question was unexpected, and the coroner just sat looking at him for a long moment.

"It's only a matter of time before I find out," Martin pointed out. "I'm legally entitled to that information."

"I supplied the necessary DNA samples," Doctor Amos admitted. "Detective Vance had his own people do the testing."

"And he just called you up, and volunteered the results?"

"I demanded the results!" He clubbed his fist on the arm of his chair, and fairly shouted his response.

"Why?"

"Because I wanted to know who the father was!"

Martin allowed a slow smile to hover around his mouth. "You mean you wanted to know who the father was not."

Doctor Amos indulged in his own guilty smile.

"I wanted their investigation to move away from you, I admit it."

"How long has he known?" Martin wondered idly.

"For a few weeks, now."

"And yet, he persists in trying to poke holes in my alibi," he mused sarcastically.

"You might as well know that I performed my own DNA test, when I learned that the detective intended to have his own people test," Doctor Amos confessed.

"Same results," he said, and noted Martin Satterfield's look of intrigue. "I just wanted to make sure the correct results were reported," he added. "But, Martin..."

He sat forward in an attempt to get him to listen. "The tests only told the police that you are not the father. It didn't tell them who is. It didn't tell me either, but I'm convinced that you know."

"What difference does it make?" Martin asked, with maddening apathy.

"It makes all the difference in the world!" The coroner was incredulous. "Don't you realize that matching the DNA to the father strengthens his position, as being the one who killed your wife?"

"Does it?"

"Yes, it does!" No one could make Doctor Paul Amos more likely to shout than Martin Satterfield, and he indulged in raising his voice once more.

"Then why are you the only one asking me who he is?" Martin inquired dryly. "Vance already knows that I wasn't the father of Darlene's baby. So, why isn't the junior detective here with his little notepad, trying to find out who was?

"I'll tell you why," he added, resting his ankle on one knee, and folding his arms, unbelievably relaxed. "Because Greg Vance would sell his own mother, if I could be found guilty instead of the real killer."

Doctor Amos narrowed his eyes, and viewed the man with pardonable skepticism. "What possible difference could it make to Vance, as long as the right person was arrested?"

"Because in his mind *I* am the only right person," Martin informed him with a sardonic grin.

"But why?"

"Because my name is Satterfield, and contrary to popular belief, we are not held in high esteem by everyone."

Martin toyed with the fringe on a pillow he had moved over when he'd sat down. "I did a little investigating, myself. It turns out that this is Detective Vance's first case."

Doctor Amos looked confused. "Why does that matter?"

"It matters, because he intends to make national headlines by arresting the heir of Hawthorn Manor, and skip to the head of the line in his department."

Martin paused, tempted to add that this was, of course, not the detective's main reason for focusing his investigation on him, but decided to let his recent discoveries remain his own.

"Can't you inform the police that you would like his senior officer to take over this case, or you will stop cooperating and lawyer up?" Doctor Amos asked.

"I could," Martin admitted, seeming to find the doctor's suggestion oddly amusing. "But where's the fun in that?"

"Fun!" The doctor shook his head. "I would think you would just want all this to be over and done! Martin, sooner or later, the police are going to ask you if you know who the father was. You're going to tell them, aren't you? They have to interview him!"

He shrugged in an infuriating manner, and then relented when he saw the doctor's helpless frustration.

"At some point," he conceded. "When I'm ready."

Chapter Six

Audra looked up from her laptop when she heard her name, and was surprised to see Dee Sanders encroaching on her personal space, and smiling down at her.

"It *is* you!" Dee fairly rejoiced.

She managed to restrain herself from pointing out that they'd just seen each other last Sunday at church, and that she doubted that she'd changed that much since then.

"I suppose it is," she admitted, silently hoping that this was all Dee wanted to say. Her hopes were dashed.

"Imagine running right into you like this, when I was just thinking about you!" the young woman exclaimed, pulling out a chair and settling down, then looking around the coffee shop with a pleased expression.

"You were just thinking about me?" Audra couldn't hide her mild surprise.

"I was," Dee insisted. "And here you are!"

Audra struggled again, but she was able to resist complimenting Dee on her flair for stating the obvious.

"What's going on, Dee?" she asked, not because she cared, but because she was hoping that it might expedite things.

"Oh, tons of things," she informed her, with a wave of her newly manicured pink nails. "But, what about you? When I found out you had moved back, I just couldn't believe it! We were all so thrilled!"

Audra smiled down at her laptop, refusing to mutter "Oh, I just bet!" and feeling pleased with her victory.

"Well, I never signed on to give my life to the mission field," she reminded Dee. "I just wanted to help my dad through a difficult time."

Dee Sanders effected a sweet smile, and sat her coffee cup down, before looking curiously at Audra's laptop.

"Am I interrupting a chat, or anything?" she asked.

"A chat?" Audra looked at her blankly. "No, I'm just doing a little research." She closed her laptop, and pushed it to one side, and gave the excitable woman her full attention. "Why were you thinking about me, Dee?"

Dee Sanders hadn't expected Audra to continue focusing on her claim, and realized that she was expecting an answer.

"Well, for one thing, Mother and I were wondering if you're just visiting, or if you're back to stay?"

Audra smiled, then sipped her coffee, looking at Dee over the rim of her cup. "I'm in no hurry to decide," she said, "so for now at least, I suppose I'm pretty well socked in with my Aunt Celeste."

"That's nice." Dee ran her fingers through her red hair, and seemed to be wanting to ask Audra a question, but couldn't quite make herself do it.

Audra decided to help her. "Is there anything I can do for you, Dee? Did you want something specific?"

She gave Audra another of her odd little smiles. "Well, to be honest, I'm a little embarrassed to even bring it up."

Dee had peaked Audra's curiosity, and she simply waited.

"Of course, all this may be unnecessary," she began, "because as lovely as *you* are, Audra, you probably have a fiancé, or at least a boyfriend."

She shook her head to the contrary, and Dee's downcast face revealed her disappointment. "No? So, that means you're available, then?"

"It depends on what you mean by available, Dee," she said slowly. "I'm available to help you paint your bedroom. I'm not available to double-date."

Audra traced her finger around the edge of her cup.

"Do you intend to try to set me up, Dee?" she asked quietly, resting her eyes on the nervous woman sitting across from her. "I really hope not, because that's the last thing I'm available for. If you have someone in mind, please give him to someone else. I'm sorry, but I'm not interested."

Dee Sanders looked confused. "Set you up?" Her face cleared. "Oh, no! In fact, just the opposite!"

"Just the opposite," Audra repeated, partly to herself. What was that supposed to mean? She folded her arms, and peered at Dee closely.

"Are you asking me to set *you* up with someone?"

"Well," The girl looked as uncomfortable as she sounded. "Maybe not set me up with someone, but maybe put in a good word for me?"

Audra couldn't help wondering why Dee's earlier question, about whether or not she had a boyfriend, had anything at all to do with Audra putting in a good word for her, but decided that the fewer questions she asked, the sooner this would be over.

"Is it for a referral? Are you interviewing for a job?"

Audra was stymied. She had no clue what Dee Sanders was inching her way toward.

"Actually, it's more of a character reference."

Audra didn't try to hide her complete bewilderment, and continue to look at Dee with a wrinkled brow.

"Who has asked for this reference?"

"Well, he hasn't asked. I was thinking of being more proactive, than waiting for him to ask."

"Him," Audra noted. "So we're talking about a man."

"Oh, not just any man!" Dee was positively glowing. "I'm talking about Martin!"

"Martin," Audra repeated, in a flat tone.

"Martin Satterfield," Dee confirmed.

Audra just continued to stare at her.

"Dee, I don't know Martin Satterfield."

"Don't you?" She looked completely thrown off balance. "But your aunt knows everyone in this town, and she and Martin's mother were such good friends so naturally, I just assumed..."

Audra was steadily shaking her head negatively during Dee's entire discourse.

"No, it's only my aunt who knows Martin Satterfield. I don't know him, and he's pretty much the last man in this town I intend to get to know," she declared with a frown.

Dee looked stunned. "Audra Campbell, why would you say such a thing?"

"I just don't like him," she admitted. "I didn't like him when I lived here before, and I don't like him now. I have no use for that man."

Dee's expression was vacillating between incredulity, and stark relief. She was beginning to realize that she could check the beautiful Audra Campbell off her ever-growing list of rivals for the affections of the recently eligible master of Hawthorn Manor.

"I completely understand, Audra, and I'm sorry for the confusion. I'm terrible about just assuming things!"

Dee practically leaped up from her chair, to report back to her mother that she was wrong to be concerned.

"It was lovely running into you," she gushed. "Let's do this again sometime. I'd better be off."

She waved her fingers, and hurried out to her car, as Audra stared after her in wide-eyed disbelief.

She looked down at her laptop with a sense of aggravation, realizing that there was no way she was going to be able to concentrate on her staging project after all this.

She sighed and gathered up her things, then drove back home with this ridiculous exchange still playing over in her head.

Aunt Celeste looked up from the kitchen counter with a smile of welcome.

"Hey there, pretty girl! I'm chopping onions, so tell me something funny."

Audra sat her laptop bag on the table, and pulled out a stool to perch on. "Don't ask, unless you mean it," she said blandly.

Aunt Celeste paused and looked at her in wonder.

"You are not going to believe the conversation I just had with Dee Sanders!"

"I'm not going to *not* believe it," her aunt countered, with a little laugh. "I'm up for anything. Whatcha got?"

"She wants me to put in a good word for her."

Audra purposely waited for her aunt to ask.

She continued her culinary task, and casually inquired, "Put in a good word with whom?"

"Martin Satterfield!" Audra practically spat the name out, and Aunt Celeste ceased with her dinner preparations, and gave Audra the shocked stare that she had been counting on.

"Did that daft girl really ask you to be a forerunner, and pave her way to Martin Satterfield?"

Aunt Celeste was dumbfounded.

"Who does she think you are, her own personal pioneer?"

"She must," Audra muttered.

"It's obvious that the girl doesn't know Martin at all," her aunt declared, raking her diced onion into a pile. "If she did, she'd realize that enlisting anyone to approach him on her behalf, with that kind of silliness, would be the worst possible thing she could do. Can you imagine Martin's reaction?"

Audra frowned with displeasure. "I imagine he would give her a scowling she would not soon forget. Right after he finishes off the forerunner."

Aunt Celeste laughed at her glum remark. "Oh, you can be sure!" She laid a paper towel over the onion, and leaned against her side of the counter, propping herself on her elbows.

"What did you tell her?"

"I told her that I didn't know Martin Satterfield, and that he's the last man in this town that I would ever want to know," her niece informed her, still annoyed by the entire thing.

Aunt Celeste studied her quietly. "Okay, we've talked about this before, Audra. I keep hearing you say that sort of thing about Martin, and I'm sorry, but I cannot understand your complete dislike for that man. You're gonna have to help me out here. Did you two have an unpleasant encounter, or anything along those lines?"

"No, thank God!" she returned fervently. "We've never had any encounter at all, and we never will, if I have anything to say about it."

"But why, dear?" her aunt was baffled. "It's not like you to just dislike a person for no reason. You're not petty."

"Apparently, I am," she sighed.

Her aunt continued to consider her beautiful, but sullen niece thoughtfully.

"I've never heard you say anything at all like that about another person, Audra, so of course, I'm absolutely stumped. Why just Martin Satterfield?"

"It's not just him," she admitted, choosing not to include Phillip March as someone else she found intensely objectionable. "If we're being honest, I disliked his trophy wife even more. And this is probably the part where you scold me for speaking ill of the dead."

"Well," Aunt Celeste began, pausing to think about the recently deceased Darlene Satterfield. "I'll admit that she wasn't exactly endearing, and I expect she cared less about people liking her, than she did about them envying her. If we're being honest," she added, with a grin.

"I just got so tired of seeing them over in their pew of choice knowing, good and well, that she was just there for everyone to admire her, and that he was only there..."

Audra stopped and grimaced. "Who, in the world, knows why *he* was there? He certainly didn't want to be. I expect Darlene just snapped her fingers and he jumped, which makes me dislike him even more."

"Nope." Aunt Celeste shook her head, and moved back from the counter to finish preparing dinner. "That part, I can't agree with, dear. I don't know why he agreed to attend church with her, but I can tell you with no hesitation that Martin Satterfield doesn't jump for anyone, especially for a woman."

"If Dee Sanders has her way, he's gonna jump for her," Audra declared, intentionally riling her aunt just to get a reaction out of her.

"Oh, Miss Dee Sanders better think again! I'd caution her and Torey Jordan, and the rest of the contestants, to meditate long and hard about what it is they think they're ready to leap into. One of them just might get what she's after, and realize that she should have been careful about what she wished for."

Audra looked up from examining a nail. "What does that mean, Aunt C?"

"It means that if there ever *is* a second mistress of Hawthorn Manor, Martin won't exactly be fanning her with palm fronds, and feeding her grapes."

"But he wouldn't be abusive to her, would he?" Audra hadn't considered what Darlene Satterfield's life at Hawthorn Manor had really been like, and now she wondered.

She could tell, just from the times that she glanced over at Martin Satterfield in church, that there was something in his eyes that gave her the chills, especially once, when he seemed to feel her glance, and rested his steady gaze on her, as if mocking her.

She had never been able to forget that penetrating stare, and had relocated to another pew after that, so that she'd not be able to see him, even if she wanted to.

Aunt Celeste looked at Audra with disapproval.

"No, he absolutely would not be abusive to her or to any other woman, Audra. You don't know him, so you'll just have to take my word for it. Martin would never express his anger toward any woman by physical means. He's a very disciplined individual, and I would never believe that of him."

"Well," Audra commented softly, "Dee Sanders and I aren't exactly buddies, but I do hope for her sake that she never puts herself in a position to find out."

Chapter Seven

Aunt Celeste sat nursing her cup of coffee, and prepared herself to have the conversation with Audra that she was dreading. She had heard her moving around in her room, so she knew she was up early.

She decided to go ahead, and tackle this right off the bat, and let the day take whatever direction it wanted to, after that. She wasn't feeling too optimistic about it, though.

Her niece had been up late the night before, poring over her design portfolio, and creating new drawings, and was feeling the effects of it now, as her yawn proceeded her actual entrance into the kitchen. She stopped and grinned at her aunt.

"I know, I know," she said, anticipating Aunt Celeste's teasing. "But I smell coffee, so all is not lost."

Aunt Celeste pushed an empty cup over to where Audra normally sat, and winked. "I brought the pot over here. I figured this is at least a two-cup morning."

Audra sat down on the stool, and lifted her long hair up and back in both hands, to let it tumble down behind her, and waited for her aunt to fill her cup before gratefully picking it up, and deeply breathing in its steamy aroma.

Aunt Celeste let her have a few sips before trying to engage her in any dialog. When she did finally begin, her words alone were enough to wake Audra up, and command her full attention.

"I spoke with Martin Satterfield yesterday."

Audra provided her with a blank stare, then decided that she really did hear her aunt correctly. "I didn't know that was allowed," she mumbled dryly.

Aunt Celeste wrinkled her forehead, wondering what she meant, and Audra smiled down into her coffee.

"I mean, I didn't realize that Martin Satterfield allows people to just speak with him. Not without him pointing his scepter at you."

Aunt Celeste sighed, and reached over to tousle her niece's hair. "Be nice," she said, repeating what she often said when Audra was prone to be critical of the controversial man.

Audra twisted her lovely face into a comical parody of rebellion, then continued to let the coffee work its magic.

Her aunt studied her tall, willowy niece with approval, grateful that, unlike Darlene Satterfield or other young ladies in their community, she wasn't overly caught up in her looks. This only added to Audra's natural beauty, and Aunt Celeste was as proud of her as if she'd been her own daughter.

She caught Audra's quirky, sideways attempt at giving her the stink eye, and laughed.

"Is the coast clear?" she teased.

Audra set the coffee cup down, and fixed her aunt with her version of a sleepy stare. "For now. But watch your step, lady."

Aunt Celeste displayed a non-threatening fist and made her grin, then hesitated a moment more before plunging in.

"Calvin Moore, and his wife listed their home with me. You remember them?"

"Don't they have something to do with the funeral home?" Audra was trying to remember.

"Indirectly. They own the monument company next door to the funeral home."

Audra couldn't imagine what that had to do with Martin Satterfield, but tried not to interrupt.

"I went there yesterday to have them sign the papers to activate the listing, and Martin was there," Aunt Celeste said. "He was arranging for a headstone for Izzy."

"I didn't try to engage him, or offer condolences on his housekeeper's passing, because Martin has no patience for that sort of thing, I've noticed."

"Or anything else," Audra muttered, reaching for her cup again. She caught her aunt's expression. "Okay, I'm sorry, go ahead."

Aunt Celeste decided that she needed that second cup of coffee, and poured it before continuing.

"As I said, I didn't try to engage him, but when I was leaving, he stopped me."

She turned to look intently at her niece. "Now, this is where I'm gonna ask you to hang in there with me, and at least hear me out."

Audra drew her brows in confusion, but silently nodded.

"Okay, I'm just gonna blurt out the bottom line, but don't overreact. Just let me finish, that's all I ask."

A weird sensation began to creep over Audra, and she somehow sensed what was coming, but she dutifully waited without comment.

"Martin wants you to work for him."

"No."

There, conversation over. Audra prepared to go get dressed, and her aunt stopped her.

"Now, Audra, you sit back down and wait! You said you'd hear me out!"

"Aunt Celeste, I love you like I loved my own mother, but I am not going to work for Edward Rochester!" she stated flatly, referencing the brooding character from *Jane Eyre*.

"You don't even know him!" her aunt protested. "You've never said one word to him."

"I don't plan to say any more than that, either," her niece said emphatically. "Let him scowl, and growl at somebody else!"

"Audra." The look Aunt Celeste gave her was so filled with disappointment, that Audra's heart convicted her. She sighed heavily, and sat back down.

"Alright, I'll listen first, and then say no," she muttered.

Her aunt studied her despondently for a moment, before she decided to try again.

"It uses your skills as a designer," she began. "He wants some things removed from the house, and he'd like someone to replace them with more appropriate, but insignificant elements, and not bother him about sentimental attachments."

"He wants a dumpster, then," Audra said blandly. She looked up at her aunt suspiciously.

"That's what this is, isn't it? He wants his dead wife's things removed from the house!" She shook her head, and leaned back, crossing her arms. "Why can't he do that, himself? *He* certainly has no sentimental attachments!"

"Listen to me," her aunt interrupted, a bit of impatience becoming hard to curb. "We're Christians, you and I, but from what his mother confided to me, Martin is not.

"The only hope he has of ever realizing a need for God in his life, is if he sees God in the lives of people around him. He's certainly not open to preaching."

"What about all those mothers, and all their daughters who want to audition as Darlene Satterfield's replacement?" Audra asked, with a touch of sarcasm. "They're Christians, too. Can't he see God in their lives?"

Aunt Celeste looked sternly at her niece. "Did you talk like that, when you joined your dad on the mission field?"

Audra looked down, and made no reply. She knew she deserved that.

"Listen to me, honey," her aunt urged, reaching over to take her hand. "I know you don't like Martin, but he has had nothing but grief for many years now, and Izzy's passing would have been devastating to him.

"I know, to you, he doesn't seem capable of loving anyone, but you're wrong. I happen to know how he felt about his parents, and the way he felt about Izzy was maybe the last source of human emotion that man had left in him.

"Regardless of how he conducts himself, Audra, I believe he feels things deeply, and right now that feeling is pain. Layer that with the fact that he's being harassed by the police over the death of his wife, and surely you can scrounge up at least a strain of compassion!"

"You know, you've listed everyone he loved, except his late wife, Aunt C."

Audra studied the countertop for a long moment, before looking up to meet her aunt's eyes.

"Doesn't that make you wonder? Are you sure that he doesn't *deserve* to be harassed by the police?" she asked quietly.

Aunt Celeste looked stunned. "Honey, why would you ask such a thing?"

Audra stopped herself just before blurting out what she knew about Darlene Satterfield and instead, tried another tactic.

"I know you said you didn't believe he could have ever killed his wife, Aunt C, but what if he did? Do you really want me to be alone in that house with him? What if I make him angry? I bet it wouldn't take much," she added, dismally.

"Audra, are you really afraid of Martin Satterfield, or is this just an excuse to get out of working for him?"

Aunt Celeste's brown eyes were flashing with displeasure. "Be honest with me."

"No, Aunt C, I'm not afraid of him," she sighed. "I just don't understand why he can't hire a professional designer, instead of asking if your niece could help.

"And why would he specifically ask for your niece? He could tell, when they came to church, that I didn't like him, and he didn't like me either. I'm pretty sure he didn't forget that."

"He didn't ask for you. He asked if I could recommend someone, and I told him that you were more than qualified," her aunt confessed. "And before you say whatever that is on your face, I'm not sorry I did.

"You are a very talented woman, Audra, and if you can add Hawthorn Manor to your growing resume, your future as a designer is guaranteed. Now, you know that's true, despite how you feel about it!"

"I'm not sure it's worth it," she retorted, before laying her hand on her aunt's and looking at her fondly.

"Aunt C, I know you did it for me, and I appreciate it, I do. But, I'll be honest with you. I'm not sure I'd last one day at Hawthorn Manor. Martin Satterfield can be counted on to be insufferable, and I don't think I have the patience for that. I'd probably tell him to drop dead!

"Okay," she hurried to correct herself, "bad choice of words, but you get what I mean."

Aunt Celeste tried not to react to her niece's outburst, but she couldn't help herself, and her niece smiled softly.

"I wouldn't really say that to him, Aunt C," she promised. "At least, I don't think I would."

"I certainly hope not," Aunt Celeste said, widening her eyes dramatically, "or you may just end up in that dumpster!"

She let out a hearty laugh at Audra's exaggerated response, and wrapped her up in a bear hug. "Kidding! I'm kidding!"

Audra reluctantly tarried on the wide, sweeping veranda, that bordered the ground level of Hawthorn Manor, and took in a few deep breaths, still not ready to commit to working here, even though she'd finally relented, and told her aunt that she would.

She decided that a few moments of silent prayer might be in order, and asked God to give her the patience to keep from reacting to any of Martin Satterfield's hostility, but she knew she wasn't praying in faith, and made herself ring the bell, if for no other reason than to put this day behind her.

She stood studying the door absently, and wondered why Martin Satterfield hadn't just taken care of throwing all of his late wife's things out himself, imagining that if he'd stopped to realize what a great amount of pleasure it would surely have given him, he most certainly would have done so, with sadistic glee.

She pulled her mouth into an annoyed grimace. There was no sound from inside to indicate that anyone was approaching to answer.

Audra briefly considered just leaving, since that was the case, and telling Aunt Celeste that no one appeared to be home, and that she'd just assumed he had changed his mind, but at least she'd tried.

Audra smiled to herself, as she admitted that her aunt would simply fix her with a discerning eye, and ask her how hard she had tried.

After another moment of being certain that her ring was either being ignored or hadn't been heard, she breathed a sigh of both impatience and surrender, and tried a second time.

"The doorbell doesn't work."

A man's deep, quiet voice startled her, but she managed to stop herself from jumping, and slowly turned to find Martin Satterfield standing behind her, looking down at her with neither welcome nor objection in his disturbing eyes.

Normally, Audra wouldn't have been able to hide her reaction, when encountering a man dressed as he was, in a loose fitting, linen tunic shirt and a thin over shirt that seemed almost medieval in style, but Aunt Celeste had said that he had spent quite a lot of time in Europe, so she supposed that he had grown accustomed to dressing for comfort or, more than likely, simply as he pleased. She reluctantly admitted to herself that it suited him, which gave her a displeased expression.

The master of Hawthorn Manor wondered if Audra's steady gaze meant that she simply didn't believe him.

"You may try it a third time if you like, but it is unlikely to work any better for you than it does for anyone else. It is, for all intents and purposes, broken."

"That surprises me," she returned evenly.

"Why is that?" He sounded mildly amused. "The house is old, or haven't you heard? Historical," he added, with a touch of irony. "Things break."

"Things get repaired," she countered, before being able to stop herself. She decided not to apologize, however. She said what she said. It was out there.

He raised one brow, and reached past her to open the door, gesturing her inside with a slight motion of his hand.

"It's not high on my list of priorities," he informed her, closing the door behind them, and waiting for her to look around the large entryway, as most people who visited Hawthorn Manor did.

She did glance briefly about her, but turned her defiant inspection back to him.

"You want to get this over with," she stated simply.

"Yes." He was fine with admitting it.

He narrowed his eyes, and remembered her after a long, unsettling moment.

"You used to attend your aunt's church," he said musingly. "You used to glare at me, and then roll your eyes."

She saw no point in denying it. "Did I? Then you must have deserved it."

"I expect I did," he returned smoothly, leading the way into the library, and indicating a chair before seating himself behind his desk. He reached for his pipe, but refrained, and glanced up at her, when he heard her say that she didn't mind if he smoked.

The suggestion of a smile settled around his mouth. "This is my home, Miss Campbell," he reminded her. "Therefore, it would matter little to me if you minded, or not."

She didn't flinch, but looked at him as intently as he was looking at her. "You're not the only one who wants to get this over with."

"Is that a fact?"

He leaned back in his chair, and regarded her with interest. "My reasons for wishing it to be so are my own, but please elaborate, Miss Campbell, on why it is that you also desire to, as you say, get this over with?"

She shrugged, and even though her green eyes had begun to sparkle with temper, she simply said, "Because I like myself."

"I see," he returned, looking down at some papers in front of him, and allowing his smile to linger. "Are you suggesting that the longer you are in my home, the less likely you are to like yourself?"

When she made no reply, he offered her another alternative. "Or could it be that the longer you are in my home, the less likely you are to like me?"

"I already don't like you," she informed him.

"Ah," he said softly. "Christian charity rears its reluctant head because here you are, despite your antipathy."

"It's not charity, it's a job," she corrected him, unable to completely keep the irritation she felt out of her tone. "Or was my aunt mistaken? Because, Mr. Satterfield, I didn't come for charitable reasons. There's no casserole out in my car."

He suppressed an abrupt response that came immediately to his lips, but that would have certainly sent the beautiful, but angry Audra Campbell storming out of his house. Instead, he simply nodded, and pushed the paperwork in front of him over to her side of the desk.

When she continued to glare at him angrily, he touched his fingertips together, and settled back in his chair, viewing her expression with cool detachment. "Yes, that's the one. That's the look I remember."

She snatched up the papers, and began skimming through them while he steadily watched her.

"Are you waiting for me to sign this?" she finally asked, putting the papers back down on the edge of the desk.

"It is, as you say, a job. In the interest of not confusing your paid assistance with charity, coming to an official agreement is advisable. Do you not concur?"

"In theory."

"If there are conditions or requirements that you find unacceptable, please indicate them."

He laid a pen on top of the papers, and waited while she sized him up to determine if he was mocking her. He indicated with a slight wave of his hand that he expected her to make her objections known.

She grabbed the pen, and began to furiously write something that was obviously much more than a mere signature. When she was done, she pushed the papers back over to him.

He picked them up, and read her added condition, as a wry grin brought an unexpected lightness to his otherwise dark countenance. *"Mr. Satterfield will remember that Miss Campbell is not a servant, and will not be spoken to, or reprimanded as if she were."*

He lifted his challenging blue eyes to hers, and held out his hand for the pen.

Audra pushed it back to him, and he initialed the addendum, returning it for her endorsement.

When they had reached a signed agreement, he placed the contract in a drawer, and stood, as an obvious indication that she should do likewise.

"It would appear that we have achieved a mutually accepted accord, or perhaps more fittingly in our case, a tenuous, but successful peace treaty."

"That remains to be seen," Audra muttered under her breath, and he concealed a look of amusement.

"Will you require a tour of the house today, Miss Campbell, or will you be content to wait until your employment begins tomorrow?"

He led the way back into the main entry, the fact that he lingered by the front door suggesting what her response to the options he offered should be.

She didn't wait for him to open the door for her, but took matters into her own hands, and did little more than fling a wave in his general direction, as she wasted no time in starting her car, and driving through the gates, and away from Hawthorn Manor.

Martin stood watching her through the leaded glass of the door's sidelights and turned, after she drove away, surprised but impressed by her taste in vehicles.

He allowed a thoughtful expression to rest on his handsome face, recalling today's angry flash of green eyes that was so reminiscent of the way he remembered her glaring at him at church. He stood reflecting, recollecting her frequent, silent displays of vivid disapproval.

He had been compelled to return fire, and had been quietly disappointed when she had apparently refused to be his target, and had removed herself from harm's way by sitting elsewhere.

"Maybe I did deserve it," he admitted to himself, with a half-hearted smile of regret.

Chapter Eight

Aunt Celeste looked up from her desk in wonder, and laid the papers she'd been shuffling over to one side.

She hadn't expected Audra to stop by her office, especially this early in the day, and immediately suspected that she had more than likely stomped out of Hawthorn Manor, after being unable to keep from entering into combat with its difficult, and challenging owner. She witnessed her niece's fed up expression with disappointment.

"You couldn't even last the day with him, Audra?"

"I haven't actually begun, yet. I was only there for him to tell me exactly what my duties are, and find out how he wants the east wing to change. Although, why he couldn't have told me all that yesterday remains a mystery," she muttered, dumping herself into the nearest chair, and tossing her hair over the back of it with a scowl.

"I drove out there for pretty much no reason."

She pushed a few loose strands back off her forehead, and leveled her eyes at her aunt solemnly. "I guess you're probably pretty busy."

"I'm never busier than I want to be," she replied, leaning back in her seat, and examining Audra more closely. "So, that's two days in a row at Hawthorn. You still work for him, then."

"You sound relieved," Audra pointed out, with a tired stretch and smile.

"Well, I am, so I won't deny it," Aunt Celeste admitted. "But you don't look so thrilled."

"I just want to get it over with," she sighed.

That was a phrase Celeste Campbell had heard often from her niece lately, and she smiled down at her desk when she heard it, yet again.

"That's hardly the mindset for you to dive in with."

Audra slumped down in the office chair, and lifted one leg over the arm of it, with no regard for either good posture or feminine etiquette.

"Is that what you wore?" Aunt Celeste asked, lifting her brows in wonder.

"What's wrong with it?" Audra glanced down at her denim overalls and tank top, and moved her right high-top sneaker up and down carelessly.

"Nothing, I suppose, if you were planning to paint or burn trash," she returned. "I mean, it's cute, honey. You could walk around in an old whiskey barrel, and still be cute. But I guess I'm just surprised. I suspect that yours are the first pair of overalls to ever cross the threshold of Hawthorn Manor."

Audra rippled out a laugh, and her aunt responded with a shake of her head, and a grin.

"Maybe that's why the illustrious Lord Satterfield looked at me so oddly," she speculated. "Maybe he's never seen overalls before."

Aunt Celeste could only imagine Martin's reaction to opening the door, and being confronted with the startling vision of her beautiful, but hostile niece, casually clad in the latest thing in garage wear.

"I expect you took his breath away," she insisted, and Audra grimaced.

"Would that it were true," she retorted. "Then he wouldn't be breathing *my* air."

"Stop it," her aunt gently scolded. "So, did you get to tour the house, then?"

"If you can call it that," she grumbled. "Rooms were indicated. Like this." She flipped her fingers toward nothing in particular. "I wasn't actually invited into any of them. I don't know how Martin Satterfield makes all his money, but it isn't by being a tour guide."

"It stems from old money of course, as many inherited fortunes do, but I seem to remember Maureen telling me once that Martin is a very shrewd investor, so I would imagine he's been able to augment his worth quite well. He's not impetuous, so I would think any investment choices he's made have been well thought out."

"Then I don't feel bad for telling him that I wasn't there for charitable reasons," Audra replied.

Aunt Celeste drew in a breath, and held it for a quick minute. "Audra, don't deliberately provoke Martin."

"Why not? I thought you said he would never threaten a woman." She looked at her from her relaxed position through half-closed eyes.

"Anyway, I wasn't trying to pick a fight. I just wanted to make sure he understood. He should be able to handle a little honesty."

"What else did you tell him?" her aunt asked, not sure if she really wanted to know.

"I told him that I didn't have a casserole in my car."

Her aunt reacted to her confession by laughing, in spite of her resolve not to. "Oh, honey, you did not!"

Audra leaned her head back, and grinned up at the ceiling. "Actually, that wasn't today. That was yesterday."

"So you started out on day one, laying down the law to Martin Satterfield?" Aunt Celeste didn't know whether to be dismayed or entertained.

"He started it," she replied. "Anyway, he was just annoyed, because I told him I didn't like him." She raised her arms up over her head, and pulled them into a stress-relieving stretch, while her aunt dropped her mouth open, and stared.

"Audra, you did not just come out, and tell him that!"

"I just thought he should know." She shrugged, and absently inspected a nail. Something flitted across her mind, and a naughty grin crept slowly across her pretty face.

"Guess who stopped by, today?" Audra challenged, an undisguised mischief dancing in her eyes. Without waiting for her aunt to participate, she supplied the answer herself.

"Torey Jordan."

"Now, you're just making stuff up!" Aunt Celeste accused. "Sit up in that chair, and look me in the eyes, and say that again!"

Audra pulled herself up straight, and leaned forward to say it again. "Torey Jordan!"

"What in the world for?" Aunt Celeste frowned. "Has that girl lost her mind?"

"I say they've *all* lost their minds, but who cares what I think?" Audra retorted with a careless wave.

"Did she see you there?" Aunt Celeste demanded, and Audra supplied the customary shrug.

"She saw my car. Kinda hard to hide it, although the day I'm expected to do that, is the day I quit."

"What happened? Did she talk to Martin?" Aunt Celeste paused to put on a face of disapproval. "By the way, you sure know how to bury the lead, young lady!"

Audra laughed. "I did hear some sort of muffled conversation, but I was up in the east hall, and I decided that I probably shouldn't come sit on the stairs and listen."

Her aunt let her know with just a look that she wasn't buying any of that, and Audra came clean.

"Okay, well, I did decide I shouldn't listen, but I might have listened anyway."

She ran a hand through her hair, and folded her arms, slowly smiling at nothing in particular.

"Torey Jordan *did* come bearing a casserole."

"No, she did not!"

"Yes, she did, too!"

Aunt Celeste was trying to decide if Audra was telling the truth, or just messing with her.

"Seriously, Audra."

"Seriously, Aunt C."

She was incredulous. "How did Martin respond to that? Was he rude?"

"Is the sky high?" Audra countered sarcastically.

"What did he say to her?"

"Well, I admit that his first remark wasn't that bad. He just thanked her, but declined it. But then, Torey started doing that whole little girl voice, eyelash batting thing, and that's when the sky got high."

"Did he yell at her?" her aunt wondered, still not sure if she believed any of this.

"No," Audra said simply. "He doesn't yell, I'll give him that. But his mouth is like a gun with a silencer, and the whole time he's staring at you, he's loading his words, and aiming them at you. He told Torey that he didn't appreciate anyone coming to Hawthorn without being invited, or having scheduled an appointment, and then he just shut the door, and walked off."

Audra pulled one foot up, and inspected the bottom of her sneaker, then began trying to dig a bit of gravel out of the treads with her fingernail.

"Actually, I do think shutting the door in her face was a little over the top. I mean, all she wanted to do was give the man a casserole, for crying out loud."

"What if Martin thinks you're the one who put her up to it?" Aunt Celeste demanded.

"Why should he think that?" She frowned at her shoe.

"Possibly because of your cute little remark on your first day there, about *you* not bringing him one."

Aunt Celeste watched the effect her words had on her niece, as she considered the fact that her employer might just connect those two events, and she couldn't resist laughing at her.

Audra rolled her eyes, and pushed herself up out of the chair, strolling over to glance out the window at the traffic.

She seemed to seriously be considering the possibility that Martin Satterfield might actually credit the arrival of any future casseroles to her influence. The thought both amused and annoyed her.

Aunt Celeste broke into her reverie. "He didn't actually rent a dumpster, did he?"

"He did," Audra admitted, "so maybe I'd better dial it back on the whole casserole thing."

"I think that might be wise," her aunt agreed.

Her niece smiled out the window, as she thought about Martin Satterfield's muttered expression, when he realized that some girl was standing outside his door with a casserole.

She decided that it was just possible that Aunt Celeste might not be too far off the mark, and that the master of Hawthorn Manor placed the blame for Torey Jordan's arrival squarely on her.

A little giggle escaped her lips, and Aunt Celeste just smiled down at her paperwork and shook her head.

It had been a long day. Martin Satterfield rose from his desk, and indulged in a stretch, before reaching for his pipe bag, and moving into the den to put his feet up. He applied himself to preparing his pipe, and actually lighting it, before allowing himself to relax, and give his thoughts free range.

Unfortunately for him, free range meant all thoughts, not just pleasant ones. His first reflection took him back to earlier in the day when that foolish Jordan girl showed up at his door with a casserole in her arms, and a gush of goodwill that tested his patience.

He had tried to simply thank her and decline to accept her offering, but she had proceeded to pout, perhaps thinking he might consider it cute. This annoyed him to the point of advising her that he did not appreciate callers who showed up unannounced, then quietly closing the door, and walking away, but not before noticing the unmistakable, and hasty withdrawal of a sneakered foot in the stairwell.

It was no surprise to him that his thoughts would inevitably gather where they seemed to camp out lately against his will, as Audra Campbell's striking, but combative eyes came to his mind.

Martin couldn't truthfully declare her to be petulant or even antagonistic, but she seemed to react, rather than respond to him.

Of course, the first day she came to Hawthorn she told him very clearly that she didn't like him. This was something that shouldn't have mattered at all to Martin, but it still managed to rankle him.

It seemed that it took very little at all to cause her to level those green eyes of hers directly at him, and say more in just a look, regardless of its brevity, than she would actually speak throughout an entire day.

It was very early on in the renovation of the east wing, so much of her time was currently spent separating what could be thrown into the dumpster, and what could be sent to charity. Martin had no indication yet of what her taste in design might be, but Celeste Campbell had assured him that her niece would remain committed to the character of Hawthorn Manor.

Martin frowned impatiently, and wondered if Audra Campbell would consider the character of Hawthorn Manor to be himself.

He thought about the way the east wing once looked when his parents were still living, and before Darlene Parks had managed to not only take the Satterfield name, but half of Hawthorn, if using the word "take" loosely meant declaring an entire wing to be her own living quarters, and immediately removing pieces that had been in the Satterfield family for decades, and replacing them with sleek, ugly, chrome and plastic creations that could hardly be taken seriously.

This was all done without his being present, and certainly without his permission, and all with no regard for Izzy's distress, and feeble protests.

Martin was determined to have it all dumped in a field, pour fuel on it, and set it ablaze, but he knew that the loud, shrill hysterics Darlene could be counted on to engage in, would be yet something else to upset Izzy so he let it be, since he had no intention of ever approaching the east wing for any reason.

He breathed a sigh of remorse and wished, as he had done so many times before, that he'd never met Darlene Parks, let alone married her.

She had just seemed to materialize, almost immediately after the deaths of his parents, and their chauffeur. All were killed when attempting to drive in what began as rain, but quickly turned to sleet.

Aware that the weather was changing, Martin's parents had decided to try to make it back to Hawthorn, before things deteriorated too quickly, rather than be trapped in their mountain cabin for an indeterminate amount of time, and had telephoned to let Izzy know to expect them.

The winding mountain roads had become treacherous, and the vehicle skid in a curve, and left the road, then plowed down a steep ravine, flipping and crashing into several trees.

Martin was in Europe when he received the news of his parent's sudden demise, and returned at once to be with Izzy.

He had been the Satterfield's only descendant, and was left alone to lay them to rest, to comfort a heartbroken, and shocked Isabelle Draper, and to deal with the tedious, and dull matters of settling the estate.

Darlene Parks had managed to make his acquaintance at a board meeting that she attended with a member who was also her employer, something Martin had found highly unusual, but hadn't cared enough about to question.

Of course now, as he sat mulling over so many things alone in his quiet den, he realized that he should have suspected right away what he later learned. Darlene didn't just accompany her employer to board meetings; she managed to stay close by at his disposal for any number of reasons, including those of a risqué nature.

After meeting the Satterfield heir, she attempted to find numerous excuses to arrive at Hawthorn, claiming to need clarification on something he had stated at a meeting, or personally relaying messages that could have very easily been delivered by phone.

After a while, she no longer bothered to come up with a work-related excuse to bring with her, but would casually just stop by, professing to be concerned about the toll that the death of both his parents was taking on him, as well as the stress of having to deal with the many tedious matters of the estate.

She soon became a regular visitor to the home, and began to cleverly try to convince Martin that, as his wife, she would be an invaluable asset to him, and a great help in assisting him to manage the large estate, as well as serving as hostess for the charity events that Martin's mother had been so well known for.

She wasn't without charm, and Martin, who had begun to feel the depressing effects of being the lone Satterfield, with nothing remaining around him, but a massive, empty house, miles of silent fields, and meadows, and the graves of all those who had left him, began to consider her proposition.

He made it clear that he didn't love her, and had no desire for intimacy with her, reminding her that what she was suggesting was only for the sake of social obligations and appearances, and for helping him deal with estate matters.

She hadn't wasted his time with any false claim to love him either so, in Martin's mind, as long as Darlene Parks was fine abiding by the structure of her own proposal, and was agreeable to marrying a man as nothing more than a practical arrangement in order to live at the estate, preside over social functions, and provide clerical assistance, he saw no harm in marrying her. He did warn her that if she continued to have relations with other men indiscreetly, or ever brought them onto Satterfield property, she would be leaving immediately.

Darlene wasted no time in stepping into the role as mistress of Hawthorn Manor, and would actively seek an invitation to any event that would allow her to be seen in that position.

Because Martin's quarters were in the west wing of the home, she cited the lack of various amenities in that part of the house, and immediately took over the entire east wing, discarding items that would have been precious to Martin's mother, and replacing them with shocking, gaudy displays of modernism.

Any charm that the woman had formerly exhibited, was immediately dispensed with after they were married. Izzy would no longer come to the east wing for any reason, unless she was ordered to appear, and Darlene seemed to enjoy making life difficult for the frail, elderly, petite woman.

Martin had been unaware of her clandestine visitors, particularly Phillip March, one of his wife's many male friends, as well as her investment banker.

When he'd begun to suspect, he waited to confront her, knowing that Izzy would have been the one Darlene took her anger out on. He could also see that Izzy was approaching the end of life, and he didn't want her remaining days to be ruined by Darlene's vindictive intimidation. He determined to restrain himself from taking action against Darlene, until after the time of Izzy's passing, vowing to deal with things then.

Martin had begun keeping frequent company with friends from his university days who had stayed in close contact with him, and who sought to include him in their hunting and backpacking trips.

He was with those friends when Darlene Satterfield was determined to have fallen down the stairs and died, and the only regret he had was that Izzy had been the one to discover his late wife's body, and to become overwhelmed with the immediate aftermath.

Martin sometimes wished he was a drinker so that he could shut his mind off, and stop all these rogue thoughts from robbing him of any chance of a peaceful evening, but he had never developed that habit, to the pride and relief of his Christian parents.

He'd never felt he could commit to a belief system he didn't understand, but he did purpose to honor them by embracing their code of moral ethics, and never giving them a reason to be ashamed of him.

His attending church with his attention-seeking wife was primarily to keep her from creating one of her ugly scenes that would invariably be visited upon Izzy in some manner, but he had also gone as a personal, unspoken tribute to his wonderful parents, that he had loved with all his heart.

Of course, as his thoughts circled back to church, the ever provoking and unfathomable Audra Campbell loomed again to take his mind captive.

Martin sighed in defeat, and climbed the stairs to go to bed, in the remote chance that sleep might bring him some relief.

Chapter Nine

Martin leaned against the doorframe of the east wing suite that his late wife had occupied, and wordlessly watched Audra kneeling, and methodically folding a sweater, before she placed it in the carton with other similar items.

She felt his eyes on her, and paused to look directly at him with the manifestation of alarm on her face.

"You seem to be waiting for me to explain my presence," he observed.

"You're blocking my exit," she pointed out quietly.

"Do I make you feel the need for an exit?"

"Please move," she asked, then bit her lip, waiting for him to oblige her.

He made an impatient gesture. "This room is vast, and you're telling me that you're feeling crowded, just because I'm standing here?"

Audra closed her eyes, and took in a deep breath.

"Please."

Something disagreeable flashed across his face. "Are you afraid of me, Miss Campbell?"

She simply shook her head, her eyes still closed.

Martin scowled at her, then began to sense an undercurrent of urgency in her manner. He stood in mute contemplation.

"Cleithrophobia, if memory serves. The fear of being trapped," he added, drawing from something he'd read during his university years.

He drew his brow, trying to determine if she was being authentic, or simply difficult.

"Do you have cleithrophobic tendencies?"

"Yes," she admitted, becoming embarrassed. "Please come in or out, but don't stand, blocking the doorway."

"Perhaps, you should have added demands of that sort to our contract," he quipped, relaxing his stance, but remaining where he was.

Martin continued to study her, and noted the color had drained from her cheeks. He began to realize that her breathing had become shallow and accelerated, then frowned and came into the room, lowering himself to kneel beside her, and assess her more closely.

"Audra..." It was the first time he'd failed to call her Miss Campbell. He said her name with a look of concern in his eyes.

"Are you indeed cleithrophobic?"

She nodded, relieved that he had ceased to obstruct her avenue of escape, and took in a deep breath, but said nothing and reached for another sweater to begin folding.

Martin lifted it out of her hands, and waited for her to look at him.

"I'm sorry," he offered simply. "Of course, I didn't know, but now that I do, I'll try not to create a situation that triggers this issue again."

She remained silent, but held out her hand for the sweater, looking away from him.

He handed the sweater back to her, and stood to his feet, letting his eyes graze her with displeasure, seeming to react to the fact that she had rebuffed his apology.

"I realize that I'm an odious and hateful creature, and I expect that will never change, but I'm not the devil, Miss Campbell."

He left as quietly as he had come, and Audra sat staring after him, confused by Martin Satterfield's momentary departure from his typical hostile and intimidating manner.

For a fleeting moment he had appeared to be sympathetic, but Audra had been unable to respond. She now suspected that this must have been the reason for his terse remark, as he was leaving.

Nothing in their contract required that she disclose any personal details about herself, and she hadn't felt the need to be forthcoming about her strange, and irrational fear of being in a situation where she was denied any access to leave.

Aunt Celeste was well aware of Audra's problem, and had sat down with her after a bad reaction, and revealed to her that when she was a small toddler, she had wandered into her parent's garage where they had left the trunk of the car open, intending to come back, and remove the rest of their luggage.

Audra had climbed into the trunk, and saw a strap hanging and had pulled it, bringing the trunk lid down to latch.

By the time she had eventually been found in the trunk, she had been crying and screaming for so long, that she'd made herself sick.

Aunt Celeste had hoped that if Audra understood the catalyst behind her fear, it might help her cope with it, and Audra thought it had. She had even become able to use elevators, and believed she was fine. This was the first episode in many years.

She asked herself if she would have been so upset today, if it had been Aunt Celeste standing in the doorway, and was forced to acknowledge that she wouldn't have been.

She knew her panic was because it was Martin Satterfield who stood between her and safety.

Audra remembered Aunt Celeste asking her if she was afraid of him, and she had been quick to say no, but now she found herself unsure.

She laid the sweater back down on the pile, and wrestled with the desire to find him and apologize, but she couldn't bring herself to do it.

She lifted herself up from the floor, and walked over to one of the large windows, and let her eyes rest on the beauty of the grounds, making an attempt to bring her rampant emotions back to some kind of calm state. She felt foolish, and that, in turn, made her irritable.

"Miss Campbell."

She turned around to find Martin Satterfield not blocking the door, but standing in the middle of the room with his arms crossed, and a somber expression in his eyes.

"I won't hold you to our contract, if you believe yourself to be unable to fulfill your duties at Hawthorn."

She covered her surprise, and steadied herself.

"Did you not say that you wouldn't create any triggers? If you meant it, then that's the only issue I have."

"Is it?" he probed. "I sense that you are still troubled, Miss Campbell. I asked you if you were afraid of me. You shook your head, but that was hardly a response. You certainly didn't look me in the eyes, and answer me."

Audra drew in a slow breath, but made no effort to reply to him, one way or another. Instead, she simply fixed her eyes on him in the manner that Martin had begun to interpret as a challenge.

He came nearer, approaching the window to share her view of the grounds, and they both stood in mutual silence before he spoke again softly, as if he were thinking out loud.

"A question hangs in the air between us."

Martin turned to look down at her intently. "Why will you not ask this question?"

Audra pressed her lips together and hesitated.

"If I do, will you tell me the truth?" she inquired, trying to read him despite his gaze making it difficult.

"Not only am I not the devil, Miss Campbell, I am not a liar." He waited.

She wished that she were able to deny having questions, but suddenly she had to know.

"Was your wife's death an accident?"

"It was not."

He stood noting her reaction, surprised that his response didn't cause her to immediately move away from him.

Something prodded him to discover exactly what *would* cause her to move away from him, and he stepped closer, and looked down into her eyes provocatively.

"If her death was deliberate, you wonder, what was the manner of her demise?"

He watched her for any sign of apprehension, but she gave him nothing. Instead, she simply returned his gaze. He smiled to himself and persisted.

"Was she perhaps hurled down the stairs, in a moment of tempestuous rage? Was she the victim of a deliberate, precisely delivered blow?"

Martin slowly raised his hands, and cradled her face gently, then trailed his fingers down to wrap them loosely around her throat, resting his thumbs just beneath her chin.

"Or perhaps, her vulnerable neck was snapped like a communion wafer."

He continued to silently regard her, before gradually removing his hands, and allowing a strange sort of reluctant approval to rest on his face.

"You intrigue me, Miss Campbell. You become stricken with terror when a potential murderer lingers in the doorway, but you stand as motionless, and as serene as a sculpted goddess when he caresses your lovely neck with his bare hands."

Audra remained impassive, and he relented in his mildly sadistic taunt, returning to the window to survey the hills and valleys of his estate with little appreciation.

After a moment, he turned and considered her with renewed interest.

"Would you like for your question to be the first of three? I'm feeling generous."

A trace of amusement flickered in Martin's eyes, as he saw her struggle with his offer.

"Don't be afraid. I will resist the temptation to engage in any further reenactments of the crime."

His smile was unexpected, and Audra was taken aback by the fleeting transformation, as his austere face softened.

"It's quite alright, Miss Campbell," he assured her. "I offered, you didn't ask."

She breathed in deeply, and exhaled with a sigh.

"I suppose question number two would have to be the obvious one."

"It seems a difficult one for you to ask. You should make the acquaintance of Detective Vance. He can instruct you on the many, obnoxious ways to ask me if I killed my late wife."

"You told him no."

She waited for his confirmation.

"I told him no."

He looked away from her, and aimlessly observed the grounds below them.

"Then, a third question is unnecessary," she said.

"What would it have been?" he wondered, smiling faintly as he continued letting his eyes travel across the meadows of Hawthorn Manor.

"Your answer would have had to be yes, to prompt a third question," she replied, glancing up at him.

He laughed quietly. "Pretend that I answered yes. My curiosity knows no bounds."

"I would have asked why," she admitted, eliciting another soft bit of laughter.

"What reason would be acceptable?" he demanded in a light tone, seeming to enjoy their dialog.

She appeared to have lost her nerve, and he glanced over at her, wondering what made her hesitate.

"I asked what reason would be acceptable," he reminded, abandoning the expansive view the window afforded, and training his eyes on hers instead.

She returned his scrutiny, but offered no response.

"You don't like that question. Very well, we'll leave it, for now. I'll ask a different one."

She managed to stop herself from looking away from him, and prepared to hear it.

"Why do you hate me?" he asked, again crossing his arms, and watching her face carefully.

"Why do you think I hate you?" she countered.

"Oh, come now, Miss Campbell. That wasn't love in your eyes, when you used to glare at me in church," he said, with a tinge of sarcasm. "You admitted the day I hired you that you don't like me. How did I earn such loathing?"

"I suggest that you have a gift for reading into things what you want them to mean," she said stiffly, causing him to clench the muscles around his mouth, and adopt a belligerent stance.

"Enough! I'm not a fool, Miss Campbell, and you're not as naive as you would have me believe! I ask again, how have I managed to deserve your apparent disgust?"

He lifted a warning finger to her lips, not allowing her to insult him by continuing to deny what was clearly evident.

"I insist on honesty!" Anger churned in his eyes. "You obviously hate me, and I demand to know why!"

"Because if *I* knew, then *you* had to know, and you just sat there beside her, every Sunday, and let that woman make a fool out of you!"

Audra had no intention of blurting out her words, but she heard them come out, and stepped back with wide eyes, lifting her hands to cover her mouth.

He became immobile, with only the clenching of his jaw, and the whiteness around his firm mouth indicating any emotion, at all.

The tension between them could be felt, and the silence all around them began to reverberate.

"Why did you make me tell you?" she whispered, tears beginning to threaten. "I didn't want to say that to you."

He continued to pelt her with his disturbing, penetrating eyes, but made no move to approach her, having not missed the way she had just taken a step backward away from him.

"What is it you think you know?" he finally asked in a tight, controlled manner.

When she wouldn't answer him, he dispensed with catering to her reservations, and moved to close the gap between them, leaving only inches of demarcation.

"If you believe yourself to know something about my late wife, please don't keep me in suspense. Do me the courtesy of not mucking about with ambiguity, and just say it!"

Audra resented the position he was putting her in. "Why do you force me to say things that make you angry?"

"Is it my anger you hope to avoid?" he demanded. "Why, Miss Campbell? Do you dread my response?"

He caught her by the arm, when she made an effort to walk away from him.

"You say that you are not afraid of me, but you lie! I see it in your eyes. I told you that my answer, as to whether or not I killed my late wife, was no, but you don't believe me.

"Very well! I don't need or desire you to believe me. And now, I ask you again. What is it you profess to know about my late wife?"

Audra looked down at his hand around her arm, then back up at his turbulent eyes, her own temper beginning to smolder and ignite.

When she attempted to jerk her arm out of his hand, it only enraged him further.

"Answer me!" he hissed, pulling her closer, and causing her to realize that, even if he were too strong for her to physically resist, she still had the ability to hurt him.

"Phillip March!"

Audra waited in agony, thinking that surely she had gone too far, and fully expected him to strike her.

Martin stiffened, then slowly released her arm, and turned his back on her. He closed his eyes, and plowed his fingers through his dark hair in frustration.

He seemed to have forgotten that anyone was in the room with him, and remained frozen in uneasy silence for a long moment.

Audra felt hot tears rush to her eyes. She certainly didn't feel like congratulating herself on having done this to him. She simply felt ashamed.

She watched him bow his head, and press his lips tightly together, and even though she knew that Martin Satterfield was a volatile and unpredictable man, she moved around to stand in front of him, a stab of pity surprising her.

"You're wrong," she said quietly. "I do believe you."

He raised his head and stared beyond her, the light from the windows illuminating a humiliating awareness in his eyes.

He stepped away from her, returning to the window, looking at absolutely nothing, and wishing that he could feel absolutely nothing.

After a long moment, he turned and stared around the room with empty eyes, that gradually began to reflect a slow, steady, sick aversion to the many cheap, repulsive trinkets and ostentatious possessions of Darlene Satterfield, and lifted a hand to indicate all of it in a brief gesture.

"Don't bother to ask me about keeping anything, including the furniture," he instructed, in a dull voice. "I want it all gone."

Audra swept her eyes around the room, seeing it the way he did, then looked back up at him with a strange compassion for him, in spite of the resentment that Martin Satterfield had so effortlessly been able to stir inside her.

"Only this room?"

"All of it!"

He made no effort to dampen the level of simmering rage in his voice.

"The entire east wing! Get it all out of here!"

He turned abruptly and left.

Chapter Ten

Audra pulled her car into a space, and glanced over at Aunt Celeste with a twist of her lips. "You know you wanna drive this car, admit it!"

She laughed. "I'd love to be seen driving it, but I'm still not clear on how to shift it, and I'm afraid I'd tear your transmission up. But, maybe I can figure it out someday."

Audra grinned, and hopped out to accompany her aunt into the grocery store. She wrestled a cart out of a tight row of other carts, then tested the wheels on it.

It passed her inspection, and she presented it to Aunt Celeste with a sweeping bow, lifting her chin, and peering at her, down her pretty nose.

"I shall allow nothing, but the finest of trolleys for the sister of my father!" she declared, with a lofty, pompous accent.

Aunt Celeste had to laugh at her preposterous dig at the upper crust, and fixed her with a knowing look. "Don't tell me, let me guess. The master of Hawthorn Manor has somehow managed to influence your perception of the privileged and powerful."

"I bet he's never pushed a shopping cart in his life," Audra said flatly. "I bet he's never even been inside a grocery store."

She stopped, observing her aunt's ironic expression.

"Wanna bet?"

Aunt Celeste nodded ahead, and Audra looked around to see that her employer had been witnessing her performance, with faint bemusement.

"What's *he* doing here?" she muttered.

"Be nice," her aunt whispered hastily, as the privileged and powerful man lifted the fingertips of one hand resting on the handle of his cart in a general greeting.

Aunt Celeste approached him with a pleased smile that he returned, as Audra remained steadfastly where she was, reasoning that someone had to stay behind, and guard the one good cart in the entire store that actually rolled, and pretended to read the fascinating label on a bag of kidney beans.

"I couldn't help but overhear your niece's entertaining observation of the elite," Martin commented lightly, and Aunt Celeste gave him a gentle laugh.

"Don't be upset with her, Martin. She wasn't referencing you by what she said. She wouldn't have made that crack about you never pushing a shopping cart, if I hadn't mentioned your name. That was just like giving a match to an arsonist, and she jumped on it.

"Audra's not mean-spirited in any way; she just likes to clown around," she informed him. "She can make me laugh, without even trying."

Martin looked surprised. He had certainly never seen any evidence to back up Celeste Campbell's claim.

"I must say, she brandishes a British accent rather well. Has she spent time there?"

"Oh, no, other than joining her father for a few years in Honduras, she's never been out of the states." Her aunt turned and looked back at her, with fondness softening her eyes. "She's just naturally funny, and has a wide range of impersonations, and I love her as if she were my own." She smiled up at him, hoping he wasn't offended.

He looked beyond her at the tall, slender, young woman, with lovely, dark hair that hung almost to her waist, and eyes that could be both irritating and mesmerizing, then indicated with a nod that Celeste Campbell should pay attention to her niece's current antics.

Audra had managed to back into an elderly woman, who was trying to make her cart turn the corner, and was now apologizing profusely, and offering to trade carts, since hers rolled so nicely.

When the small, white-haired woman seemed hesitant to accept her offer, Audra hurried to move all her items over into the good cart. In no time at all, the lady was laughing at something the beautiful girl said, and patting her on the cheek, seeming to cherish the chance encounter.

Audra watched her roll the cart down the aisle, then tested the cart she was left with, and a scowl of displeasure crossed her face, as she dragged it to one side, and sat down in the middle of the floor to figure out what was locking the wheel up.

"Okay, now that's funny, Martin, admit it!" Aunt Celeste demanded, her eyes full of laughter.

"It does have an element of comedy, I will concede that much," he said, with a soft look.

Martin had begun watching this exchange with humorous intrigue, but when the elderly woman began to remind him of his Izzy, he felt a pang of sorrow, and wished in vain that she could have known Audra.

He believed that even though this vexing, confrontational woman seemed to be bent on fostering a consistent disapproval of him, she certainly would have tried to put that same sweet, happiness on Izzy's face.

Aunt Celeste looked up at him with her smile fading, as she caught his look of regret. "Martin, are things not working out with Audra? You're probably not used to her blunt way, but she means no harm."

He seemed surprised that she would ask, and hesitated, causing a greater look of concern to cross her face.

"I wouldn't declare it to not be working out," he began cautiously. "She just takes a bit of getting used to. She does work hard," he added, glancing down at Audra's aunt. "But she seems to maintain a devoted bias against me."

He took on a somber expression. "I would assume that Audra related today's unpleasantness to you?"

She shook her head. "I can't remember her saying anything, but Audra holds her cards close." She laid a hand on his arm, and he looked down at her. "Did she do something wrong, Martin?"

"I'm afraid I triggered her phobia, when I stood in the doorway." He decided to stop there, and not mention anything about their intense interaction that followed.

Audra's aunt let out an audible sigh. "Well, maybe she should have told you about that, Martin. She was locked in a car trunk when she was a tiny, little thing, and I'm afraid she still lives with the effects of that, even though she doesn't remember the reason. Of course, it was an accident, but that hardly matters."

A surge of deep regret at the way he had goaded her about her reaction to his presence in the doorway, rushed into his eyes as he looked back at Audra, who was now chatting with a bag boy, and easily persuading him to lend her his box cutter, so that she could cut a thick mop string off the cart wheel.

"She's much better, Martin. It takes a lot more to trigger her, now that she's older." She followed his gaze to her niece, who had managed a successful cart repair, and was celebrating by free spinning the wheel with her finger, and grinning up at the impressed bag boy.

Aunt Celeste gave Martin's arm a light caress. "I imagine Audra and I can get on with our shopping, now that she's managed to provide the finest trolley for the sister of her father."

She caused him to laugh quietly at that, and he rested his hand on her shoulder in a warm gesture.

"I suppose I should return to Hawthorn, and apply myself to dinner."

He forced himself to look away from Audra, and gave her aunt's shoulder a light pat. "Do have a nice evening, Miss Campbell."

She wished him the same, and watched him depart with a quiet sigh.

Martin sat alone in the kitchen that Izzy used to warn him to stay out of, and pushed his fish around with his fork, deciding that he wasn't that hungry.

He was actually a very good cook, having learned from different professionals when he was abroad, but there had been no need to use those skills after he'd returned. Now that the kitchen was completely at his disposal, he seemed to have lost his willingness to take advantage of it.

He spent a few moments tidying up the evidence of his efforts, and smiling at the memory of Izzy fussing at him, whenever she caught him anywhere near her stove.

Martin glanced around to be sure that things were left to Izzy's standards, and began to make his way to the den, but paused as he passed the rarely used, but beautiful formal living room. He stood in the wide, arched entry, looking around it, thinking of his mother.

He moved slowly about the room that had once been the cheerful center of their family home, but now sat like some museum exhibit, only lacking a velvet rope across its entrance.

Martin let his eyes roam around, and fancied hearing strains of old laughter, and music that seemed to be trying to escape and return to him, from somewhere in time, before all became quiet, and the moment was gone.

He stopped at the large grand piano, and slowly lifted the lid. After idly touching a few keys, he lowered himself to sit down, and let his fingers wander lightly over them, softly playing a rendition of Moonlight Sonata, as if his mother were seated next to him, as she had often been when he played, listening with her eyes closed, and a sweet smile on her lovely face.

He slowly left off playing and just sat, staring down at his hands for a long while, before finally closing the piano lid, and rising to leave the room.

He turned to look around it again, and listen for what he thought he'd heard before, but there was nothing. He turned off the light, and the darkness rushed in to replace it.

He finally settled down in the den, after stirring the embers in the fireplace, and adding some wood, and used his favorite pipe as a prop to think with.

Martin hadn't told Celeste Campbell anything else about today, other than the incident with Audra's reaction to his blocking the door. He'd not mentioned his return to the room, and the heated exchange that followed.

He silently rebuked himself now for intentionally setting out to unnerve her, by resting his hands around her neck while suggesting, in his low, persuasive manner, that she was in danger of perishing by the same method his late wife had.

He had no acceptable justification for why he had done such a thing, other than the fact that she frustrated him beyond reason with her brave, unflinching coolness, and her steadfast denial of the animosity toward him, that persistently rested in her eyes, and in her manner.

He couldn't pretend that he wasn't vexed by the beautiful Audra, when he lifted his hands to intimidate her, but he also had to admit to himself that her refusal to give him the satisfaction that he desired was impressive.

He let the ghost of a smile flit across his lips, before it vanished, and a weary, disappointed frown replaced it.

Martin reclined his chair, and rested his head back, staring at the ceiling, and remembering the rest of the day with remorse.

He had stormed out of the upstairs room, after barking some order at Audra. He couldn't remember what he'd actually said. He'd gone into his library, and shut the door.

When Audra had come downstairs to leave, of course she found his library door closed, and apparently determined that it was his way of telling her that he had no wish to speak further.

He had sensed her proximity, and felt that she was lingering just beyond the library, perhaps wavering between an apology and a rebuke. In any event, he had no intention of entertaining either.

He had lifted his feet up to rest them on his desk, and folded his arms, glaring at the door, as if believing that his hot stare could penetrate its surface, and reach her.

It had become apparent to Martin, when Audra had finally admitted what she knew about Darlene and Phillip March that, faced with the threat of his aggression and anger, she was simply trying to fight back with the only weapon she had.

Her immediate regret made it clear that she had intended to hurt him, and she thought that she had, but had instantly been overwhelmed with guilt.

Martin knew that she believed that his stunned reaction was because it had reopened a wound caused by his late wife's infidelity, but what she didn't know was that, in order for that to have hurt him, he would have had to care.

That wasn't the cause for his dismayed response, when she finally told him what she knew. It was Audra, herself, who had become his source of pain, with the injury she had inflicted on him by a sudden revelation of what had been behind her hostilities toward him, when she would look at him with such repulsion.

Martin had sat brooding in his library, still feeling the mortification of realizing that all those glares and gazes Audra had aimed at him as they sat in church were not simply because she disliked him or found him to be disagreeable, but she had leveled them at him because she despised him for what she concluded was his pathetic weakness, and pitiful willingness to be made a fool of.

Her angry answer to his demand that she tell him what she knew, proved to be shameful and degrading to him, but only because it revealed her true evaluation of him.

As he sat fuming behind his desk, a renewed fury was stirred in him, sparked by his inability to simply not care what she thought of him, one way or another. He did care, and he hated himself for it.

Martin could hear the slight movement of her nearness to the door, and had leaped up to come over and jerk it open, still agitated following their explosive skirmish, and the clashing of their verbal weapons.

Audra hadn't flinched when the door opened, but stood looking at him steadily and calmly.

"I'm leaving," she had said quietly.

"Go."

His response had been chilly, and she had continued to evaluate him for a long moment, before speaking again.

"I see."

She had turned and walked out of the house, not looking back, not lingering, and simply drove away.

Martin had watched her disappear past the gates of Hawthorn Manor with a strange uneasiness welling up inside him. What did she mean by saying "I see" in that unsettling manner, and then just driving away as she had?

He had thought she simply meant leaving for the day, but had she been telling him that she was truly leaving?

Martin impatiently moved a hand through the air now, as if trying to force this unpleasant recollection to disperse, and leave him alone.

He had been confused this evening, when he encountered Audra and her aunt at the market, and she registered no discomfort, no regret, and seemed to actually be lighthearted, as if none of their conflict had occurred.

He'd kept hoping that she would at least look at him, so that he could read her intention in her eyes, but she had seemed to look anywhere, but at him.

She must still be angry with him, then. He laid his pipe down with a sigh, and told himself that he'd probably seen the last of her, and that she had just been keeping up appearances in front of her aunt since, according to Celeste Campbell, Audra hadn't mentioned anything about it.

Perhaps she wasn't ready for her aunt to know that she wouldn't be returning to Hawthorn Manor.

Martin stood and looked around his massive, cheerless dwelling, with a sadness stealing over him that he had been hoping would leave him alone tonight.

He climbed the stairs to go to bed, knowing that it would follow him to his room.

Chapter Eleven

When Martin Satterfield opened the door, the look in his eyes reflected at least some level of surprise, and perhaps the slightest hint of relief, although he did his best to conceal it.

"I wasn't expecting you," he admitted, then stepped back to allow Audra to enter.

"I wasn't going to come." She moved past him, pausing as he closed the door behind her.

"Why did you?" he challenged. He let his eyes travel lightly over her, as he waited for her answer.

"Because you never actually said I was fired."

"And you came to discover if you are, in fact, fired? A simple phone call would have accomplished that."

"I came prepared to work, if I'm not," she replied.

He looked closely at her, trying to detect her bearing, and her attitude toward him.

"Perhaps you thought it might be more difficult for me to fire you, if you were standing in front of me," he suggested, silently appreciating the beauty of Audra Campbell, as if seeing her for the first time. "I suspect there is some merit to that."

They stood waiting in the stillness around them, each trying to read the other.

"There's a term for this sort of awkwardness between us," he remarked, making no move to lead the way into the library as he typically did when she arrived, but lingering in indecision.

"Unfinished business," Audra replied.

"Yes."

"Do you want me to leave?" she asked.

A sudden awareness that he did not want her to leave startled the master of Hawthorn Manor, but he simply indicated the door of the library with a raised hand. She moved ahead of him, and took the chair in front of his desk as he seated himself, and settled back to fix her with a searching look.

"Are you here to remedy the state of our unfinished business, then?"

"If you're willing."

"I'm more than willing, provided you haven't concluded from our last discourse, that there's no point to it."

"I suppose we should at least make the effort."

She glanced down at the floor for a moment, before raising her eyes to find him watching her carefully. "Would you like to warn me of the kinds of things we're not allowed to talk about?"

He smiled down at his pipe, picking it up and toying with it, but not lighting it. "All things are permissible."

Audra raised her brows, and looked at him with a fair amount of skepticism. "You say that *now*."

"Try me," he suggested flippantly. "I intend to be on my best behavior, in a belated attempt to repent of my recent unpleasantness. Ask your bravest question. If we survive that, our chances of success increase exponentially."

"And if we don't?" she wondered.

"You are closer to the exit than I," he informed her with an ironic smile.

She pursed her lips, and gave him a pointed look.

"If we don't, it won't be because of me," he stated flatly. "I am committed to satisfying your every curiosity."

"I don't ask because I'm curious."

"You ask because you're trying to determine if you're safe alone with me in my home," he surmised, laying the pipe down, and lacing his fingers together.

"I ask because I don't want to have to keep walking on eggshells around you, never knowing if I'm about to commit some egregious blunder, and have you school me in the art of glaring," Audra said dryly, causing him to give in to a quiet laugh.

"And have you been walking on eggshells around me, Miss Campbell?"

"You wouldn't believe the billowing oceans of restraint, I've successfully navigated," she returned sarcastically, generating another smile.

"You may dispense with caution," he replied. "I pose no threat to you. Ask your many questions."

"I don't have many."

"Whatever the number, let's proceed," he instructed.

"Please remember that you agreed to this," she said with a bland expression.

He simply nodded and waited.

"How did your wife die?" Audra hoped he hadn't noticed the uneasy way she asked this, but she had to know.

"She was strangled," he answered calmly. "I would have thought, from my rather convincing demonstration, that you would have gathered that."

He noted her reaction. "I can see that the manner of her death surprises you."

"It seems so far removed from the account of her falling down the stairs," she said, unable to mask her confusion.

"According to the coroner, she was made to appear as if she'd fallen down the stairs. I believe law enforcement sums up such an attempt by using the word 'staged.' In any event, she did not die by falling down the stairs."

Audra seemed dissatisfied, but made no further comment.

"Do you not feel the need to ask me if I am the one who strangled her?" Martin asked mildly, when she failed to reply.

"Didn't we cover that already?"

"If you consider our last conversation as covering it, then I suppose so, since we'd only be repeating ourselves."

"You said you didn't need or desire for me to believe you," she reminded him.

"You chose to believe *that*, then." He smiled down at his hands with an odd wistfulness, and Audra wondered if this was his way of telling her that he did need for her to believe him.

Martin reached again for his pipe, and appeared to be examining it, as if it were a rare artifact.

"I still see questions in your eyes," he said quietly, "and if that was your bravest one, we seem to be off to a fine start."

Audra felt that her next question must surely be her bravest one, provided she could bring herself to ask it.

"Did you love her?"

"Isn't that what you thought, when you tried to strike me down by using Phillip March's name as your weapon of choice? Your apparent concern for me immediately afterward, seemed to indicate that this was your belief."

"The question is still on the table," she said, waiting.

He continued to stare stubbornly at his pipe for a long moment, and she began to wonder if he intended to reply.

"I did not," he admitted.

He looked up at her with a dejected smile hovering over his lips. "Is this the point where you decide that you hate me, after all?"

She shook her head, and exhaled in a show of frustration. "It's not that I hated you, Martin. Mr. Satterfield."

"Come now, Audra. We're about to share our deepest, darkest secrets. Surely that warrants a level of camaraderie that lends itself to the use of our given names."

"It's not that I hated you, Martin," she repeated. "I was just angry with you."

"Were you? What did I do to stir that sort of passion in you, I wonder?" He lifted a hand to check her response. "I let her make a fool of me. I remember now."

He sat forward in his chair, and rested his forearms on the desk, having moved past his offense at her unpleasant estimation of him, but still examining her with curious intrigue.

"Why would that have mattered to you on any level, let alone made you angry?"

"I was younger then, and fresh out of high school. I was probably fostering some naive resentment. Please don't judge me now, by my adolescent desire for justice back then."

"Justice. You wanted me to humiliate her."

"I suppose I did."

"So, it was Darlene you actually hated."

"I despised her," Audra admitted.

"Should I call Detective Vance?" he asked, submitting to a rare grin that lit up his striking features. "He might consider that to be a motive."

Audra sat absently braiding a tress of her hair, which was a habit she had whenever she was deep in thought. She raised her eyes to meet his.

"He was at her funeral."

"Yes."

"So was Phillip March."

"I saw him, yes."

He watched her fingers unconsciously capturing strands of beautiful russet hair, and plaiting them, and waited for her to continue, with the faintest flexing of his jaw.

Audra drew in a breath, and paused to thoughtfully assess his demeanor.

Martin recognized her open analysis, and leaned back in his chair, resting his head as if he were relaxing.

"You're safe from any unbridled reaction on my part," he assured her, with only a trace of mockery. "Your bravest question has been asked. Surely, it's all downhill from here."

"Why did that man come to her funeral?" Audra took him at his word, and asked her question, a scowl of disapproval washing over her face.

Martin noticed it, and felt slightly gratified.

"He was supposedly a friend, and Darlene's investment banker," he commented with a shrug. "I imagine it would have seemed odd to the community, if he'd avoided her funeral."

"I think he was there to determine how much you knew," she returned with a frown.

"Do you?"

"Yes, and I can't generate much enthusiasm for Detective Vance's investigative skills, if he can stand right next to him, and not be curious about him."

"Why should he have the need to be curious about him?"

"Shouldn't any halfway competent detective, even that one, take an interest in who is in attendance at a murder victim's funeral?"

He raised a brow, and seemed to find humor in her description of Detective Vance as being halfway competent.

"I sense that you believe Phillip March killed Darlene," Martin observed quietly.

"Don't you?"

He shrugged again, and observed her from his laid back position with half-closed eyes. "I have my theories."

He drew his brows and looked curiously at her.

"What do you imagine his motive to be?"

"I don't know, but someone killed her, and why is it so impossible to believe it could have been the man she was having an affair with? He's married, if I'm not mistaken. Maybe she threatened to tell his wife."

"Or perhaps my late wife was pregnant," Martin said slowly, waiting for her reaction.

She hesitated, resting her perceptive eyes on his. "*Was* she pregnant?"

"According to the autopsy results," he replied. "The question rankling our zealous, halfway competent investigator is whether or not I had foreknowledge of her condition."

She lifted her brow, and waited.

"I did not."

She looked down at her hands, and he could tell by her flush of color what her next question would be, but waited to see if she could actually bring herself to ask it.

"Could it have been your child?" It was almost a whisper.

He watched her steadily, noting her discomfort, and seeing her seem to dread hearing his response.

"What do you want my answer to be?" He quietly baited her, aware of what he was hoping for.

Audra wrestled with admitting to him that she hated the very thought that he could have cared, even a little, for such a shallow, self-absorbed, and faithless creature as his late wife.

"I want you to say no," she confessed, not looking at him, and unable to see the thin veil of pleasure her words gave him.

"In order for the child to have been mine that would have necessitated my being intimate with a woman who, as you pointed out, was making a fool of me."

He paused, until she finally raised her eyes to his.

"Do I strike you as desperate, Audra?"

She shook her head, and her noticeable relief caused his dispassionate expression to give way to a soft smile.

She asked the next question tentatively, hoping that it wasn't insensitive.

"Martin, how could Phillip March have been with her in this house, without Izzy knowing?"

"Why do you assume Izzy didn't know?" he queried, not missing the effect his question had on her.

"She would have told you!"

He made no reply, but she could tell that her words stirred an unusual sort of unrest in his manner.

"Wouldn't she have?" She pressed him, unable to believe otherwise.

Her question produced another shrug.   "Perhaps not, if she thought I was unaware of... the situation."

"She would try to spare you, then," Audra sighed.

"I expect so, yes.   Izzy actually loved me, if you can believe that," Martin said, with a sadness drawing his face.   He sat up straighter, and absently touched his pipe again.

"No accounting for taste," he quipped, and the temptation to comfort him surfaced, as Audra realized that he was simply saying what he felt.

"Aunt Celeste said that Izzy doted on you all your life," she offered gently.

His face mellowed for a moment, before something harsh and bitter left its mark.   "Darlene killed Izzy," he said, causing Audra to stare at him, clearly startled.

He saw her expression, and waved an impatient hand.

"She worked her to death! She treated Izzy as if she were her own personal slave, and kept her running up and down the stairs for any ridiculous reason, while she lounged lazily about the house, as if she owned it.

"And, to finish her off, she allowed her selfish carelessness to present the occasion for Izzy to discover her dead body, at the foot of the stairs."

The anger that burned in his eyes could be felt, and Audra remained quiet.

"Izzy's heart never recovered from that," he finished in a dull, listless voice.

After a long moment, he looked up at Audra to find tears brimming in her eyes.

"I've upset you, yet again," he observed.

"It's not about me," she denied, brushing her fingers across her cheek impatiently.

"What is it about, then?"

"It's just that I'm really sorry, Martin, but I'm not allowed to say that, am I? Because you don't accept any form of sympathy."

"Is that my reputation?" His smile was without feeling.

They both sat reflecting for a long moment, before Audra felt she was ready to venture another question.

"I understand why Izzy would try to spare you, but if Phillip March was in this house the night Darlene died, I can't get a grasp on why she wouldn't have immediately told the police that. I mean, it's not like she would have wanted to protect *him*, of all people."

"I see you're following the bread crumbs of all my musings," he remarked calmly, lifting his pipe again and cradling it in his hand.

"Save me the trip," she suggested, watching him trace the line of his pipe, quietly startled at the sudden thought of his long, elegant fingers, now so gentle and sensitive, being the same threatening ones that he had curved around her bare throat.

"If I'd had no alibi, I've no doubt that Izzy would have immediately advised the police of his presence," he replied, an aspect of tenderness settling on his sad, handsome face at the thought of his beloved Izzy. "But she knew exactly where I was, and that it was indisputable. I'm sure that's what stopped her from sharing that information."

He raised his eyes to hers. "Izzy wouldn't have wanted Darlene's extra-marital activities to develop into fodder for the gossip mill, and force me to become the local object of pity, if it could be avoided, even after Darlene's demise.

"I allow myself to speculate that Izzy wouldn't have cared who killed Darlene, as long as she knew that I didn't."

"So, she would have just kept all that to herself, and hoped for the best?" Audra forced herself to stop watching his hands.

"I won't chide you, if you find that hard to believe," Martin said quietly. "You didn't know her."

"I wish I had," she sighed, making him think of his own wish, as he'd watched her encounter with the elderly woman in the market.

"We must also remember the impressive size of Hawthorn Manor," its owner reminded her, indicating it with an inclusive wave, and a dour expression.

"Darlene's body was found on the back stairwell which, in itself, is unusual, and suggests that she received her visitor at the back entrance, perhaps anticipating his arrival. It's not hard to conclude that Izzy was simply never aware that someone else was with her."

Audra considered this without comment. Another tangible silence filled the room, before she attempted to stand. His upheld hand halted her.

"Am I to be allowed a question this morning?" he asked.

"You're not going to interrogate me about why I hate you again, are you?" Audra demanded, her humor laced with sarcasm.

He crossed his arms, and stared vacantly at nothing, with a rueful smile.

"I don't expect either of us wants to revisit that theatrical bit of drama."

She smiled in agreement and waited.

Martin's smile faded, and a wondering look took its place.

"Audra, how did you find out about Darlene and March?"

"I saw them," she replied simply. "I was grabbing lunch for myself and Aunt Celeste, and when I looked up, on my way back to the car, they were coming out of the motel across the street from the restaurant."

"And you immediately assumed?" he asked, letting his gaze drop to his desk.

"I didn't have to assume. And, maybe we should leave it at that," she advised.

He looked up quickly at her, and a mutual understanding passed between them.

"Perhaps that's best," he conceded.

Martin rested his hands in front of him, and seemed to be taking a moment before speaking.

Audra had been about to stand again, but the simple lifting of his fingers on one hand caused her to wait. He raised his eyes to search her face for a moment.

"Don't be alarmed. I haven't changed my mind. I'm not preparing to revisit why you hate me," he said softly, with a little grin, and a wry smile curved the edge of her lips.

She watched him appear to struggle with something.

"Martin, can *I* say it?"

He glanced down again, as a pensive frown washed across his face. "I'm not sure if that's a good idea."

He looked back up at her with uncertainty in his eyes.

"You possess the rare ability to wield a certain amount of power over me, simply by your assessment of me. I'm not sure I'm comfortable with that. I'm not sure why it matters, and I'm not necessarily pleased that it does."

Their bitter exchange in the east wing came back vividly to Audra, and she felt a sting of regret. It was true that she had intended to hurt him, but it was becoming clear to her now that his reaction had nothing to do with his late wife, and everything to do with her.

She tried to return his gaze before lowering her eyes, and letting out a sigh. "You won't let me apologize?"

"It wouldn't change anything, would it, Audra? You see me as you see me."

Audra wasn't sure what it was in his eyes, but it wasn't anger. She almost thought she would feel better, if it were. This felt more like disappointment.

Tears began forming, and she glanced toward the window. "So, I'll never be forgiven?"

Her whispered question took him by surprise.

"Will that mend us, do you think?"

She looked over to see him smiling gently at her.

"I was wrong, Martin," she admitted. "Aunt Celeste tried to tell me. In fact, she was upset with me, because I was forming conclusions, without even knowing you. She kept telling me that it wasn't like me, and it wasn't."

Audra looked back toward the window and bit her lip, as she fought to keep her emotions in check.

"The truth is, I'm not sure why I was so angry. It shouldn't have mattered to me who you married, or what sort of arrangement you had."

"But it did?" Martin seemed startled by her words, and he couldn't keep the confusion out of his eyes.

"I just didn't want it to be her," she sighed, in a small voice.

"You didn't think me weak and pathetic?" His question was asked hesitantly, as he tried to work through what she seemed to be telling him.

She looked down and shook her head, then raised her eyes to him with unguarded candor. "It was just that I felt that she had talked you into marrying her, and I guess just the idea that she could do that made me angry with you."

He raised a brow in surprise. "So, that's a yes, then?"

"No, Martin!" She seemed frustrated. "Again, I was just a silly, high school girl. Girls are stupid," she mumbled, causing him to grin, in spite of his still being clueless.

She began to feel embarrassed, and threw her hair back over her shoulder impatiently, then snapped at him, becoming a little irritated. "I mean, I can't say that I was angry with you for marrying her, because she didn't deserve you, without sounding like I'm about to pull a casserole out from behind my back!"

His smile quickly grew into laughter, causing her to lean back in her chair, and regard him with unamused, but lovely eyes, as her lips twisted into a little scowl.

Martin folded his arms, then lifted one hand to rest it over his mouth, regarding her in silent appraisal, the effects of his laughter causing something light and restful to begin to settle in his eyes.

"We'll forgive each other, Audra, and begin again. Yes?"

Her scowl relaxed into a smile, and an expression of gladness lit up her beautiful face. "Yes, please."

"Our hard-fought battle would appear to be over. I think we are still intact, for the most part," Martin commented lightly. "On with our day, then."

"I suppose I'd better continue to box everything up." Audra hoisted herself up from her chair, then hesitated.

"But first, I guess I still need to determine if I'm fired."

"That depends," he advised, slowly pushing his chair back and rising.

He paused, then came around his desk to hover close, and look down at her, capturing her eyes with his, and attempting to interpret her reaction to his nearness.

"On what?" she wondered, looking up at him.

"On whether or not you're afraid of me."

She waited in stillness, and submitted to his deliberate intention to examine her thoroughly, before finally speaking.

"I'm absolutely terrified."

The laughter in her beautiful eyes betrayed her false claim, and he recognized her lighthearted effort to tease him.

He gave her a slow smile of relief, before flicking his fingers toward the upper east wing, in a careless wave of dismissal.

Chapter Twelve

Aunt Celeste stood looking around the beautiful home of Martin Satterfield with fond recollection, and genuine appreciation. She'd come by, after her niece called to ask if she would be anywhere close, and could bring her portfolio.

Martin had informed Audra that he would be out for much of the morning, and had indicated his approval when she'd asked if he minded her aunt dropping by. He did express his desire that Audra only grant access to her aunt, and that she not answer the door for any other caller.

"It's very much the same as I remember," Aunt Celeste observed with pleasure, taking a seat. "I was afraid that Martin's late wife would have changed everything, and filled the house with garish, dreadful, modern art."

"I don't expect he gave her much leeway in this part of the house," Audra speculated, settling on the divan in the den, and looking around, herself. "In fact, her redecorating attempts were restricted to the east wing upstairs."

She normally began her day in the library, to be told by Martin what he wanted her to do, then went straight up to the east wing to carry out his instructions. She had been escorted through the house on her first day at work, but Martin hadn't gone out of his way to do much more than indicate a room's purpose from its doorway, and move on to the next one. She'd never actually been inside the den.

She glanced over at her aunt with a resigned expression.

"That's the main reason this job has been taking so much time. Darlene claimed the entire east wing for herself, and it was literally filled with, apparently, every tacky thing that woman ever owned."

Aunt Celeste looked puzzled. "What do you mean, she claimed the entire east wing for herself?"

Audra hesitated, before answering. "It didn't take me long to realize that she had her part of the house, and Martin has his. I've not seen any evidence that any of his personal effects were ever located in the east wing, and his instructions were to completely empty it of everything, including the furniture. He arranged for a moving company to transfer it all to a charity, so I'm finally down to a clean slate."

Her aunt made a sound of disappointment. "That's too bad. It sounds as if there must have been some friction between them, then."

Audra almost gave in to the temptation to confide to Aunt Celeste about Darlene Satterfield and Phillip March, but she stopped herself, with a great effort. She somehow felt that Martin would be extremely displeased with her, if she did.

"Maybe," she replied, with a shrug.

"Well, you seem to be much more at ease, honey," Aunt Celeste commented, laying her hand on her niece's. "I was afraid that you'd let all the speculation about Martin's late wife's death create suspicion, and make it difficult for you to be here."

"No, I'm not bothered by any of that," she assured her aunt. "I admit, I did wonder about it, but I know him a little better now. Better than not at all, I mean," she laughed.

"Of course, no one really gets to know Martin Satterfield to any real degree, but I realize now that you were right, when you said that he had been through a lot, in a short amount of time. I have no problem being sure that he had nothing to do with Darlene's death."

"That's a relief!" Aunt Celeste declared. "I still feel that Martin is very much a Satterfield, with the same goodness and decency in him, that his parents were known for. If you're beginning to see that for yourself, then I'm glad."

"I can see that he's not completely unkind," Audra confessed. "Of course, he's so matter-of-fact about most things, and even though we've had some actual conversations, I would still describe him as stoic. But not unkind," she repeated.

"I've never perceived him to be," her aunt agreed. "Physically, he's a fair blend of both his parents, which gives him those arresting, blue eyes, with those dark good looks. Maureen had beautiful, dark hair, and Martin's father had very kind blue eyes. Both of them were tall, so of course, Martin is tall.

"He's a remarkably handsome man," Aunt Celeste added innocently, not at all implying that Audra should notice for herself. "I'll be so happy for him, if he can put all his loss behind him, and have a good life, in spite of everything."

"I wish everyone felt that way," Audra replied. "Greg Vance seems to be going to extremes to completely ignore the fact that Martin was nowhere near this house, the night his wife died. In fact, as far as I can tell, he's only concentrating on Martin, and not even entertaining other suspects."

"So, the autopsy results are in?" Aunt Celeste looked carefully at her niece. "They must be, for him to still be treating this as a homicide."

"It *is* a homicide," Audra finally admitted, getting the expression of shock and dismay from her aunt that she knew was surely coming.

"Did someone push her down the stairs then, Audra?" her aunt asked breathlessly.

"She was strangled, and it was made to appear that she had fallen down the stairs."

Aunt Celeste's surprise was in her eyes. "That is the last thing I expected you to tell me!"

"That's the last thing I expected Martin to tell me," Audra agreed. "He said the autopsy listed it as cause of death.

"That stupid Greg Vance is only concerned with proving that Martin is the killer, with no evidence to suggest it, and massive amounts of evidence to prove where he was, and who he was with, that night."

"I ought to call the police chief and complain, since he happens to be a friend of mine," Aunt Celeste threatened, with an annoyed expression. "But I don't suppose Martin would be too appreciative of his mother's friend jumping in to fight his battles for him."

Audra couldn't help laughing at her aunt's fierce scowl.

"I imagine you're right, Aunt C, but he would probably be pleased to know that you're so loyal to him."

"Well, I *am* loyal to him," she stated firmly. "He would have to look me in the eyes, and confess to killing his late wife, and even then, I wouldn't believe him."

She glanced at her watch, and made a face. "I have to be at some silly board meeting in less than a half hour. One of these days, I'm going to step down from every organization that has roped me into serving on their boards, and just quit them, all at once. That'll show 'em!"

She stood up, and gave the lovely room one more fond glance. "I see Martin spends a lot of time in here," she observed, indicating one of his pipes next to an easy chair.

Audra smiled, imagining him holding his pipe, but being so deep in thought that he never remembered to light it.

"Maureen and I used to have some good chats in here," Aunt Celeste said softly. "I really miss her."

Aunt Celeste began to move toward the entryway, then turned to walk over to the large, arched access to the formal living room. Her eyes fairly danced with memories.

"Honey, I wish you could have seen how this room looked, when it was decorated for Christmas! This whole room would be filled with people and laughter, and of course, music."

Audra took it all in, as it was yet another room that had been merely indicated, but not entered. "That's a beautiful piano," she commented, indicating it with a nod.

"Has Martin played it for you?" her aunt wondered, continuing to glance around the beautiful room with satisfaction.

Audra looked at Aunt Celeste in disbelief. "Has Martin what?" She looked at the piano again, and back at her aunt, clearly surprised.

"You didn't know he plays?" her aunt asked lightly.

She just shook her head slowly, and Aunt Celeste laid a hand on her arm.

"Well, he does, baby, and I'm not talking Chopsticks! Maureen used to talk him into playing for her, and even though he didn't seem to want to at first, she was always finally able to get him to do it. I've heard him, and he plays beautifully! You should ask him to, someday.

"Of course, he was much younger, then. I suppose he became an even better pianist, when he was in Europe," Aunt Celeste mused. "I'd love to hear him again, and find out."

Audra thought about Martin's fingers, and it was easy to imagine them moving over piano keys. Of course, thinking of his fingers immediately caused her to remember them resting lightly around her throat, and she felt her face begin to flush.

She looked over at the piano again, then took in a breath, and finally just gave a little shrug, deciding that the list of things she actually did not know about Martin Satterfield, was far longer than the things she did know.

"If that rascal was home now, I'd make him play for us," Aunt Celeste informed her, moving away from the room's entrance reluctantly, and beginning to feel her time constraints.

She paused, as they made their way toward the front door, and indicated the stairway with the big question in her eyes.

"The back stairs," Audra said, and her aunt laid a hand on her throat with relief.

"I'm glad of that!" she exclaimed fervently.

Audra grinned, and gave her a hug, then walked with her to the door. "Thanks for bringing the portfolio, Aunt C."

"Oh, I'm glad you asked. It was nice being at Hawthorn again." She gave her niece a pleased smile. "So, all the clearing out is done, and you're ready to actually design."

Audra sighed. "Now comes the hard part."

"Oh, stop, you know this is where you shine," Aunt Celeste insisted. "This is when the fun begins."

"Well, let's hope so. I worry that I'll finish it all, and end up having him just glare at me, when it's done."

"He can trust you *not* to fill this wonderful home with ugly, modern art, Audra, so you can stop worrying. You understand all about maintaining original character. It'll be lovely."

"Are you sure you can't stay, and follow me around the east wing telling me that?" she laughed.

Her aunt reached to pat her cheek affectionately, and promised to see her later at home for dinner, before making her way out to her car.

Audra watched her drive away with a little smile, then closed the door, remembering to keep it locked as Martin had insisted, and headed back to retrieve her portfolio from the den.

Martin Satterfield watched Phillip March fidget nervously with a paper clip, deciding that he would actually feel sorry for him, if he didn't detest him so much. His objection to the man was not so much that he had been having an affair with his late wife, but that he had been engaging in his hedonistic activities inside the Satterfield family home, which was, in Martin's view, an affront to the dignity and moral values of his parents.

"You don't know what to say to me," he observed, covering him with a shrewd expression.

"I guess I'm wondering why you're here, Martin," he admitted, in a voice that sounded as if he needed to clear his throat. "I was your wife's banker, but you and I have never done any business together."

Martin allowed a slow smile to find its way across his lips. "Did you enjoy being my late wife's... *banker*, Phillip?"

"What do you mean?"

"Does that question have more than one meaning to you?" Martin's face was void of any emotion, with the exception of his piercing eyes.

Any doubts that Phillip March had ever possessed, as to whether or not Darlene Satterfield's husband was aware of their affair, were brutally destroyed, and he began to fidget under his icy stare.

"Martin, I'm sorry about your wife's passing, but..."

He stopped short when his former girlfriend's husband lifted a hand, almost if he thought he might strike him.

"You can spare me the false sympathy, Phillip. You know fully well why I'm here. In fact, the only thing you're unsure of is why I waited so long."

Phillip March opened his mouth to deny this, but the warning in Martin's eyes arrested him.

He finally looked down at his hands, his shoulders drooping, and waited for the angry man seated across from him to continue.

Martin observed him with uncanny perception, knowing that, of two men, Phillip March was not the one who would ultimately be in his crosshairs, but he seemed to take a certain amount of pleasure in denigrating him, as he proceeded to either include, or exclude him, as the man who fathered his late wife's child, a detail that only mattered to Martin as it related to his efforts to lay the foundation for the actual killer's motive. In fact, Martin would be best pleased if Phillip March proved not the father of Darlene's child, as it would result in complicating matters, if he were found to be.

He continued to fix the man with his unwavering gaze. "Shall I indulge in false sympathy as well, Phillip, and tell you that I'm sorry for the loss of your child?"

Martin watched as he drew his brows in confusion, before looking up at him with a convincing display of ignorance.

"What do you mean?" he asked, his look of astonishment causing Martin to peer at him closely, in an attempt to determine its authenticity. "I don't have a child!"

He seemed completely baffled, and Martin sat studying his face, again considering two equally plausible possibilities.

"Are you telling me that Darlene never managed to share her exciting news with you, that you were going to be a father?"

"What?" The banker fairly shouted his shocked response. "That's impossible!"

"And why should I believe that?" Martin pressed. "I suggest you come clean with me now, Phillip, because the longer this takes, the angrier I'm sure to become. I don't advise pushing me to that limit."

Phillip March let out a deep breath, and drew another in. "I thought I knew why you were here... I mean I do know," he stammered, "but you're wrong about Darlene carrying my child. I made sure that was surgically impossible, years ago!"

"And you're willing to provide evidence to back up your claim?" Martin asked, as he continued to drill his stare into his late wife's lover.

"Are you asking for medical records?" Phillip March seemed all too eager to provide them.

"I require a DNA sample," Martin informed him, letting him know with just a look, that he was deadly serious. "A man with nothing to hide shouldn't have a problem with that." He leaned forward to watch the man's face carefully. "Do *you* have a problem with that, Phillip?"

"What will it be used to prove?" The banker asked, not bothering to try and hide his agitated state.

"If you are not the father of the child Darlene was pregnant with, it will absolve you," Martin stated flatly.

"Why are you so sure that you're not the father, Martin?"

He wished immediately that he hadn't ask the question, as Martin Satterfield stood to his full height, and looked down at him in disgust.

"Do you imagine I would ever have been intimate with any woman, after your hands had been all over her, March?" His face displayed his contempt. "Did you think I was oblivious to your recurring trysts with my late wife?"

He waited for a response, but Phillip couldn't seem to come up with one.

"What is your alibi for the night Darlene died, March?"

"Alibi?" Again, his face reflected genuine bewilderment. "She fell down the stairs! Why would I need an alibi?"

"Am I correct in interpreting your apparent confusion to mean that you've not been made privy to the autopsy results?" Martin asked quietly.

"Me? Why should *I* have been given autopsy results?"

Martin was beginning to conclude that the obvious indication, as to who actually fathered his dead wife's child, was the correct one.

He came around and sat on the corner of Phillip March's desk, only adding to the man's sense of foreboding.

He watched him silently, while reaching into his coat's inside pocket, noting, with dry amusement, the man's relief when Martin pulled out a packet rather than a gun.

"You imply that you were not on the premises the night Darlene died."

"I wasn't, I swear it!" Phillip March said hurriedly. "I haven't been asked for an alibi by anyone, but I can check my calendar, and show you where I was. I wasn't there, Martin, I swear I wasn't!"

"If that is true," Martin continued, in measured words, "and if you are indeed not the father of the child she was carrying, there should be no reason why you would not voluntarily provide the DNA sample that would absolve you."

Phillip March wasn't enthusiastic about what he was expected to do, but he knew that, one way or another, Martin Satterfield was going to get what he came for. He breathed out a heavy sigh, and nodded in defeat.

Martin retrieved two swabs from the packet, and held them up for him to see. "Do you have gum, or anything else in your mouth?"

Phillip shook his head, and Martin proceeded to have him open his mouth, taking his time and carefully collecting saliva from both sides of his mouth, then placing the swabs in the protective container. He tucked everything back into the packet, returning it to his pocket, then stood looking down at the banker with an expression in his eyes that the man couldn't identify.

"I'm sure that you've reached the obvious conclusion by now, March, that the woman who was unfaithful to me was also unfaithful to you."

The man looked up at him in stunned realization, and for a fleeting second, Martin felt pity for him.

He turned and left quietly, without further comment.

Chapter Thirteen

Martin paused in the large hallway of the east wing, remembering not to stand in the doorway, but watching Audra sitting among piles of fabric samples, her face hidden by the long drape of her hair, its silky texture causing it to insist on tumbling around her, regardless of how often she threw it back.

She was unaware that she was being observed, and he indulged in a smile of appreciation at the way she sat on the floor, with her legs crossed like a kid at a campfire, and held up each swatch before either looking thoughtfully at it, and placing it in one group, or frowning, and sometimes making a face at it, and dropping it onto another. Once, she actually stuck out her tongue at a reject, and Martin had to make the effort to suppress his laughter.

"I hope I informed you about my strong dislike of polka dots, and shades of neon," he said lightly, and she looked up at him with an amused smirk.

"Am I creating any triggers, standing here?" he wondered, prepared to move if she asked him to.

She looked at him thoughtfully, for a moment. "No, I seem to be fine. I'm beginning to think it's a trust issue," she admitted, looking back down at her samples.

Undisguised pleasure rushed over Martin's face, and he entered the room to stand and witness her process, as she continued to systematically sort through her samples.

"Have I won your trust, then?" he inquired, watching her make her silent decisions.

"Should I admit that, or should I keep that card up my sleeve?" she returned, glancing up at him with what Martin had once called her "Mona Lisa" smile.

He gave her a smile of his own. "In which pile are the rejects?"

"If you can't tell, then I'm beginning to wonder about your tastes," she laughed. "So, no suggestions from you."

Martin looked down at her beautiful face, as her engaging eyes reflected her state of ease and contentment, and allowed a small sigh of regret to escape him.

"I have some business in town," he said quietly. "I'm not sure how long I'll be away, but some issues may delay me. Will you be alright here alone, or would you rather come back at a time when I'm at home all day?"

She studied him carefully, then braced her arm against the floor in order to stand. He reached down and lifted her up, an enigmatic emotion shimmering in his eyes, as he slowly and reluctantly released her.

"I don't believe in ghosts," she informed him, looking up at him with a self-conscious grin. "I'll be fine here."

He continued to rest his eyes on her, as he reached into his pocket and brought out a key.

"Your access to Hawthorn Manor," he offered, with an embellished flourish. "You should have it, so that you can come and go as you please."

She let him lay the key in her hand, then looked up at him with uncertainty.

"Does this mean that I've won your trust, as well?"

"It does," he said simply.

She had been teasing, but now she looked back down at the key, and the threat of tears rushed to her eyes.

Martin noticed, and reached to lift her chin with a fingertip, wondering what it meant.

"It's nothing," she protested, feeling a little embarrassed. "I guess, I'm just surprised. I didn't think you trusted anyone."

"I trust *you*, Audra."

He was gazing at her so intently that she looked back down, knowing that whatever she felt would be seen in her eyes.

"Thank you," she simply said.

"Are you sure that you're fine for me to leave you?" he finally asked in a low voice, as he realized that his study of her was making her feel vulnerable. "I'm afraid it can't be avoided."

She seemed to appreciate his returning to his previous remarks, and glanced up with another little smile.

"I'm fine, I promise. Now that I don't have to worry about being locked out, I may even head to another fabric store, if I don't see what I want here."

"You're not going to find it in all this?" He laughed, and his eyes lit up with rare humor. "What are you looking for, the Shroud of Turin?"

She found that actually funny, and had to laugh with him, and it seemed to dispel the charged atmosphere around them.

"I wonder if it comes in neon?" she mused, and he shook his head with a smile, and moved to depart.

"I'm locking the door behind me, Audra, and you have my number if you need me."

"I do," she confirmed.

He paused at the entry, and looked at her with something tender in his manner, then simply waved his fingertips at her, and left as silently as he always seemed to arrive.

She watched him depart, and drew in her breath, able to feel that her cheeks were flushed with warm color. Almost immediately, she gently scolded herself, and began giving herself sensible advice not to become affected by Martin Satterfield's captivating presence, but to stay firmly focused on what she had been hired to do.

Doctor Paul Amos closed the door to his office, after motioning for his friend to have a seat. He came around to his desk and lowered himself to sit, fixing the man across from him with an expression of complete intrigue.

"Why do I feel that the sample packet you provided me with a few weeks ago, will have no surprising results for you?"

Martin simply allowed a hint of amusement to rest on his face, but offered no insight.

"And why do I feel that the second sample you brought me will also have no surprising results for you?"

The coroner's second question actually brought a smile.

"Before we proceed, Doctor, I must ask you for a favor."

His friend gave him a knowing look. "You want me to keep these results to myself, and not inform law enforcement."

Martin touched his fingertips together and gave him a nod.

"From the time DNA tests ruled me out as the father of Darlene's child, our renowned detective has shown no interest at all in determining who the father actually was. A likely candidate was suggested. His name was ignored."

Doctor Amos couldn't conceal his surprise. "That makes absolutely no sense!"

"It depends on your perception," Martin replied. "From my viewpoint, it makes perfect sense."

Doctor Amos continued to look mystified, but Martin made no attempt to enlighten him as to his viewpoint.

"Law enforcement did not request any further testing, regardless of the names of potential persons of interest that were provided to them," he continued. "I obtained those samples on my own. Yes, Paul, I am asking you that the results are not shared. It's not simply a matter of my being fed up with them. It's a matter of timing, and it's vitally important."

He sighed in resignation. "Very well, Martin. Since law enforcement didn't ask for these tests, I feel no obligation to notify them. I do, however, hope that you will, or perhaps have your attorney do so."

Martin relaxed in his chair, and gave him a grateful smile.

Doctor Amos eyed him shrewdly.

"You will not be surprised to find that one result is an exclusion, and one result is a match."

"I will not be," Martin admitted.

"I labeled them as *A* and *B*, with *A* indicating the sample you obtained most recently. *B*, of course, is the sample you collected initially, but held onto."

The coroner reached for his reading glasses, and pulled a document from his desk files.

"Just out of curiosity, Martin, where did you learn the proper method for the collecting and storing of DNA samples?" He grinned, as he posed the question, since he didn't expect an answer.

Martin waited, while he pored over the paperwork and looked back up at him.

"I exercised the proper amount of caution to ensure that the samples were not mixed up. *A* is assuredly *A*, and *B* is absolutely *B*."

He seemed to be tempted to ask a question of Martin, but also seemed to accept that he wouldn't be given the answer, so he applied himself to simply giving the man what he'd come for.

He adjusted his glasses, and began. "Sample *A*, identified as the most recently collected, excludes the donor from having fathered the child of Darlene Satterfield."

He glanced up to see no change in Martin's countenance at all, and proceeded, after passing the paper over to him.

"Sample *B*, identified as the earlier collected of the two, indicates that the donor's probability of paternity is ninety-nine point ninety-nine percent."

He handed the document over to Martin, who folded it and placed it in his coat pocket, without looking at it. His expression was impossible to read, and the coroner waited in vain for him to comment.

"Of course, Martin, only you know which sample belongs to which donor. Are you really not going to advise law enforcement of the results of Sample *B*, especially in light of the fact that he is, in all probability, Darlene's killer?"

"I'll have to process these results, and give the matter more thought," he said quietly, causing his friend to raise his brows in astonishment.

"Don't you want him to pay for what he did?"

Martin lifted his eyes, and rested them on the coroner's face, before standing and offering him his hand.

"Thank you, Paul, for this." He hesitated, then allowed him a bit of assurance. "When the time comes, I'll see to it that he answers for it."

Doctor Amos nodded with relief, and stood to return Martin's handshake.

"Be careful with this, Martin," he advised, in all sincerity. "That man is walking around free, out there. He's killed once, what's to stop him from killing again?"

Martin paused at the door, and smiled. "Me."

Audra came downstairs after hearing a knock, and peered through the sidelights of the front door of Hawthorn Manor. A rush of anger immediately darkened her face.

She didn't stop to remind herself that Martin had explicitly told her that she was to allow no one in, and if she'd not been so upset at this moment, she also would have remembered that he didn't want her even coming to the door.

She opened the door only enough to speak through it.

"You don't have an appointment," she said flatly.

"Do I need one?" Greg Vance confidently brandished his badge, as if she would be impressed.

"Yes! Come back when you have one."

She moved to close the door, and he immediately put his foot in the frame.

"This is official business. Tell Martin Satterfield I'm here."

"Move your foot," she said, slowly and distinctly.

He made no move to do so, and she glared at him. "Mr. Satterfield is not in, presently. Please do me the courtesy of removing your foot, if you don't want to lose it."

"Are you threatening an officer?" He stood regarding her with amusement. "I saw you at the funeral. You were with Celeste Campbell."

"Do you think I have amnesia?" Audra demanded. "I see no need for you to stand here making small talk, when it is obvious that I have no wish to talk to you."

"And, exactly why is that?" he asked, with a smirk. "You don't know me, so how can you possibly know if you wish to speak to me, or not?"

"Move your foot!" She tried to slam the door against it, and he grabbed the edge of it, and attempted to push it inward.

"Aren't you going to answer my question?"

"Trust me, I know who you are," she informed him, coldly. "You're that hack detective, who draws his own lame, idiotic conclusions, and then tries to stack the evidence to support them! I said move your stupid foot!"

"And what if I don't move my foot?" he jeered. "Are you gonna make me?"

"No, but I will," a quiet voice promised, and the detective spun around to find Martin Satterfield standing behind him, an unpredictable flame beginning to burn in his eyes.

"You've been warned not to return to Hawthorn. Did you come to test me?"

Greg Vance's foot was no longer in the doorway, and Audra stepped out onto the veranda, and pulled the door closed behind her, positioning herself in front of it, and crossing her arms, as if daring him to try to enter the house.

"I have a few questions for you, Satterfield," he informed him, despite his flustered state, and reached into his pocket for his notepad.

"It's too late for that sort of thing." Martin cut him off abruptly, then stepped around him, and stood as a barrier, between the officer and Audra. "You're trespassing."

He appeared unsure of himself for a moment, then demanded, "Do you intend to use force? You do know that would be a felony offense, Satterfield."

"Do you think I care?" Martin challenged, stepping closer to him. "Leave," he suggested, his cold voice filled with venom.

"I'll be back," Detective Vance promised. "With a warrant, if that's what it's going to take!"

He turned, and strode back to his vehicle, then sped through the property gates, seething and cursing under his breath.

Martin stood watching him, anger causing his respiration to increase, and his muscles to tense up.

He turned, and reached around Audra to open the door, gripping her arm to compel her to go back inside.

When he closed the door behind them, he stood staring down at her with heated reproach, then shocked her by crushing her to himself, and wrapping her up in his arms.

"You are not to ever do that again!" he scolded, closing his eyes and pressing her close. "You have no idea how dangerous that was. Don't ever try anything like that, again!"

Martin continued to clutch her protectively, and she could feel his heart racing.

"Didn't I ask you, Audra, not to even answer the door? Why did you not listen to me?"

He tightened his hold on her for a moment, before slowly releasing her, and looking deep into her eyes, his anger dissolving into concern.

"I appreciate your attempt to stop him, Audra, but if I hadn't walked up when I did, he certainly would have managed to force his way in. You couldn't have prevented it."

She stood looking up at him wordlessly, bewildered by his emotional and desperate reaction.

"I expect the worse that could happen is that he would just keep waving his badge at me, and talk me to death," she joked, trying to get him to smile. Her attempt failed, and seemed to only agitate him.

Martin gazed down at her with a troubled countenance, reaching to lift a strand of her long hair over her shoulder, and brushing her cheek with his fingertips.

Audra had never seen the look in his eyes that he rested on her now, and she became aware of her quickening pulse, and tried to steady herself.

"I won't be leaving you here alone, again," he said shortly, with a harshness in his voice, before turning quickly and heading into the library.

Audra remained where she was, clasping her upper arms in a reassuring embrace, and trying to understand Martin's strange behavior.

She'd expected him to tease her maybe, once they were inside, but she was stunned at the way he fiercely hugged her, and reprimanded her, at the same time.

She realized that she had begun to shake, and took a few breaths to slow her heart rate, and calm down.

She came to the library door, nervous and compliant.

"I'm sorry, Martin," she offered meekly.

He looked up, while locking something into a drawer, and stood to come around and rest against the front of his desk, folding his arms, and giving her an apologetic smile.

"Perhaps I overreacted," he proposed.

"You never overreact," Audra said, frowning in confusion. "In fact, you're far more likely to have no reaction, at all. I know Greg Vance is a colossal pain though, so who could blame you for being upset?"

"I suppose we all have our limits," he remarked, traces of his anxiety still faintly visible, despite his attempt to cover it.

He glanced over at the clock against the wall. "It's about the time that you normally head home," he pointed out. "I have some business over your way, so don't be alarmed when you leave, if I seem to be tailing you. It's purely coincidental."

"I'll just grab my things," she said, and he watched her head upstairs, his smile fading.

"He wasn't kidding," Audra mused, as Martin's car stayed right behind hers until she turned onto her aunt's street. He tossed her an airy wave and drove on, turning a few blocks later, and pulling onto the main road that would take him back to Hawthorn Manor.

He breathed out a sigh of relief that no one else had followed her.

Chapter Fourteen

Aunt Celeste looked at her niece with surprise, as she made her way into the kitchen, before leaving for the office.

"Honey, aren't you supposed to be at Martin's house, by now?" She reached for a cup, gratefully realizing that Audra had already brewed the coffee.

"Apparently, today is my day off," she shrugged, looking down into her coffee with undisguised disappointment.

Her aunt came over to rest on the stool next to her. "Did you two have a disagreement?"

Audra shook her head, which did nothing to remove the puzzled look from her aunt's face.

Aunt Celeste simply waited, until her niece stopped staring into her cup and looked over at her.

"He had to be in town this morning, and he doesn't want me alone at his house when he's not there."

Aunt Celeste frowned at her. "You were alone at his house when I brought your portfolio," she pointed out. "What did you do, move a paperweight on his desk?"

Audra smiled, in spite of her moodiness. "I didn't do anything. He just said that he wants to be there from now on, if I'm there."

Her aunt continued to regard her with suspicion. "You're keeping something from me," she accused, still frowning.

Audra blew out a breath she was holding, and gave in to her aunt's prodding.

"He's just still upset at me, I think, because that stupid Greg Vance showed up at his house last week, when Martin wasn't there, and shoved his foot in the door, when I tried to close it."

Aunt Celeste's face registered her dismay. "Did he end up getting inside the house?"

Audra shook her head again. "I wouldn't let him in, and Martin just happened to walk up, and told him to leave."

Her aunt had a look of disgust on her face. "Greg Vance is a bonafide creep!" she declared. "I'm surprised Martin didn't punch his lights out."

"I thought he was going to," Audra admitted. "But he ended up leaving."

She glanced over at her aunt. "Martin just said that from now on, he doesn't want me there alone. In case he comes back, I suppose. He's afraid I'll say something to make him angry, but what do I care? Stupid Columbo wanna-be," she muttered darkly.

Aunt Celeste sat listening to all this with a feeling of unrest. "Well, honey, I'm sure Martin is just trying to protect you, even if you don't feel the need for him to. I think you can safely file this in the Lancelot category."

Audra laughed at that. "So, Martin Satterfield has now been elevated to Sir Lancelot in your eyes. I'll have to inform him of that, he'll be so pleased!"

Her aunt smiled, and finished her coffee. "Well, it's not *my* day off unfortunately, or I'd whisk you away to the mall, or out to lunch. But I'm showing a house in an hour, and I have a closing this afternoon."

She stopped, and regarded her niece closely. "What are your plans, honey?"

"I guess since it's my day off, I'll work on some designs," she replied.

Aunt Celeste nodded, and a faint bit of relief hurried across her face. "That sounds great. I can't wait to see what you come up with. I'll be in early, right after the closing, so if you get a sudden urge to go to town, how about waiting for me, and we can go together? Maybe do some shopping, and go to that Italian restaurant for dinner?"

Audra lifted her brows, and shrugged. "Okay, Aunt C. I'll wait for you, then."

She returned her wave, and Aunt Celeste headed off to her duties, with an aggravated expression in her eyes, and her frown returning.

A short time later, she pulled her car onto the property of Hawthorn Manor, after delegating her house showing to one of her agents, and was relieved to see Martin's car still in the drive.

When he answered the door and recognized her, he immediately registered alarm.

"Is Audra alright?" he demanded impulsively, without a word of greeting.

"You tell me," her aunt challenged in a gruff manner, still wearing the unhappy expression she'd left home with.

She stepped past him as he stood to one side, and turned to face him in the entryway, looking up at him with a glint of determination in her fearless, dark eyes that indicated her intention to get some answers.

"Martin Satterfield, is my niece in danger?"

He stood evaluating her displeasure for a quiet moment, before inviting her into the library and indicating a chair. Rather than move behind his desk, Martin pulled a chair close to hers, and sat facing Celeste Campbell, his eyes searching hers.

"Is Audra alright?" he repeated softly.

"So far," she answered, not missing the enormous relief that flooded his countenance. She repeated her question.

"Martin, is my niece in danger?"

"I would never hurt Audra, Miss Campbell," he said quietly, disappointed at her question.

"Oh, I don't mean you, Martin, stop it!" she fussed, reaching over, and giving him a motherly smack on the arm. "You're the last person I'd consider to be a threat to Audra."

He looked at her gratefully, then glanced over at the clock, and she laid a hand on his arm to make him focus on her.

"I'm sure I'm interrupting some big power meeting, Martin, and I apologize for that. Audra told me you were going to be gone today, and I wasn't sure I'd find you here. What time must you be out the door?"

"Within the next few moments, I'm afraid, and I can assure you that if it wasn't vitally important, I would simply reschedule. For now, I suppose the best use of our time is for me to reassure you that Audra is not in danger, but she has to refrain from antagonizing Detective Vance."

"She refers to him as a stupid Columbo wanna-be," her aunt informed him, with a flash of humor.

A smile lit up his eyes, as he thought about the way Audra had barricaded the door with her body, crossing her arms, and letting Greg Vance know, with just her glare, that she knew how to hurt him.

"Your niece, as charming as she is, can be a bit of a loose cannon. I've decided that when I'm away, she must not be here. Detective Vance is famous for showing up unannounced, without an invitation, and can be a bit obnoxious. Audra has Chihuahua tendencies, I've noticed."

"Tiny dog syndrome?" She thought about the ferocity of that breed, that was always ready to compensate for its small size by threatening to mix it up with a big dog, and laughed. "I see your concern," she admitted. "Audra is no pushover."

He nodded, relieved that she seemed to accept his explanation for his decision regarding her niece, with no further need for him to elaborate.

"She's worked so tirelessly, that I had assumed she would welcome a day to relax," he said. "I hope I haven't upset her."

"She didn't seem upset, just a little bummed. It's clear that she'd much rather be here, to be honest. But I've managed to convince her to go shopping, and to dinner with me this evening, and she promised to stay put until I get home, so hopefully she'll relax."

Something gentle rested on Martin's face, as he heard Audra's Aunt Celeste say that she would rather be at Hawthorn. He had begun to feel lonely without her here, and this small comment had an uplifting effect on him.

"Miss Campbell," he said, reaching to touch her hand with reassurance, "I do intend to hire security for Hawthorn. It's not something I've felt the need for before, certainly not for myself, but with the death of my late wife, and with your niece now frequenting my home, I've decided that it's necessary. I can't always be here, and from what you've said, Audra seems to be disappointed, when she's forced to stay away.

"I'll make it a priority today, while I'm taking care of other matters. Once I've attended to that, she will be able to continue with her work without interruption, regardless of any obligations that create the need for me to be away.

"She's doing an impressive job with the east wing," he added, standing and smiling, as Audra's aunt did the same. "You must come by when she's ready for the big reveal, and see her handiwork."

"Don't say that, if you don't mean it," she replied, lifting a harmless fist.

He laughed softly at her comical threat. "I insist."

He escorted her back to the front entrance, apologizing again for his need to leave, and watched her drive away, setting his jaw with determined resolve.

Martin stoked the fire in the den, and coaxed it into a comfortable blaze, before settling down in a leather easy chair, and reaching for his pipe. He added his tobacco, and lightly tamped it with no awareness of doing so, as his thoughts ran rampant.

After a while, he held the pipe in one hand, following one particular thought to its conclusion, before finally lighting it, and quietly drawing on it.

His reflections took him back to his conversation with Audra in his library, when the two of them attempted to settle what they agreed was unfinished business. He silently reproved himself now, as he admitted that he hadn't been completely honest with her about Izzy.

He had pardoned his hedging by offering himself the excuse that her questions, regarding whether Izzy would have told him about another man being in the house with Darlene, were directly related to Phillip March.

He let out a sigh of remorse, but had already determined that he would continue to let her think that what he'd led her to believe was the truth. It hadn't been the main focus of their discussion, he told himself, and there was no need to revisit the question. There would be time for that later.

The night he received the phone call about Darlene being found dead, he immediately left the lodge, to return to Hawthorn and check on Izzy. He returned early the next morning, having driven through the night in the company of one of his hunting companions, who had the foresight to advise him that having someone with him as he traveled back to his home, would make it difficult for law enforcement to reject or manipulate his alibi.

He arrived to find the house still being occupied by a few forensics team members, crime scene investigators, and of course, the inept and bothersome Detective Vance.

He'd heard someone address him by only his first name, and turned to see Doug Michaels, an investigator Martin was personally acquainted with, who managed to stop him, as he moved toward the west wing stairs.

He quietly let Martin know that he was the officer in charge, and that he would appreciate his being available to him in the next day or so. He advised him that he was about to depart to check on another case, but that he was leaving another detective, who would take his statement. Martin liked and respected Doug, and agreed to contact him, then hurried away.

After gruffly waving away anyone else's attempts to question him, he had turned, halfway up the stairs, and forcefully ordered that no one was to approach the upper west wing. Martin's friend stopped on the first step, and planted himself in a position to make sure no one did.

He had found Izzy sitting alone in her room, pale, and in a state of quiet agitation. She had clearly been up all night, after being interrogated relentlessly, and was now clutching a damp, and well-used handkerchief.

Martin had knelt in front of her chair, and had taken her hands into his, gently inquiring about her condition, and checking carefully to make sure she was alright.

126

He had removed the handkerchief from her hands, and touched it to her fresh tears, then raised himself up, and leaned close to hear what it was she indicated she needed to say to him.

She spoke in the faintest whisper, and Martin listened in stunned silence, as she told him who she had seen in the house with Darlene Satterfield, and that she had seen him there before. She began weeping, and asking him to forgive her for never letting him know, and he continued to soothe her, and assured her that he was not upset with her, and that he accepted her reasons. She confided to him that she had told no one else.

Izzy timidly confessed something else to him, then reached her trembling, old hand into her apron pocket, and gave something to him that was concealed inside a folded piece of paper. He tucked it in his own pocket, being very careful with it, quietly thanking her, and dropping a soft kiss on her forehead.

Martin spoke to her in hushed tones, and she understood that he expected her to act as if she had no knowledge of anyone being with his late wife.

She willingly agreed, and their pact was made. She clung to his hand, and he spent quite some time quieting her anxiety, before insisting that she go to bed.

When he was assured of her wellbeing, he made his way back down to the main floor.

The coroner had left a few hours before Martin's arrival. Darlene's body had already been transported to the morgue, and forensics had allowed the stairwell to be cleaned and the police tape removed, after Inspector Michaels informed them that Mrs. Isabelle Draper had a heart condition, and that he didn't want her coming downstairs, and seeing it all still there.

Detective Vance wasted no time flipping open his notepad, and firing off his questions.

Vance was, apparently, a chain smoker of cheap, discount cigarettes, and had created a stench in Martin's beautiful home that only added to his level of irritation.

Martin had exerted every bit of strength he possessed, to keep from grabbing the useless, and intrusive detective by his neck, and throwing him out of his home.

His friend, who'd arrived with Martin, drew him aside to quietly advise him to simply let the investigator's questions proceed, in order to be done with him, and he finally stopped pacing about, and stood solidly in front of the investigator, folding his arms, and glaring down at him with frosty precision.

This seemed to have the effect of unnerving Detective Vance, and he closed his notepad, and muttered something about returning later, then took his leave.

Martin's friend had remained throughout the ordeal, and when the house had finally been cleared of its unwanted occupants, Martin asked him to assist in an urgent, legal matter, and afterward arranged for him to fly back to the town where the hunting lodge was.

The days to follow were filled with the pushy, aggravating antics of the detective, a term Martin used loosely.

Martin had contacted Doug Michaels, as he'd requested, and he told Martin that the police chief thought he should give Detective Vance a chance to prove himself, so he'd taken a step back, in order to let him handle things, but that he was still the officer in charge, and that Martin was to call him anytime, if he felt the need to speak with him about his late wife's death.

Martin had listened to all of this with a growing sense of indignation, and quietly determined that there would be no more interviews with Detective Vance.

He sat now, idly tapping his finger on the stem of his pipe, and silently fuming over the fact that the fool had, once again, attempted to access his home. After finding him on his veranda, trying to force his way past Audra, Martin's temper was still aroused, even days later.

A darkness passed over Martin's face like a storm cloud, as he told himself that if Vance had hurt her in any way, he would have had no problem earning the charge of assault on a police officer, and that he would have been sure to make it worth his efforts.

He'd spent part of today having another visit with his friend Doctor Amos, to inform him that he had humored him by granting at least one of his requests, and had met with the police chief, and Doug Michaels to deliver the ultimatum that the coroner had suggested, regarding Greg Vance.

In fact, although he had kept these details to himself, Martin, and the police chief, who had known both of his parents very well, actually had quite a long visit, and Detective Vance was officially barred from the investigation, and reprimanded for his unwarranted and provocative behavior toward Audra, who, as Martin had pointed out, had no connection to, or relationship with his late wife, or her death.

Doug Michaels would be taking possession of anything Vance gathered during his investigation, and would contact Martin if he had any further questions.

He had mentioned the rogue detective's threat of returning with a warrant, and the police chief advised Martin that he did attempt securing one without consulting the lead officer, but had shown no probable cause, and that the warrant had been denied, especially since Martin had never interfered with any requests to search the residence for anything related to his late wife's death.

Their visit had been a long one, but ended with a clear understanding between them, and Martin had returned to Hawthorn Manor tired, but resolute in his assurance to Doctor Amos that Darlene's killer would not go unpunished, although fulfilling the promise was more about obtaining personal satisfaction, than avenging his late wife.

He saw no sense in trying to fabricate any sense of grief or regret that simply did not exist, and Martin Satterfield was not a man to engage in a particular code of behavior, merely because society dictated it.

He felt what he felt. He did not feel what he did not feel.

Martin stretched in his chair, and decided to abandon his unpleasant meditations, then looked down at his dormant pipe, a smile of irony settling on his face. Once again, his need for comfort had outlasted his pipe.

Chapter Fifteen

Audra glanced up from her list, after she realized the car was still sitting in the drive, and found Martin looking over at her with an amused smile floating around his lips.

"What is it?" she asked, when he seemed to be expecting something from her.

Rather than tell her, he leaned close and reached around her, capturing her seatbelt, and sliding it across her lap, his face inches from hers as he clicked it into place. He lingered a few seconds, playfully chiding her with his eyes, then sat back and shifted the black sedan into gear.

She grinned and returned her attention to the list. "Can't take me anywhere," she quipped, and he laughed quietly.

"Where shall we begin?" he asked. "The town, if not the world, is your oyster."

"Big pieces, so furniture," she replied, looking up at him as a thought occurred to her. "Do you have a favorite store for that sort of thing?"

"I do," he admitted. "I have some old family friends who sell beautiful pieces, and many of the items you see at Hawthorn are from them."

"Let's start there," she suggested, and Martin dutifully drove in that direction, glancing over at her from time to time, to watch her continuing to edit her list, and mutter different versions of "what was I thinking?" under her breath.

"Why do I feel that you will be holding an entirely new list in your hands, by the time we arrive?" he asked, glancing around for cars, before pulling onto the main road.

"Because I probably will be," she admitted with a rueful expression, flipping it toward him, so that he could see how many times she had crossed through an item, wrote something new and then, many times, crossed through that, and returned to her original choice.

"I see that you adhere to the 'woman's prerogative' credo." he observed lightly.

She made a comical face, intended to be the equivalent of "oh, yeah?" and he grinned, and disciplined himself to focus his attention on the road, rather than on the lovely woman sitting next to him.

When Martin pulled into a parking space, Audra looked up at the furniture market with a look of disbelief, then turned to stare at him in wide-eyed delight.

"The Markhams are your family friends?"

Martin raised a brow, and shared her surprise. "Have you managed to make their acquaintance?"

"I have!" She couldn't hide her excitement. "I've actually been here, looking for some ideas for the east wing, and I must have stayed over an hour. They're both fascinating people! I could have talked to them all day."

He seemed pleased with her assessment of both his dear friends, and came around to open Audra's door, with a little smile on his lips.

She felt his hand on her back, as he reached around her to also open the door to the Markhams' store, and she was instantly spotted by Edith Markham, and embraced by the enthusiastic elderly woman.

"Our little friend is back!" she announced to her husband, then looked up at Martin with nothing less than joy.

She had an embrace for him, as well. "Did you two come in together?" She was clearly surprised, but pleased.

"We did. Audra is the designer for a renovation at Hawthorn, and she's concentrating today's efforts on choosing furniture."

Martin looked down at Edith Markham with fondness, then raised his eyes as her husband greeted Audra first, before moving toward him in welcome.

"Young Martin," he greeted, clasping his hand. "Isn't this a fine start to our day?"

Like his wife, his accent was still flavored by British origins, despite their having been in America for many years.

A flash of teasing washed over Audra's face, when she heard the master of Hawthorn Manor referred to as "young Martin". He acknowledged it by affecting a mock expression of fierceness, and she laughed softly.

Clive and Edith Markham both noticed their lighthearted interaction with approval, and the look they exchanged with each other promised an interesting conversation between them, when they stopped for tea later in the day.

During her last visit, Audra had spotted a particular piece for what she had decided should become a reading room in the east wing, and she was visibly thrilled when she learned that it had not been sold.

She rushed off in that direction, and Martin watched her go with a contented smile, which was also noted by the Markhams.

"I suppose I should discover what she has in mind," he remarked, resting a light touch on Edith Markham's shoulder before leaving them to join her.

She glanced up at him from where she knelt beside an old Victorian spring platform rocker, made with rich, dark wood, with beautifully intricate upholstered fabric, depicting scenes of a foxhunt.

She flashed him a childlike smile, and rocked it gently with one hand, then reached under it to pull out the attached footstool, padded with the same upholstery.

"If you turn these," she informed him, indicating the wooden knobs on the sides, "it becomes a recliner, and you can lock it into position."

She waited, holding her breath, and he could tell that she was silently praying for him to like it.

Martin lowered himself to kneel beside her, and touched the beautiful piece with his fingers, before looking at her with a softness in his eyes that made her feel lightheaded.

"It's lovely, Audra," he said simply, enjoying the way her face lit up. "We'll have it."

She thanked him with her eyes, and he stood and reached for her hand to lift her to her feet, before signaling to the Markhams that this piece was to be marked as sold.

Audra continued to consult her list, and discover more beautiful pieces of furniture that would be seamlessly integrated into Hawthorn Manor, as if they had always been there, which was exactly what she was hoping to accomplish.

They ended up spending almost two hours in the Markhams' store, taking their time, and being so in agreement that Audra accused Martin of just letting her have her way.

He had actually been pleased to discover though, that Audra's tastes in design seemed to lean toward more subtle, and masculine touches, rather than the outlandish, and modern blight that the east wing of Hawthorn Manor had suffered, over the past few years.

After Martin had purchased their choices, and arranged for delivery, they lingered a few moments more, visiting with the Markhams.

Martin allowed them to express their regrets at Izzy's passing, and rather than respond in the typical stoic, and cool manner that he normally displayed when sympathy was offered, he embraced them both, and quietly thanked them.

He escorted Audra to his car, and when he slid behind the wheel, he found her looking straight at him with happy mischief in her eyes, and raised his brow, waiting.

"Young Martin?" she asked, a ripple of laughter escaping.

He grinned, and glanced over to check her seatbelt before easing the car out into traffic.

"You'll hear all of the remaining generation who knew the senior Martin Satterfield refer to me as young Martin," he explained. "The fact that I'm forty doesn't seem to phase any of them."

She tilted her head back, and viewed him with critical analysis.

"You don't look forty," she decided, and he laughed.

"What should forty look like, to you?"

She thought about it for a moment.

"Okay, whenever you're glaring at me, you might become a little fortyish."

This produced another quiet laugh, as Martin secretly acknowledged to himself that he couldn't remember having ever enjoyed a day, as much as he was enjoying this one.

Audra pursed her lips, and turned to look back between them, then up at Martin with the light of pending interrogation in her eyes.

He glanced up at the rear view mirror to determine what she had been looking at.

"I've never seen anyone, including the ever vigilant Detective Vance, display the fact that I'm about to be questioned thoroughly about something, as clearly as you do, fair Audra," he commented lightly.

"Did you mean to miss that exit, back there?" She somehow felt a change of plans unfolding.

"I did." He waited with a little smile for her to add another layer of questions, something he had come to learn that he could expect from her.

"Why didn't you take it?" she finally asked, tilting her head and studying him closely.

He couldn't stop himself from reaching over, and tapping the end of her nose with his fingertip. "Why don't you just skip to the last question, and ask me where we're going?"

"That's not the way Detective Columbo Vance does it," Audra declared, mimicking the way he was known to whip out his important notepad, in a cavalier manner, and posing a vital question to him.

"How much wood, would a woodchuck chuck..."

Martin's burst of laughter kept her from having to finish the whole thing, and she flashed him a sly grin.

"So, where are we going, young Martin?" she demanded.

"I'm kidnapping you," he replied airily. "When we get to the border, I'd better not see you trying to tip anyone off."

This time, it was Audra who gave a shout of laughter, and Martin changed lanes to take the next exit, with leftover merriment still in his eyes.

"I'm taking you to lunch," he finally told her. "I don't care for many of the places in the downtown area, and I find it worth the extra bit of driving to eat at a place I enjoy."

Audra clapped her fingertips together, in the manner of her Aunt Celeste whenever she was excited.

When Martin pulled his car around in front of a beautiful inn, that Audra had never known existed, in spite of her having lived in the area for several years, her excitement became genuine.

"This is beautiful," she breathed, and Martin seemed happy with her reaction, as he came around to open her door.

She stood glancing around at the many vehicles of people who had also discovered the inn. "But it looks like we may be in for a wait."

"I would assume that some of those cars represent guests of the inn, but in any event, I don't anticipate waiting."

He reached for her hand, and tucked it under his arm, and nodded to the doorman, before escorting Audra inside.

She paused to take in the warmly lit ambience, and the soft, subtle music in the background, then let her eyes appreciate the high ceilings, and tasteful decor, as a host recognized Martin, and immediately came forward to greet them.

He murmured a table location preference to the host, and rather than seat them in an area where most diners hoped to sit, he showed them to an out of the way table, in a less occupied section, but one that Martin knew Audra would prefer.

A waiter was quickly sent to their table and, after their meal was ordered, he relaxed back in his chair, and watched her continue to appraise the room with fresh eyes, and with a genuine appreciation for a new experience.

He was enjoying her innocent delight in every facet of her new discovery, and even though she was casually dressed in her jeans and sandals, she looked completely at home in her surroundings, and Martin had not missed the admiring glances that others cast her way.

"I don't even care if the food is good or not," she admitted with a happy grin. "I love this place!"

She continued to allow her gaze to wander, before looking back at him with a soft expression, as the lighting only enhanced her beauty. "Thank you, Martin."

"You're so welcome," he returned quietly, holding her eyes with his for a moment, before indulging in a faint smile.

"Which of your attractive limbs must I be forced to twist, in order to have you tell me more about yourself?"

She grinned, and held out her pinkie finger, and he caught it with his own.

"The pinkie," he observed. "Suitable for swearing, and for twisting for purposes of eliciting information."

She gave him a slight roll of her eyes, and looked away with amusement. "What do you want to know?"

"Is there a limit to the number of questions you're willing to answer? If so, perhaps I should skip to the last one." He smiled at her playful attempt to scowl.

"I was born at a very young age," she began facetiously, and he reached to hook her pinkie with his own again.

"Don't compel me to use force," he warned, with a mischievous suggestion of punitive strength.

"Fine then, I'll behave," she surrendered. "Go ahead, you ask, and I'll answer."

"Your parents?"

"They were missionaries. Dad still is. My mom passed away several years ago, and my dad came back here for her memorial service, and then went back. Later, I joined him for a few years, then came back to live with Aunt Celeste, again."

Martin processed this silently, then looked up at her with faint surprise. "You became a missionary?"

"No, that's not me. I just felt that my dad needed his only child to be with him, after losing my mom, so I went to stay until he ran me off."

She grinned when she said this. "I guess I did missionary work, but only to try to help him. I was never called to that sort of life."

"But you're religious," he pressed.

"I hope not."

She noted his reaction. "I mean I love God, and I'm all set for eternity, but even Jesus had no use for religious people. I'm definitely not anyone you would want to emulate, as far as being good. I have a temper, and I've been known to shoot my mouth off, but..."

Audra stopped, and gave his arm a thump. "Watch it," she threatened playfully, when he seemed to agree with all that.

"I don't beat myself up too badly about it, though," she told him honestly. "My salvation doesn't hinge on anything to do with my performance, so I stopped trying to depend on the whole good works versus bad works thing, years ago. "

"What *does* it hinge on?" he wondered, asking as if he were simply trying to be a good listener, but secretly wanting to know the answer.

She gave a slight shrug. "Just believing what Jesus said about Himself, and agreeing that you can't save yourself, and that you need Him to do all that."

"How could something with such crucial consequences be as simple as that?"

Audra saw that he wasn't mocking her, and there seemed to be a childlike wistfulness in his question, as if he wanted to believe she was telling him the truth.

She looked at him intently, in a way that she never had, before answering him.

"Martin, will you be offended if I make an observation about you?"

He smiled fondly, and reached a finger to touch her chin. "Not unless you offend me."

She returned his smile, then seemed to be reading him, trying to identify what it was she was seeing.

"Am I wrong, if I think that you seem to be adrift, since you lost Izzy, and your parents? I realize that I didn't know you, when your parents died," she hurried to add, "but sometimes, when I see you, I see a man who's lost his anchor."

He lowered his gaze, feeling that she was seeing too much. "Very perceptive," he murmured.

"The only hope you'll ever have of being with them again, is by putting your trust in the same Savior that they did."

He sat quietly, still looking down at the table, and she began to wonder if he was even listening to her.

"Izzy spent her last few words telling me the proper thing to pray," he finally said. After a moment, he looked up at her searchingly.

"Audra, do you really accept what Christians say, about Jesus being the Son of God?"

"I have absolutely no problem at all accepting that," she admitted with ease.

"And you believe He can save you?"

"He'll have to, because I sure can't save myself. I just accept His sacrifice, and let Him do all the heavy lifting. All of that to say no, Martin, I'm not religious, and I don't want to be."

He seemed to be weighing her words, and Audra could tell that he was processing them, for authenticity.

She waited until their food was placed before them, and offers to refill drinks were made, then looked at him shrewdly.

"You don't like religious people, either."

"I don't," he admitted. "I do quite enjoy your aunt, and I like Pastor Reynolds, but I don't view either of them as religious. I believe they're honestly who they seem to be. I suspect they both would also say that they're all set for eternity, as you say you are."

His face took on a poignant cast, for a brief instant. "Izzy wanted me to make sure I was all set for eternity, and I'm sure I disappointed her, in the end. But I wasn't in a place to think about anything like that. I was only concerned with keeping her with me, on this side of eternity, if it even exists."

Audra rested her hand on his without realizing it, regretting his lapse back into sadness, when he had spent so much of the day seeming to be relaxed and free of stress.

"Do you sit and think about deep things like eternity, when you're playing around with a pipe you never actually bother to smoke?" she asked, getting him to laugh.

He turned his hand over, and cradled her fingers loosely in his palm. "I do smoke it. I just try to refrain from inflicting that on you, despite my claim to not care whether or not you mind."

"I don't, actually. I was being honest about that. Pipe tobacco smells amazing."

"I'll bear that in mind the next time I'm tempted to seek its comfort."

"Oh, so it's a magic pipe!" she exclaimed, and his laughter dismissed the sadness from his eyes.

"Perhaps it is," he conceded.

"How long have you been smoking a pipe?" Audra asked. She had idly wondered before, but never thought to ask. "Is that something you picked up, when you were in Europe?"

"It would be very refined of me, if I could make that claim, I suppose," he commented, enjoying their relaxed conversation. "But I'm afraid I acquainted myself with the tranquil aspects of pipe smoking, when I was a student at the university.

"It provided me a more respectful vice than attending keggers, and kept me from becoming a party to inevitable fraternity pursuits, such as cow-tipping, or panty raids."

He grinned at Audra's comical attempt to draw back, and thoroughly inspect him, while trying to imagine him involved in such common pursuits.

She suddenly thought of something she'd meant to put on her list, and the subject of his pipe reminded her, but when she put her hand into her purse to fish out her list, her fingers came in contact with something else.

She pulled out the house key he had given her, and stared down at it for a moment, then laid it on the table, looking up at him with a reluctant expression.

"Did you want this back?" she asked quietly.

Something like hurt appeared in his eyes, as he raised them to hers. "Have I somehow made you feel that I no longer trust you, Audra?"

His question surprised her.

"No, but you said... I mean, you don't want me at your house when you're not there, and I know me. If I were to drive up, and you weren't home, I would be very tempted to just let myself in anyway, and go to work.

"But you said you don't want me to be there alone anymore," she finished, unable to cover up her regret.

Martin realized that he'd forgotten to inform Audra that he'd arranged for security at Hawthorn. He knew he should just tell her that now, and not tease her, but he didn't seem to be able to resist.

He looked down at the key as if in deep thought, hoping that a smile wouldn't betray him.

"I suppose I should hang onto it," he said, implying that he was considering it.

He raised his eyes to meet hers, and allowed a moment to pass in silence, and the sadness around her lips allowed him to see that she expected him to pocket the key.

"But then again, I may decide to fall in love with you, and if that happens, I'd just end up giving it back to you."

He smiled at the rush of color in her cheeks, and caught her pinkie with his again.

"I've hired security for the estate. In fact, tomorrow will be their first day on the job."

He took her hand, and let the house key rest in her palm, before gently folding her fingers over it.

"Audra, you may come and go, as you wish. I'd very much like for you to keep it."

She looked steadily at him, with undisguised happiness in her beautiful eyes, as she slipped the key back into her purse, and completely forgot about her list.

Chapter Sixteen

Aunt Celeste stopped in the hallway, and looked toward Audra's door curiously. It was partially open, and she could tell that her niece was home, instead of at Hawthorn Manor, which was where she'd expected her to be.

She gave the door a light tap before opening it, and stood staring at her niece, who was laying on the floor on her back, with her legs straight up in the air, moving them back and forth, as if she were walking.

"Honey, what, in the world, are you doing?" her aunt demanded, and Audra simply grinned over at her, and pulled herself up to sit cross-legged.

"Exercising," she informed her.

"Okay," Aunt Celeste said slowly. "Why are you here exercising, instead of at Hawthorn, decorating?"

"Lord Satterfield ordered me to go to my room, and think about what I did!" Audra snapped hotly, feigning outrage.

"Oh, he did not!" her aunt replied dryly, relieved when Audra immediately made it obvious that she was kidding, by her droll expression.

"What's going on though, Audra? I thought it was okay now for you to be there, when Martin is away."

"Are you trying to get rid of me?" she demanded.

"I'm trying to get you to tell me what the deal is," Aunt Celeste said, laughing. "But I'm doing a miserable job of it."

Audra pushed herself up from the floor, and settled on the foot of her bed.

"I moved some rooms around, as far as what they'll be used for, since he seemed to want as much change as possible.

"I'm making the last rooms at the end of the east hallway into a master suite, so some plumbing has to be moved.

"Martin said this is the time to do that, before furniture begins to be delivered, so there's really nothing for me to do, until he calls to tell me that the plumber's done. So here I sits and thinks," she finished, with another little grin.

Aunt Celeste came over to settle down beside her, and gave her leg a little pop. "Well... you *could* sits and thinks, or you could go with me out to the Vanleer place, and give me your ideas for staging it."

"Did I leave you high and dry, Aunt C, when I stopped staging to work for Martin?"

"No, honey, but I'm curious to see what your thoughts are, before I have other stagers come in. That way, when I argue with them, I'll know what I'm talking about. That house is going to need a miracle," she sighed.

Her niece gasped, and grabbed her hand, jumping up and tugging her toward the door, with exaggerated slapstick urgency.

"Then, what are we waiting for? To the Batmobile!"

Aunt Celeste laughed, and swatted her on her seat. "Don't pull on me, I'm an old woman! You need to change out of those ratty gym shorts, and get some shoes on, and I need to bring Dexter in, and lock up the back, so it'll be a few minutes."

Audra padded into her bathroom to change, and do a light, quick cosmetic job, knowing that all her outings with Aunt Celeste invariably ended up at the coffee shop, or somewhere for lunch.

She glanced up into the mirror, then looked back up at it again, more deliberately, examining her face and realizing that she seemed to look different today, even though she could find no obvious reason as to why she should.

When she came outside, and got into her aunt's very nice SUV, she turned and faced her, lifting her chin, and waiting. "Do I look different to you, Aunt C?"

"Different how?" Aunt Celeste studied Audra's lovely face carefully.

"I don't know," she admitted. "Has the lighting in my bathroom changed?"

144

She shook her head, and lifted Audra's chin to examine her again. She did see something different, and as she began to realize what it was, an odd expression worked its way across her face, but she kept her observation to herself.

"You look like your beautiful self, daughter of my brother," her aunt declared, with her own variation of Audra's grocery store histrionics. She patted her cheek lightly, before driving in the direction of the house she wanted her niece to see.

"I've already been in the Vanleer house, of course," Aunt Celeste remarked, "and I know the first thing you're going to say when I open the door, but I'm hoping for the most economical approach, so bear that in mind."

When Aunt Celeste retrieved the key from the lock box, and opened the door, she glanced over at Audra with an affected look of dread, before leading the way in.

Audra stopped, and opened her mouth. "It's..."

"Orange," her aunt finished, with a grimace of distaste. "And that look on your face is the same one that my potential buyers are going to have on theirs."

Audra nodded slowly. "Where does the orange end?" she asked, as her eyes kept seeing it.

When her aunt crossed her arms, and gave her a knowing look, she drew in a sharp breath.

"The whole house?"

"The whole house, sister," Aunt Celeste said grimly. "Now, Audra, I know what you're going to say, but let me stop you there, and just let you know that the sellers want it listed as is, and I do not have the time to paint this entire house, nor do I want to put that kind of money into it."

She laid her hand on Audra's arm, in a desperate manner. "Is there any possible way to get around all this orange?"

She stood taking it all in, and her aunt let her process.

"The good news is that it's not neon." When she said this, her face lit up with a smile, as she remembered Martin's aversion to neon colors. "It's actually a burnt orange, so that's helpful."

"I don't see how," Aunt Celeste sighed doubtfully.

"This light Berber carpet is also helpful," Audra noted, looking down at it. "Are all the floors like this?"

"They are, and the carpet is actually fairly new," her aunt said, beginning to feel more hopeful, as Audra took on a thoughtful expression.

"You definitely want to distract from the walls, and with this carpet already helping to do that, I'd make a grouping of furniture away from the walls, toward the middle of the room. It's a large space, so there's plenty of room for that.

"I'd add some big pops of complimentary colors that are surprising, but in a nice way, and draw the buyer's notice to those first."

Aunt Celeste stood thinking about it, with her finger tapping her chin. "So, don't cover the walls up with art?"

"I mean, you could, Aunt C, but you really don't want to draw the buyer's eye to the walls, and that's what would happen. I'd skip the artwork, and draw as little attention to them as possible.

"That way, they'll read like a neutral, and you could just float your colors down low, and away from the walls. Get a rich teal green sofa, and maybe accent that with a very light shade of that same color, then add some orangish-red pops with things like vases, and fill them with something like tall silver curly ting branches, or some dried pampas grass."

She stood, mulling it over. "Actually, a few silver accents would be nice, and a little navy blue would work with the teal, but not too much of it.

"I'd get a couple of tall, modern floor lamps. You know what I mean, with the slender black stem, and a simple white shade. Maybe put those, and small end tables, on either side of the sofa, and maybe some accent pillows that have only a trace of this wall color in them, but mostly a repeat of all the accent colors. Maybe an oversized, really unique coffee table with a few nice, colorful magazines."

She glanced up, while moving her palm in a circle, toward the floor. "Anchor it all with a cowhide rug. I'd use a palomino one with a white background."

Aunt Celeste looked surprised. "A rug on top of carpet?"

"Cowhide works anywhere," Audra replied absently, still looking around and thinking.

She gestured over to the windows. "Those plantation blinds are nice, but the windows also need drapes. They need to be similar in color to the Berber, and hung really close to the ceiling, and slightly puddle on the floor to take the eye up, and bring attention to the high ceilings."

Aunt Celeste had begun jotting down Audra's comments, and the worried look she had come in with, finally began to smooth away.

"Well, honey, I believe if I can get people to bite on this downstairs area, then I won't have to work that hard to sell the upstairs, so I think I'll just concentrate most of my efforts down here, and hope for the best."

Audra stepped around to the kitchen, and made some additional comments, before they headed back outside.

"Thank you, Audra, for weighing in on this," Aunt Celeste said, locking the door, and giving her a grateful smile. "Let's go grab some coffee, and think about the rest of our day."

After a quick stop at the office, so that Aunt Celeste could give Audra's notes to her personal assistant, who was scheduling the staging for her, they made their way to the square.

Aunt Celeste brought their coffees over to Audra's usual table of choice, and looked at her oddly as she sat down.

"What's wrong?"

Audra grimaced. "If looks could kill, I'd be six feet under right now."

"What are you talking about?" She glanced around the room, then looked back at her niece with exaggerated wide eyes, and a little grin.

"Oh, my! That does not bode well," she agreed, after she'd spotted Dee Sanders glowering at her niece from her own table. "It was nice knowing you."

"I want all white lilies, and John Denver songs," Audra informed her facetiously.

"I'll probably just shove you in the freezer," her aunt laughed, playing along.

"Here comes my killer," Audra announced tightly through her teeth, in the suppressed manner of a ventriloquist.

Dee Sanders paused by their table, and after a brief nod to Celeste Campbell, favored her niece with an angry frown.

"Why would you just sit there, and lie to me, Audra Campbell?"

"Pull up a chair, Dee," she invited, curbing a smile after her aunt donned another big-eyed expression.

"I prefer to stand," she returned stiffly.

"Very well."

Audra slowly rose to her full, lovely height, and looked down at Dee quietly. "Refresh my memory. Exactly how did I lie to you?"

"You sat right there, and told me that you didn't know Martin Satterfield!" Dee accused, after having a slight reaction to Audra's intimidating stance.

"Where is the lie in that, Dee?" Aunt Celeste asked quietly.

"Well, she obviously *does* know him! She's at his house every single day!"

"You asked me to approach a man I had never said one word to in my life, and give you a character reference," Audra reminded her calmly. "I told you that it was my Aunt Celeste who knew Martin, not me."

"Exactly!" Dee snapped.

"Exactly what, Dee?" Aunt Celeste asked, deciding to stand, as well. "When you meet someone for the first time one day, is it not correct that you didn't know that person the day before?

"Audra had only ever seen Martin and his late wife in church several years ago, but she never met him, or said one word to him, until I ran into him, and he asked me to recommend a designer for Hawthorn. That was well after you talked to Audra about him."

"She also said that she had absolutely no use for him!" the irate girl persisted.

"Again," Aunt Celeste pointed out rationally, "because she had never met him, and had already drawn conclusions about him. She's made those same remarks to me."

Dee looked away sulkily, and crossed her arms, but made no comment.

"I know him now, Dee," Audra said thoughtfully, if not slyly, stubbornly refusing to look at her aunt, who was sending her a silent rebuke.

"Do you still want me to talk to him?" she asked, with childlike innocence, despite Aunt Celeste giving her a pointed look that accused her of being up to no good.

Dee Sanders brightened up immediately, and morphed into sweetness and light. "Would you, Audra?"

She shrugged carelessly. "Sure, why not? What do you want me to say?"

She steadfastly ignored her aunt's attitude of reproof and waited, while Dee clasped her hands together in delight.

"Oh, I don't know, but maybe just make me sound interesting. You know what I mean?"

"I do know what you mean," Audra replied lightly, "and I can absolutely do that."

"Oh, thank you, Audra," her would-be killer sang out, taking her hand with a little squeeze. "I'm sorry for thinking that you had lied to me," she offered, with an ingratiating smile.

"I've been accused of lying before, Dee," she assured her, with a careless wave of her hand. "No worries! I am the very back of a duck."

"I'm sorry?" Dee Sanders asked in confusion.

Audra shook her head. "Nothing important. It was nice seeing you, Dee."

"You too, both of you!" The girl practically danced her way out to her car, and Aunt Celeste wasted no time fixing her niece with a stern look of disapproval, as they sat back down.

"I don't even know where to start!"

"Start at the end, and work your way back," she suggested, still in her flippant mood.

"That was not very nice, Audra, even if it *was* Dee Sanders."

"Dee thought it was nice," she replied, with a lazy grin.

"You're not seriously going to talk to Martin about that girl, are you?" her aunt demanded in disbelief.

"I gave my word," Audra declared, striking a noble pose.

"What, exactly, are you going to say?"

"Whatever comes out."

Another careless shrug paired with her answer, to give Aunt Celeste even more reason to frown, before leaning back, and eyeing her niece curiously.

"You told her you've been accused of lying, before. Who made that accusation?"

"Martin."

"In what context?" she demanded.

"It was when I first began working there. It was no big deal, Aunt C, he was just angry and acting out, because he knew I didn't like him."

"Details," her aunt requested dryly.

Audra took a moment to recall their early days of saber rattling, before donning a severe expression, and deepening her voice to sound like the master of Hawthorn Manor.

"You say that you are not afraid of me, but you lie!"

"Audra!" Her aunt was floored. "Did Martin really think that you were afraid of him? I asked you if you were, and you told me you weren't!"

"I wasn't, for the most part, but you have to admit, he's a pretty intense man, and for the first few days, he was a living, breathing paradox. He'd deliberately try to intimidate me, and then get angry, if I was intimidated."

She glanced out the window, with a little smile. "It's not an issue anymore, Aunt C. We worked it out."

Aunt Celeste had laid a hand over her mouth, and was still staring at her niece. "Was he really yelling at you, Audra?"

"No, Martin doesn't go for volume, when he's angry. He just says his words as if he's pushing them through a meat grinder, then flings them at you."

Audra thought about the way Martin's piercing eyes had flashed at her, as he breathed out his heated utterances, and despite that, something tender wandered across her face for the briefest moment.

Her aunt caught her expression immediately.

"And there it is," she said quietly.

"There what is?" Audra asked. She looked puzzled.

"You asked me this morning, if you looked different," Aunt Celeste reminded her. "And it's that little look on your face, right there, that is different."

Audra drew her brows in uncertainty, and her aunt finally reached over, and clasped her hands.

"Audra Campbell, you have fallen in love with that man!"

Aunt Celeste said this with a look of worry in her eyes. Right now, she wasn't too sure she was happy about it.

Chapter Seventeen

Martin hung up the phone with a blend of pleasure and regret. He had felt a small, pleasing surge of emotion, when he'd told Audra that it would be at least another day before the plumbing on the east wing was completed, and she was unable to hide her disappointment from him. This was coupled with a sting of sadness, as he keenly felt her absence.

Audra Campbell had an enchanting way about her that seemed to dismiss the gloom and loneliness from the hauntingly beautiful, but isolated Hawthorn Manor.

She infused it with youth and light, whenever she breezed through its door, with her first whimsical comment of the day landing on its owner's ears. It lifted his grave countenance with his first smile, that would pave the way for him to later surprise himself with the sound of his own laughter, as they each went about their appointed tasks, and had their chance encounters.

Martin meditated on the captivating young woman, who had once viewed him with undisguised contempt, but who looked at him now with soft eyes, and complete trust.

He devoted a few more moments of allowing his thoughts to dwell on her, before opening his safe, and retrieving a document folder that he slipped a small, flat, cardboard box into.

He peered into the folder, and thumbed through all its contents, assuring himself that nothing was missing, then checked the time before leaving to run an important errand, and to attend an even more important meeting afterward.

Martin stopped his car at the gates of his estate that he'd determined would remain closed from now on, only to be opened after a visitor's identity, and purpose had clearly been established and approved.

The head security guard approached Martin's car, as he rolled down his window.

"Good morning, Mr. Satterfield."

"Good morning, Rob. I don't want any other car allowed in today, even if they're on the list and check out. The plumber's already here, of course, and he may need to come and go, but you're already familiar with him. Of course, the groundskeepers occasionally need to leave and enter. You've met them as well. I expect to return in a few hours."

"Sure thing, Mr. Satterfield." The armed man nodded, and acknowledged Martin's wave, then returned to his post.

The employees of his security company were all bonded, and had all worked for the Satterfield estate before. They were handsomely paid for their dedication to their job, and Martin was confident that no one would trespass, now that their services had been retained, particularly Detective Greg Vance.

Martin had reason to suspect that the obnoxious, ambitious man would not simply go away, regardless of his having been suspended from the investigation into Darlene Satterfield's death.

As a matter of fact, Martin speculated that his having been reprimanded might even renew his hostilities, and incite him to feel the need to confront him. The thought caused him to smile dryly with anticipation.

He covered the distance to the downtown area quickly, and attended to his first errand by stopping at his bank. He was immediately welcomed, and the bank manager escorted him to the vault and assisted Martin in opening his safe deposit box, by providing the second required key.

He showed him to a private room, and waited outside the door until Martin was ready to return the box to the vault. When Martin was satisfied, the manager walked with him to the door, and pleasantly wished him a good afternoon, always glad to see the bank's largest account holder, whenever he made a rare, personal appearance.

Once Martin had accomplished this simple, but necessary task, he checked the time, and drove around to the opposite side of the square, to park and wait for a few minutes, before heading into his attorney's office for a meeting.

Martin was a consistently punctual individual, but he hated arriving anywhere ahead of time, and being forced to listen to sappy elevator music, or endure a bored receptionist's attempts to make his acquaintance.

He sat quietly in his car, then raised a brow as he saw Celeste Campbell coming down the sidewalk, trying to sort through a sheaf of papers, and walk in a straight line in high heels, at the same time.

He noted her sense of frustration, and smiled to himself as his late mother's good friend muttered abstractly, and frowned down at her papers, clearly aggravated about something.

Martin exited his vehicle, and came around to rest against the hood, waiting for her arrival with a sense of pleasure. He straightened quickly, and reached out a protective hand, when he saw that her foot was about to miss the edge of the sidewalk in her oblivion.

"Careful, there!" he cautioned, catching her with a little smile, as the busy woman came close to falling, and ending up with a sprained ankle, or worse.

She grabbed onto his hand, and looked up at him in alarm. "My goodness, Martin! I almost bought it, didn't I?"

She flashed him a smile of relief, and looked down to make sure she was on solid ground. "Thank goodness I didn't lose all these papers. I wouldn't go back into that county records office today, for half your kingdom!"

She continued to check around herself to make sure nothing had fallen out of her arms, and looked back at him with wide, brown eyes that reflected her annoyance.

"That's the last time I feel sorry for my assistant, and offer to pick up records for her. That place is a madhouse, and the lunatics are the ones behind the counter!"

Martin looked down at her fondly, then glanced around, disappointed that Audra didn't seem to be with her.

She knew who he was hoping to see, and gave him a little laugh, in spite of her irritation, as she straightened her papers.

"That niece of mine is probably either rearranging all my furniture right now, or braiding my dog's tail. She gets up to all kinds of mischief when she's bored."

"Then it's just as well that she's bored there, rather than at Hawthorn today," he grinned. "She wouldn't be able to work with the plumber there, and the last time she was forced to stop working and wait for something, I caught her sliding down the banister, barefoot."

"You did not!" Aunt Celeste stared at him in amazement.

"Oh, I assure you, I did. I kept hearing something odd, and when I came out of the library to investigate, I saw her at the top of the stairs, throwing her leg over, and getting ready to take off, like a subway.

"Apparently, she had already done it several times, which explained the recurring, whooshing sounds. She didn't realize I had come into the entry, and when I grabbed her at the end of the rail, she let out a yelp, and tried to take me out. Ever the Chihuahua."

Audra's aunt continued to stare, and covered her mouth with her hand, in dismay at the thought of her niece pummeling the master of Hawthorn Manor, before she gave in to a hearty laugh that he shared with her.

"She didn't actually land any punches, and once she realized that it was I, she appeared to be mortified."

Martin's face lit up with the memory of Audra's embarrassed grin, and the way she had dashed back up to the east wing, as if nothing had happened. He had remained there, watching her run upstairs, willing himself to maintain a stern frown, but had paused and smiled quietly on his way back to the library, when he'd heard her giggling to herself like a naughty, unrepentant child.

Aunt Celeste stood shaking her head in amusement. "I'm glad we don't have any stairs, then. But I do have a pool, and I wouldn't be surprised to come home and find it filled with three feet of soap bubbles, which was one of her school girl methods of dealing with boredom."

She clasped Martin's arm lightly. "Thank you for stopping me from breaking a hip, Martin. You were exactly where I needed you to be."

Martin gave her shoulder a light embrace, then watched her make her way to her SUV with much more caution, and waited to return her wave, before he reached back into his car for his folder, and allowed the purpose of his meeting to cause his smile to fade.

Audra lay on her back on the living room carpet, with her feet propped up on the couch, and vacantly stared at some design show on television. She absently munched an apple, occasionally waving Dexter away.

"I'm not hurt, Dexter! Go away, and stop trying to rescue me!" She employed one of her long legs as a barrier to his good intentions, sweeping it toward him, and forcing him to seek an alternate route of approach.

"What is it with animals not leaving people alone, when they're on the floor? Sheesh!"

She took another swipe at him, then they both looked up as Aunt Celeste came in, immediately stopping to kick her heels off, and tossing her armload of paperwork onto a chair.

"I am never going outside this house again!" she declared, indulging in a bit of hyperbole to underscore her aggravation.

Audra flipped around onto her stomach, and braced herself up on her elbows. "You look beat."

"I *am* beat!" she complained. "I stood in that silly county records office for half an hour, if I stood there a minute, and then when I finally got someone to look up at me, she told me I was at the wrong counter, and seemed to think I was going to go stand in another line, and start all over again.

"I pitched a fit! There are no signs, telling you which line to be in for what. I let them know that I wasn't budging, and finally, thank God, Wade Hearn came out of his office, and saw me. You remember Wade?"

Audra shook her head, but Aunt Celeste hadn't waited to find out if she knew Wade Hearn or not.

"I let him know that I was not pleased, and he personally helped me out. All I wanted was a septic map, for crying out loud, and a perc report! You'd think I was asking for sealed court documents.

"And then, to top it off, on my way out, I dropped all the papers, and just scooped them up in my arms, and took off down the sidewalk, trying to see if I had them all, and almost stepped right off the edge!"

Audra frowned. "But you didn't, right?"

"No, thank God again, because who should be standing right there, as my foot was getting ready to miss the edge, but Martin Satterfield? He caught me, and probably saved me from ending up on crutches."

Aunt Celeste was still blustering about, and failed to see the sweet rush of pleasure that Martin's name caused to sweep across her niece's face.

She swirled around to plop herself down in a chair, and closed her eyes, completely done with being a real estate broker, for the rest of the day.

"I guess the plumber is still at the house?" Audra asked.

Her aunt removed the hand she had resting over her eyes, and looked up vacantly.

"What was that, baby? Did the plumber do what?"

"Is he still at Martin's house?"

"Oh, I guess he is, because Martin said it was a good thing you were here instead of there, because you couldn't do any work with the plumber there. You'd just be bored."

Aunt Celeste folded her arms, and fixed her niece with a long look that Audra had trouble interpreting.

"He also advised me of the sort of mischief my darling niece can get up to, when she's bored."

Audra pushed herself up from the floor, much to Dexter's glad relief, and hopped onto the couch, hugging a pillow and frowning. "What did he say?"

"I'm sure you already know what he said, and you're just waiting to tell your side of it!"

Audra did know what he'd said, and a slow grin betrayed her. "Well, I'm not sorry, it was fun."

"Oh, I bet it was a blast and a half, especially when you ended up being captured in the arms of Sir Lancelot," Aunt Celeste returned sarcastically.

Her niece drew her pretty mouth into a little pout.

"I can't believe he ratted me out!"

Aunt Celeste smiled, and returned to resting her eyes a moment, and trying to think about food. At this point, even the notion of calling for pizza delivery seemed not to be worth the effort of picking up the phone. She was exhausted.

Audra took the opportunity of assessing her closely while her eyes were closed, and knew that she was fretting about what dinner would end up being.

"Aunt C, want me to whip something up tonight, while you have a hot bath?"

She looked across the room at her sweet niece, and considered it. "I can't think of what there is, that wouldn't be frozen, and have to be thawed out," she said, trying to remember the contents of her fridge.

"We can have breakfast," Audra decided, "which is about all I can cook, anyway. You go get a bath, and I'll fry some eggs, and bacon, and wait to put some pancakes on the griddle until after you're done, so they won't get cold."

"And coffee?" Aunt Celeste asked hopefully. "Can there be coffee?"

Her niece leaped to her feet, and raised an authoritative finger toward the ceiling, with impressive solemnity.

"Henceforth, shall no good thing be withheld from the sister of my father!" Audra decreed, with exaggerated dignity. "And for the crime of visiting their ineptitude, and lack of respect, upon her person, none who are gainfully employed in the house of county records shall escape my wrath unscathed! Off with their heads!"

Aunt Celeste stopped on her way to her room to grab her silly niece, and squeeze her in a bear hug. "I love you, you ditzy broad!"

She headed off down the hall, and Audra watched her go with a little grin, wishing she could have been hiding behind a tree today, when Martin found it necessary to tell on her.

She began humming softly, as she took the eggs and bacon out of the fridge, and plotting her revenge.

Martin pulled his car to a stop, as his entry gates opened for him, and leaned out the window, waiting until his security guard stepped over to him.

"All quiet, Rob?"

"For the most part, Mr. Satterfield. The plumber had to make a run into town and back, and two of your groundskeepers left to go pick up a truckload of mulch.

"Some guy pulled up in a cute, little, red SUV, probably his kid's car, and claimed to have an appointment, but we told him that no one was entering the property. He flashed his cereal box badge at Mike."

Rob grinned, remembering the man's assumption that his badge was a golden ticket, and that the gates would just magically swing open.

"Mike told him it was very pretty, which really hacked him off. He did turn around and leave, though. He tried to squeal his tires, but his little four cylinder couldn't make that happen."

Martin had frowned quickly when his guard mentioned Greg Vance's attempt to return, but couldn't stop himself from laughing at Rob's rendition of the episode.

"Blitz, here, won't be half as nice the next time, will you, boy?" Rob reached down and roughed up the impressive German Shepherd's coat. "He's pretty sensitive to our reactions, and has a keen instinct."

Martin got out of his car in an easygoing, non-threatening way, and knelt down in front of the beautiful animal, holding out the back of his hand for him to smell, before giving him a light scratch behind his ears.

"I used to have a Shepherd," he said softly, remembering his beloved dog with a bit of emotion. "He was with me all my life until he got old, and left me."

He stood up, and regarded the noble animal with a sad smile, before looking up at Rob.

"A young lady will be a frequent visitor here, Rob, pretty much every day. Her name is Audra Campbell, and she drives a blue, sixty-nine Karmann Ghia Coupe." He grinned at Rob's peaked interest in that fact.

"She's overseeing the renovations in one of the wings here. Once you see her, you won't forget her, so she'll become easy for you guys to recognize. Long hair, green eyes, relaxed attitude. You'll probably have to make her turn down her radio to hear you. I think this week, it's Boston, or Kansas. She tends to mix it up."

Rob laughed in appreciation. "Nice!"

"When she comes through here the first time, if Blitz is around, would you ask her to hop out and meet him, and let Blitz get a sense that she's okay to be here?"

"Sure thing, Mr. Satterfield!"

"And Rob..." He paused, and drew in a breath, his eyes roving around, as he thought about what his guard had told him. "You've trained Blitz as an attack dog?"

"Yes sir," the ex-Marine said proudly. "He's fully trained."

Martin nodded, looking down at the dog with approval, before glancing back up at the guard.

"Regarding that cop who tried to get through the gates today... as far as Blitz is concerned, that man is a walking bite suit. He is to be considered the aggressor."

"Understood, Mr. Satterfield," Rob replied soberly.

Martin got back in his car, and pulled through the gates, after giving them a wave. He stopped in front of his house, and sat still for a moment, fuming over Greg Vance's attempt to once again enter his property.

Vance knew that Martin had been informed of his suspension, so he could hardly claim the need to question him, but Martin knew that asking questions was hardly the reason for his continued efforts to gain access to Hawthorn.

His face took on harsh lines, as he recalled stepping onto the veranda, just as the man was clearly about to force his way past Audra.

Martin knew Audra well enough to realize that Vance would have had to hurt her to succeed.

He wished now, that he hadn't made his presence behind him known, but had simply caught him by the neck, and beat him to a pulp. Whatever the consequences, they would have been worth it.

He mulled over informing the police chief about this latest appearance, but decided that he'd rather just deal with Greg Vance, himself.

Chapter Eighteen

Martin stopped short, and gazed into his library in surprise, the fact that he was startled clearly evident, in his unbelieving eyes.

The last thing he'd expected to see when he came down from his shower, still in his robe, having not even gone into the kitchen to start a pot of coffee, was his designer, balancing on the front corner of his desk, slumping forward, swinging her feet back and forth, deep in thought, as she focused on her sneakers.

Her hair, as usual, refused to stay behind her back, and had fallen forward to hide her face, keeping her from realizing that she had been discovered.

"I see you used your key," he remarked softly, once he had sufficiently recovered.

She smiled down at her feet before sitting up straight, and reaching to toss her disobedient hair back.

"I see you still haven't fixed the doorbell," she charged, noting his morning attire, and lifting her brows. "Are you just now getting out of bed? Wakey, wakey!"

He wasn't sure if he wanted to scold her, or embrace her. As glad as he was to find her back in his home, he did manage to be slightly annoyed.

"I have been up for hours, but I remained in my quarters until now. The doorbell, as you point out, does remain in disrepair. I'll make a note to attend to that."

Audra tilted her head back, and studied him through lazy eyes. "You wake up gripey," she finally observed. "You haven't had any coffee."

"I have not." He came into the library, and approached her slowly before crossing his arms, and favoring her with an inquisitive look.

"How long have you been perched on my desk in this nonchalant manner, Miss Campbell?"

"Ah," she responded, seeming to find humor in his return to addressing her formally. "My Lord Satterfield, I have been in your lovely home for, lo, these..."

She broke off, and looked over at the clock, calculating it. "Forty-seven minutes."

He stood looking intently at her, but made no reply.

"Forty-seven minutes of sheer bliss," she continued, tilting her head back, and closing her eyes, gently swaying, side to side. She stopped, as she remembered her mission.

"By the way, do you know who Dee Sanders is?"

Her abrupt transition rattled him.

"Should I?"

"She has attempted to cross over your threshold on at least two occasions, although she would prefer you carry her."

Martin smiled sarcastically.

"If her attempt to cross over my threshold was with the intention of forcing yet another casserole upon my person, then I have, more than likely, made the effort to deliberately *not* remember her, so please do not endeavor to undo the progress I seem to have made."

Audra's eyes danced with playful rebuke.

"Oh, you must try, Lord Satterfield, otherwise I won't be able to keep the sacred vow that I made."

She leaned toward him, precariously close to falling forward. "Dee... Sanders..."

Martin began to feel that she was making him dizzy.

"Is the name Dee perhaps an abbreviated form of some other name?"

She screwed up her lips in deep thought, and leaned back to think about it.

"Maybe," she shrugged.

Her mouth relaxed to imply a solemn manner, regardless of what her eyes were doing. "She's interesting."

"Is she?" Martin came around to lean against his desk next to her, and glanced over at her, a smile insisting on undermining his attempt to frown.

He hadn't seen her lovely face for a couple of days, and he had missed her. "And what is it about Dee Sanders that makes her interesting?"

He glanced down absently at her sneakers, as they continued to swing idly, and waited for her to enlighten him.

"I'm not exactly sure," Audra said slowly, narrowing her eyes, as if she'd find the answer written out in front of her, if she squinted hard enough. "But I am tasked with the chore of making her sound interesting, and I have given my word."

She turned to look at him as he continued to rest against his desk, close to her, and regarded him with a mischievous light in her eyes.

"I always keep my word."

"Do you?" He was returning her gaze. "I'm impressed."

"Don't be," she warned. "Because that would make *me* interesting, and I'm here on behalf of Dee Sanders."

Martin nodded gravely. "Do continue, fair Audra. Who has tasked you with this apparent mission of goodwill?"

She gave him an exasperated look.

"Dee Sanders, sheesh! Keep up!"

He laughed softly.

"I'll try. What I understand, thus far, is that someone named Dee Sanders, whose first name may, or may not, be an abbreviated version of some other name, has dispatched you on her behalf to inform me that she is interesting."

He bumped her shoulder lightly with his own. "How am I doing, so far?"

"I'm pleased with your effort," she commended graciously.

Martin seemed to be exploring the color of her eyes for a long moment. "If I agree to accept your claim that Dee Sanders is interesting, may we dispense with making her a part of this conversation?"

She appeared to consider it, contemplating her shoelaces, and remembering that Martin told her aunt about the banister incident, before looking up at him provocatively.

"No. You deserve this."

"I must have wronged you grievously, to deserve *this*," he muttered dryly, and Audra laughed.

He compelled her to look at him.

"Is it your wish that I find this woman to be interesting?"

She seemed to struggle with that.

Martin leaned close, his lips touching her ear.

"Say no," he whispered.

She grinned, and brushed his ear with her whisper. "No."

He smiled tenderly at her, and gave the tip of her nose a gentle tap.

"Tell her that you fought hard for her, but that I was distracted beyond all hope."

He lightly tugged a strand of her silky hair.

"Apparently, you charmed my security guards, and they let you breeze right through the gates."

"They seemed to already know me," she admitted. "They have a cute dog."

"Blitz, cute." Martin laughed at that.

He forced himself to stand away from the edge of his desk, and paused to look down at her, taking her hands in his.

"The furniture is being delivered today."

He tugged her slightly forward to indicate that he wished for her to stop using the desk as a chair.

Her face lit up, and she landed on her feet, clearly excited.

Martin continued to smile down at her, and she looked up contentedly at him, still bent on harassing him.

"I hope you don't intend to embarrass me when the delivery men get here, by running around half-dressed."

He gave her a wry grin. "I propose that you find the kitchen, and brew us a pot of coffee, while I array myself in a manner conducive with maintaining your dignity."

She started to move in that direction, when he caught her hand and enticed her back toward him, surveying her closely.

"Audra, I've missed you."

She almost replied with her usual folly, but instead, gave his fingers a light squeeze.

"I might have missed you, too."

She rested happy eyes on him, then turned and headed out to the kitchen.

"I *might* have.   A little.   I find that interesting."

She continued tossing random, fading, little remarks over her shoulder until she was out of his hearing.

He watched her go with a deep sense of joy.

When Aunt Celeste heard Audra letting herself in the front door, having returned from Hawthorn, she hastily dabbed her eyes with a tissue, and sat waiting for her to go drop her things off in her room, as she always did, before coming out to look for her.

She heard her before she saw her, because Audra had already begun telling her about the furniture arriving, as she was still walking through the hallway.

When Audra reached the den, she continued with her humorous story, tossing a throw pillow to one side, and dropping down on the couch with a bounce.

Her account of the day's events trailed into silence, as she saw her aunt's face, red from crying. She laid a hand on her throat, staring at her with a feeling of dread.

"What happened?" she demanded breathlessly.

She hopped up, and came over to kneel in front of Aunt Celeste, and grabbed a fresh tissue to tuck into her hand. "What is it, Aunt C? You're scaring me."

Aunt Celeste reached to take her hand, and offered a loving smile, in spite of her tears.

"I'm sorry, baby, I don't mean to scare you. But I do have some bad news."

Audra had an immediate flashback to this same scene that had played out between her aunt and herself, when her father called to say that Audra's mother had passed.

She looked up at Aunt Celeste with those same anxious eyes now, and made herself ask the question.

"Is it Dad?"

She nodded, but had to wait to add anything more. She took a few deep breaths, and prepared to finish, but Audra stopped her.

"Don't say it," she whispered.

Aunt Celeste looked at her helplessly, then burst into fresh tears, her heart broken.

Audra raised herself up higher on her knees, and pulled her aunt's head onto her shoulder to just hold onto her, while Aunt Celeste wept over the loss of her twin, and part of herself.

She stared past her at nothing, her eyes wide with shock, and continued to silently comfort her aunt, not knowing what else to do.

It was some time before Aunt Celeste leaned back in her chair, and looked vacantly out through the sliding doors, where Dexter was rolling around on his back with a chew toy in his mouth, and clutched her tissues in a tight fist.

"Was it his heart?" Audra asked in a small voice, already knowing the answer.

"It was, sweetheart," the sister of her father answered softly. She flashed Audra a bittersweet smile.

"We both tried to make him stay here, honey, but Jack wouldn't hear of it. He knew the risks, but he wanted to finish what he and Glenda had committed to do."

She looked down at Audra's beautiful, solemn face, and stroked her hair lovingly.

"I'm so glad you got to go be with him when you did, Audra. That was such a sweet gift to him."

"But I should have stayed," Audra said in a trembling voice. "I shouldn't have let Dad talk me into leaving him."

A single tear made its way down her face, warning her of others to come.

"To be honest, Audra, I believe that's why your dad was so insistent that you return to the states," Aunt Celeste supposed, quietly marveling at the young woman's composure, but knowing that it was simple shock that caused her to remain as calm as she seemed to be.

"I think he knew that this day was coming sooner than he'd hoped, and he wanted to spare you the hardship of being left alone in a foreign country, having to deal with the aftermath his death."

Audra nodded slowly, not knowing what to say.

Aunt Celeste reached for her hands. "Honey, I got the call late this morning. I decided to wait until you returned to tell you in person for several reasons, and I hope you can forgive me for doing that.

"Things have to move quickly in Honduras, when a U.S. citizen passes, especially when the family wishes for their loved one to be repatriated.

"I spoke with the U.S. Embassy, who put me in touch with a funeral home that provides cremation services, along with facilitating repatriation.

"Of course, when your mother passed, Jack was still in Honduras, and he could oversee all that himself from there, as the surviving spouse."

Audra continued to simply nod and say nothing, and her aunt watched her processing everything for a moment.

"Your father's ashes are to be brought home, just as your mother's were, and we'll have them interred at the columbarium in the double niche, next to hers. Unless you want to change any of that, sweetie, but since your mother's body was cremated, and I knew that was Jack's wish, I did go ahead and authorize it."

She reached to stroke her niece's beautiful, long hair and gave her a loving look of concern.

"Your father and mother made me the executor of their wills, when you were just a small girl, Audra, but if you feel any resentment at all, at not being consulted, just tell me how you want any of it to change. You're no longer a small child, and if you would like executorship to be handed to you, I completely understand, and I'm glad to do it."

She shook her head slowly, and turned to look out at the fun Dexter was having, all by himself, and remained silent for a long while, before looking up at her aunt with a shaky smile.

"Thank you, Aunt Celeste, for taking such good care of Dad." She looked back out at Dexter, and the unshed tears in her eyes made them luminous, and even more beautiful.

"The sister of my father," she whispered to herself, just before they escaped, and found their way down her cheeks.

She laid her head on her aunt's lap, and Aunt Celeste sat stroking her head, deep in thought.

"Sweetheart," she finally asked softly. "Do you want to call Martin, and let him know? I wouldn't think you'd be up to working tomorrow."

She lifted her head, and took a deep breath, before raising her eyes to her aunt's in sad petition. "Would you do it, Aunt C? He'll be really kind to me, and I'll just start crying."

"I absolutely will, baby. You go get a hot shower, and I'll take care of it."

They both stood and shared a comforting hug, before Audra went to go stand in the shower, and cry alone.

She cried for the guilt she felt over leaving her father by himself. She cried over losing her faithful audience of one, who laughed, and cheered for his beautiful daughter, whenever she insisted on telling him all about something that had happened at the mission, by adding her own clever impersonations, and unique spin, sending him into fits of laughter.

She cried all over again, for the loss of her beautiful mother, who could dance like a ballerina, and who was always ready to take a bit role in one of Audra's impromptu plays, and who wrote funny notes, back and forth with her during church, while her father put his hand over his mouth to hide his grin, and pretended to be upset about it.

She cried for the future, when Aunt Celeste would leave her as well, and those tears might have been her most bitter, because it was a sorrow that still loomed before her, like an ominous threat.

When she was weary from crying, she found her ratty old gym shorts and a faded sweatshirt, and pulled them on, then sat down on the foot of her bed, and just stared at the floor.

She kept her gaze pinned to the rug, when she heard a light tap at the door, and mumbled, "It's not locked," in a dull, weary voice.

The door opened slowly, and she looked up to see Martin standing there, with his heart in his eyes.

Audra immediately ran to him, and he gathered her close, remembering the sting of this particular pain. He stroked her hair, and whispered soft things in her ear, then laid a kiss on her forehead, soothing her, until she grew quiet and still, in his arms.

When she raised her face to look up at him, he softly traced his fingertip over her lips. It took every ounce of discipline he had not to kiss those lips, but he wouldn't allow himself to take advantage of how vulnerable she was in this moment, or to add confusing emotions to the ones that were already overwhelming her.

He let his eyes linger gently on her sweet face, and they silently told her the things she needed to hear, before he drew her closer into his protective embrace.

Chapter Nineteen

Myra Hepplewhite nervously waited for someone to answer the door, tightly holding on to the bundt cake she'd made, in case the big dog that had come around the house to greet her tried to get it.

"Now, you get down!" she commanded Dexter, who hadn't made any attempt to jump up. He looked at her in confusion.

"You just run on back where you came from," the old lady admonished him. "I didn't make this for you!"

She was still fussing at a bewildered Dexter, when Aunt Celeste opened the door, and appeared startled to find her neighbor standing on her porch.

"Miss Myra!" She stared down at the bundt cake in wonder, then back up at her old, white-haired neighbor's face. "Come in," she hurriedly said.

She pulled the door open wider, and stood to one side to allow her to pass through, carrying her cake.

Miss Hepplewhite made her way slowly toward the kitchen, as Aunt Celeste motioned for Dexter to go back around the house, and placed her baking efforts on the counter, turning to acknowledge Audra, and eyeing the handsome man next to her with obvious surprise.

Aunt Celeste had followed her in, and saw that she was unprepared to encounter a stranger. She hurried to introduce Martin Satterfield to her, and Miss Hepplewhite actually smiled at him, when he graciously offered his hand, and greeted her.

"I'm afraid we've only just returned from a funeral," Aunt Celeste apologized. "That's why we're a bit more dressed up, than usual."

"I read about it in the paper," the old lady informed her. "I'm sorry for your loss," she added.

"Thank you," Aunt Celeste returned quietly, still thrown off balance by her neighbor's unexpected kindness.

"I had a brother once," she continued, with a rush of surprising emotion brightening her faded, blue eyes.

"Of course, he wasn't a twin to me, he was the baby. It broke my heart when we lost him, and I imagine for you, it would be even worse, being a twin, and all. I sure am sorry, Miss Campbell."

Aunt Celeste didn't know what to say, so she simply gave her neighbor a gentle hug, and a smile.

She turned, and focused her gaze on Audra, and her normally inquisitive, critical expression that was most often leveled at the young woman, was replaced by soft regret.

"I sure am sorry about your daddy, young lady."

Audra impulsively got up, and came around the counter to give the old woman a hug. "Thank you, Miss Myra."

"I met your daddy, once," she added. "He and your mama were visiting over here, and you were just a little thing.

"A big wind had come up, and took my trash can down the street, and I guess he saw it. He took off running after it, and brought it back to me. I always thought that was a nice thing for him to do."

She sized Audra up with smiling approval.

"I guess I've only ever seen you from across the street. My, aren't you a beautiful thing?"

Audra didn't know how to respond, other than offering a whispered, "Thank you." She gave her another hug.

Miss Hepplewhite gestured over toward the bundt cake, with a frail hand.

"Now, that's lemon. Some people don't like lemon, but I always think lemon makes a good bundt cake. It goes good with coffee or milk."

"It's beautiful, and it smells really good," Aunt Celeste said sincerely. "It was so sweet of you to think of us."

"Well," Miss Myra said, waving the compliment away, "I expect you'll have people stopping by to pay their respects, and it might be nice to have something to offer them. Don't worry about the dish. When I need it again, I'll come get it."

She moved toward the door, but stopped to turn, apparently remembering something.

"I noticed some of your company came already, but I guess he got tired of waiting. I expect he'll be back."

Aunt Celeste looked at her with a confused expression. "Was it anyone you recognized, Miss Myra?"

"I can't say that I did," she admitted. "He was in a red car, kind of like yours, but real small." A look of indignation flashed across her face.

"He threw a cigarette butt out, right on your driveway! I'd pick it up for you, Miss Campbell, on my way back, but I fall easy," she apologized.

"Oh no, Miss Myra, don't try to pick it up. I'll go out in a minute, and get it, myself," Aunt Celeste protested.

She rested her arm around the old woman's shoulders, and walked with her back to the door.

"I can't tell you how much it means to us, for you to come by, and bless us the way you did," she told her, unable to resist another light hug.

She stood watching her neighbor make her slow way back across the street, then decided to go on out now, and pick up the cigarette butt, knowing it would please the disapproving lady.

Audra had come back over to reclaim her place next to Martin. She noted his stony countenance, and his tightened jaw, and touched his hand with hers in a light caress.

"Maybe it wasn't him," she offered softly.

Martin made no reply, but turned his hand over to lace his fingers into hers, his eyes fixed firmly on the countertop with a quiet anger settling in them.

Aunt Celeste came back in, and tossed the nasty cigarette butt into the trash, then stood washing her hands at the sink.

Martin spoke to her quietly. "Miss Campbell."

She turned to look back at him, while drying her hands on a paper towel.

"Yes, Martin?"

"Would you know Greg Vance, if you saw him again?"

"I certainly would know that little weasel!" she scowled, before looking at him strangely. "Why do you ask?"

"Your neighbor just described him," he replied, and she came over to take a seat across from him.

"What, in the world, would Greg Vance be doing here?" she demanded with a frown. She glanced over at her niece with a look of dread.

"Audra, have you had any more run-ins with that man?"

She shook her head. "I haven't seen him since he showed up at Hawthorn."

"Well, this is just harassment, then. He knows it will get back to Martin."

Aunt Celeste crossed her arms, and expelled a deep breath.

"If he comes back again, he'd better not get out of his car. I'll call 911, I don't care if he *is* a cop."

"Do that," Martin advised quickly. "But don't admit to them that you know he's a police officer. Just imply that he's a stalker who's been aggressive toward Audra.

"The quickest way to get someone over here, is to advise the 911 operator that you have a gun, and that if you feel threatened, you intend to use it, whether you actually do or not. That should result in an immediate response."

"Well, I wouldn't be lying, if I did say that," Aunt Celeste returned dryly. "And I definitely *would* use it if I had to. That wouldn't create a conflict with my theology, at all!"

Martin had to smile faintly at that, as he looked down at Audra's hand in his, and gave it the slightest squeeze.

"I still need an answer to my question, Martin," Aunt Celeste reminded him, not missing her niece gently returning a soft pressure to his hand.

"Do you think Greg Vance is just doing this to get to you, or is Audra in any danger?"

"I intend to find out," he replied. "In any event, I'll take care of it." He slowly released Audra's hand and stood up, preparing to leave.

"Thank you for allowing me to accompany you and Audra to the funeral, Miss Campbell."

"Thank you so much for making the time to be with us," she said, with a tired smile.

Martin gave her a hug, then compelled Audra to walk him to the door, by simply resting his hand on her back.

She stepped out onto the porch with him, and stood facing him with her arms crossed, and a worried look shadowing her eyes.

"What are you planning to do, Martin?"

He looked down at her with only a hint of a smile, and crossed his own arms.

Martin had teased her a few times about the way she had planted herself in front of Greg Vance with her arms crossed, and she knew that's what he was doing now.

"Stop it, I'm being serious," she said, reaching to give his arm a light punch.

He smiled and caught her hands, then gave her a pleased, soft look. "You were being flirtatious with me in there, Miss Campbell, and right in front of your Aunt Celeste."

She tilted her head back, and treated him to a little wink. "Like that?"

Martin laughed softly, reaching to comb his fingers through her hair, and rest his eyes on hers.

"Is Miss Hepplewhite watching us?" he asked. Audra had once entertained him with several minutes of parody, involving their elderly neighbor, and her binoculars.

She glanced over toward her house, and shook her head. "Nope. That walk across the street and back probably tired her out. Who knew that she could be such a sweetie? I feel bad for picking on her, now."

"As well you should," Martin reproached lightly.

They stood quietly, intently aware of each other, before Martin slowly leaned close to whisper in her ear.

"Miss Campbell, I find you very interesting."

Audra giggled, and he grinned, glad that he could make her laugh, especially after her tearful past few days.

She looked away, and he could see her thoughts reflected in her eyes, when she gazed back up at him.

"Martin, what are you planning to do?" she asked again.

"I have the same question that your aunt has, regarding Detective Vance's unwarranted appearance at your home" he replied lightly. "And I'm going to get an answer."

She stared up at him, knowing that it would do her no good to try to talk him out of it. It had been an emotional day, and her eyes began to brim over. She lowered her head.

"None of that," Martin gently scolded. He lifted her chin to make her look at him.

"There's no reason to be upset, Audra. I don't expect to run into his little red car by simply driving around looking for it, so I'll return to Hawthorn for now, and decide how I wish to proceed."

"I won't sleep at all, tonight," she mumbled, still upset.

"Yes, you will, if I have to come back over here, and blow sand in your eyes."

She smiled, then studied him, remembering his question. "Why did you ask me if Miss Hepplewhite was watching us?"

"Because I'm thinking of kissing you," he enlightened her, watching her tilt her head to consider that.

"You never have," she replied, suspiciously.

"No."

"Why now?"

He shrugged. "I only said I was thinking of it."

She appeared to be put out with him, and gave him a little frown. "Well, I'm going back inside, and leave you to think."

"Come back here," he growled playfully, catching her hand, and gently persuading her.

He was entertained by Audra's half-hearted attempt to appear reluctant.

"Watch and learn."

He slipped a hand behind her waist. "I saw this once in an Errol Flynn movie," he informed her, scooping her rapidly, and firmly up against him, into a snug hold.

She was unable to suppress a small gasp.

"Not too shabby," she approved breathlessly. "Then, what happened?"

"Well, after that he kissed her, of course," Martin said, matter-of-factly. "But I didn't approve of his method."

"Didn't you?"

"I did not. I found it all a bit frantic."

"What would you have done differently?"

He gave her a slow smile.

"Why, Miss Campbell, I suspect that you are baiting me."

"What gave me away?"

"For one thing, your willingness to remain pressed tightly to me, like Scarlett O'Hara, in a vintage 'Gone With The Wind' poster."

She lifted the corner of her mouth in a little smirk, but remained exactly where he'd put her.

"It's only a matter of time, before Aunt Celeste begins to wonder what's taking me so long to come back in."

"I'm not afraid of your aunt," he scoffed.

"Prove it," Audra challenged, trying not to laugh.

"Are you daring me?"

"I'm double dog daring you," she replied.

He drew his brows, in an effort to reminisce.

"I suspect that I haven't been double dog dared, since I was a lad in grammar school."

"I'm calling you out, Satterfield!"

He found her squinty eyes, and western drawl immensely funny, and laughed quietly before reaching to stroke her chin.

"This is to be our first kiss," he murmured.

"I don't remember any others," she agreed.

"And, how have you imagined our first kiss to be?"

She gave him a deadpan look. "Kind of like Errol Flynn."

"Ah. Frantic, it is."

Audra knew that it wouldn't be, when his flippant demeanor subsided into a more serious intensity, and a rush of adrenaline began to take her breath.

Martin slipped his hand up the back of her neck, and into her hair, then prolonged anticipation, by allowing his eyes to play with hers for a long moment.

He was intentionally taking his time, before bringing her lips to his and, with meticulous deliberation, he very slowly, and thoroughly proceeded to stun her.

When he finally released her, he turned her around, opened the door, and watched her with a smile, as she gradually groped her way back inside.

He slid behind the wheel of his car, and sat thinking about her for a moment, before finally starting the engine, and breathing a casual observation to himself.

"That's what she gets, for calling me out."

Chapter Twenty

Alan Carr waited outside the door of Hawthorn Manor, peering down at his phone, and glancing up absently, when his client opened the door to admit him.

"Come in, Alan." Martin moved to let him pass.

His attorney quickly finished reading a text message, before putting his phone away, and looking up at him.

"Good evening, Martin."

He recognized Doug Michaels, as his eyes traveled across the entry out to the den, and looked back at Martin with a question in his eyes. "I hope you didn't begin this without my being present."

"I did not."

Martin gestured toward the den, and followed his attorney in. "I believe you and Doug are already acquainted?"

Alan reached for the investigator's hand. "Absolutely. How are you, Doug?"

The senior police office stood, and acknowledged him pleasantly, then settled back down, intrigued to learn why Martin had requested this meeting, but patiently waiting.

"Your security officer is very devoted to you, apparently, Martin," Alan joked. "Even though you told him I was coming, and I checked out, I thought he was going to make me get out of my car, and frisk me."

Martin smiled at that. "Rob is a good man. All of them are, and they've worked for me before."

He returned to the chair he'd been sitting in earlier, and reached for his pipe. "Did you see Blitz out there?"

"You mean Rin Tin Tin?" Alan laughed. "I wouldn't want to get on *his* bad side."

Martin smiled again, remembering Audra's estimation of the trained attack dog as "cute".

Alan laid his briefcase on the table, and removed a small recording device.

"Doug, against my counsel, Martin has insisted on informing you of his actions, that are directly connected to the investigation into the death of his late wife."

He noted the investigator's raised brow before continuing. "If you have no objection, I'd like to record this meeting."

Doug indicated with a dismissive lift of his fingers that he didn't mind, and leveled his eyes at Martin, making no remark as the attorney spoke the time, date, and the names of those present into the device.

Martin studied the pipe in his hand for a moment, before looking up to meet the investigator's steady gaze.

"I have to admit to you that I have deliberately withheld evidence, Doug."

Martin respected Doug Michaels, primarily because he took his duty as a police officer seriously. He knew that if the investigator felt that Martin's failure to turn over evidence rose to the level of obstruction, he would charge him, regardless of their friendship.

The officer remained silent for a moment, as Martin's confession placed him in a difficult position.

"I suppose I don't have to explain obstruction of justice to you, Martin."

"No."

He continued to study Martin thoughtfully, and began a series of questions, in an attempt determine his motives for withholding evidence, in the hopes of avoiding an obstruction charge.

"It is not exculpatory evidence, I would assume."

"It is not."

He nodded, and studied the back of his hand, seeming to not want to ask his next question. Finally, he raised his eyes to Martin's.

"Did you conceal this evidence to protect yourself?"

"No, Doug, I did not," he returned quietly, not missing the quick relief that swept across the officer's face.

"Did you conceal this evidence to protect the killer?" He looked sharply at him.

"No, certainly not."

Doug Michaels leaned back in his chair, and mutely considered Martin Satterfield, clearly recalling the morning he'd returned to Hawthorn, after receiving the call about his late wife's death, and his urgent desire to be allowed to continue up the stairs to the west wing.

When he addressed Martin again, it was quietly, and with a note of compassion. "Did you conceal this evidence to protect Mrs. Isabelle Draper?"

Martin dropped his gaze down to his pipe for a long moment, before looking back up at him.

"Not in order to cover any guilt on her part," he said, a hint of sadness resting on his face.

"In order to keep her from being interrogated?" Doug asked, watching the man seem to wrestle with the anger that began to stir inside him.

He looked up at Doug Michaels with disgust in his eyes. "Greg Vance was not going to be allowed anywhere near her."

His attorney flashed a look of caution at his client, but Martin steadfastly ignored it.

"She was a weeping, incoherent, badgered, old woman by the time I found her, and all because Vance continued to harass her until she fell apart. Izzy had a heart condition, and that fool could have killed her. There was no way, in hell, that insufferable hack was going to be allowed to say one more word to her!"

Greg Vance's senior officer emitted a sigh, and nodded.

"I understand that, Martin, but it's unclear to me how that factored into your decision to conceal evidence." He paused, then looked up at him, with a growing suspicion in his eyes.

"Martin, was Mrs. Draper in possession of this evidence?"

"She was," he admitted, almost too softly to be heard.

The investigator considered this silently, processing it, before attempting to proceed with his questions.

Martin sat regarding him with watchful eyes, waiting to be asked before supplying anything further.

Finally, the officer leaned forward, and rested his inquisitive gaze on Martin.

"Is this evidence something that Mrs. Draper removed from the crime scene?"

Martin laid his pipe down, and met his gaze steadily. "It had not yet been declared a crime scene."

"So, it was removed before calling the police."

"Yes."

Doug Michaels hesitated, realizing how protective Martin had been of Isabelle Draper, and not wishing to upset him. Finally, he pushed ahead, still needing to understand Martin's reasons for what he had done.

"Did Mrs. Draper conceal the evidence in order to protect you, Martin?"

"No, Doug, she did not." Again, Martin could see the investigator visibly relax.

Another possibility began to present itself to Doug Michaels. "Did Mrs. Draper conceal the evidence because she was afraid?"

"She was terrified," Martin said darkly, and the investigator sat back in his chair, with a feeling of uneasiness settling on him.

"She felt threatened?"

"Yes."

The detective exhaled, and shook his head, then reached to run his hand through his hair, indicating his slight frustration.

"I do understand your need to protect your housekeeper, Martin, but I can't understand why you didn't immediately provide this evidence, after she passed. You no longer needed to protect her. Why hang onto your evidence, if it could have closed this case?"

"Because I didn't want this case closed," he replied simply.

"Why, in the world, not?"

Martin paused before answering. "In, and of itself, I find the evidence to be compelling, but I wanted to determine what other facts it might lead to. I was determined to not let him get away with it."

"Him," Doug Michaels repeated flatly.

"Yes."

He breathed out a mild oath. "Martin, you can't just go out, collecting evidence on your own. You aren't the detective investigating this case!"

"And that idiot, Vance, is?" Martin glared at him, enraged. "He is the *last* person I would have given any evidence to!"

"I realize that he's certainly not the most likeable guy on the force, but..."

Martin's angry scowl, and his clenched fist, caused the investigator to look at him in surprise, without finishing.

"I didn't meet with you and the police chief, to demand that he be barred from the investigation, simply because he's not likeable, Doug."

"Alright," he responded quickly. "I think it's time you told me exactly what the evidence is, or better yet, show me."

"That's the reason I invited you here, tonight," Martin agreed. "I've known all along, that I would certainly turn the item Izzy gave to me over to your custody, Doug, but I had my reasons for making sure that when the time came, you alone would be the only one to know about it."

He leaned forward, and viewed the investigator in a manner that let him know just how serious he was.

"I would very much appreciate your being especially cautious with whomever you decide to share this with. I realize that I can't insist, but I'm asking."

Martin paused, before adding, "I'm afraid you aren't going to like this, Doug."

The officer studied his friend with intrigue.

"Let's have it, Martin."

Alan Carr lifted a hand to interject, before speaking into the recorder. "For the record, just to establish chain of custody, the evidence was retrieved by Isabelle Draper, and given directly to Martin Satterfield. He, in turn, placed the evidence in his safe and, when it became clear to him that Detective Vance would not relent in his efforts to try to gain access to his home, the evidence was then placed in a safe deposit box at his bank.

"As his attorney, Alan Carr, I met with Mr. Satterfield there today, and witnessed that it was just as he'd left it. He retrieved it, and brought it back to Hawthorn in order to turn custody of it over to you, Officer Doug Michaels."

The investigator listened to all of this, and silently indicated his approval, before addressing Martin again.

"You said that you wanted to see what other evidence the concealed item would lead to. In addition to that item, do you have other evidence then, that has come to light?"

"I do," Martin admitted. "I would consider one last bit of evidence to be helpful, and that could be easily obtained by you, Doug, with little effort."

He stood, and gestured toward his library, and the two men followed him, waiting for Martin to access his safe.

He removed a packet and a small box, and brought them over to his desk.

Inspector Michaels came closer, and waited.

Martin began by opening the sealed packet, and removing one item.

"My late wife's phone. It was located after everyone left this house, the day following her death. I did not turn it over to Greg Vance.

"He did return, insisting that I had it, and demanding that I give it to him, but I looked him straight in the eyes, and lied. He was not going to be allowed to have it, nor to gain access to my home to search for it."

He laid it on the desk, rather than handing it to the investigator.

"I'll put everything back in the packet before giving all of it to you, together."

Officer Michaels looked puzzled. "Is this phone the item we've been discussing?"

"No," Martin said simply. "But I intend to give it to you, along with everything else. I think you should know, however, that I had someone clone the SIM card, and I will retain that. The phone contains text messages, voice messages, and photos that will be of interest."

He reached into the packet, and retrieved a document.

"In addition, my late wife's phone records. I have a copy of them. Essential information has been highlighted."

He pulled another document from the packet.

"A copy of the autopsy, which I'm sure you already have, but one is included in this grouping for your convenience."

Martin flashed a faint grin at Doug Michaels when he said this, and he smiled, and nodded.

"Very considerate."

Martin paused briefly, looking into the packet, and slowly bringing out two paper-clipped documents.

"I was told that Detective Vance ordered a DNA test to establish whether or not I was the father of the child my late wife was carrying."

"You were ruled out," Doug replied, "but I'm sure you know that."

"I do know that," he confirmed quietly, "which is why I also requested a couple of DNA tests."

Martin had expected the look of astonishment that Doug Michaels now gave him.

"Where did you get the samples?" he inquired curiously. "And how did you know whose samples you needed?"

"All this evidence was gathered after Izzy gave me what she had discovered," Martin explained. "Because of that, I knew what I was looking for.

"I asked Doctor Amos to sign a statement itemizing the types of samples used, and how they were collected, and stored. That's included in the packet."

He laid the first of the two papers on the desk.

"Sample A, with results indicating that the donor is ruled out as having fathered the child. This man's name was given to Vance, early on. He failed to order a DNA test to determine the man's likelihood of paternity. In fact, he did nothing, at all.

"The fact that I was assuredly not the father presented the substantiation of my late wife's ongoing activities. It was not difficult to assume that my late wife, herself, did not know with a certainty who had fathered her child.

"Testing Sample *A* was merely the first step in a process of elimination. It allowed me to be even more confident that the testing of Sample *B* would provide the result I was expecting."

The officer nodded, and waited as Martin placed the second test result on top of that one.

"Sample *B*, another candidate for whom no DNA test was ordered, other than by me, with results indicating that the donor's probability of paternity is ninety-nine point ninety-nine percent."

Doug Michaels raised his brows, and leaned over to see the results for himself. He looked up at Martin inquisitively.

"Will your late wife's phone and her records connect to the donor of Sample *B*, Martin?"

"They will, but I realize that fathering a child or phone records are not enough to establish a murderer's guilt."

"That's true," Doug agreed. "But, knowing you, I suspect you aren't done."

Martin reached for the small cardboard box, and held it in his hand for a moment before speaking.

"After I give this to you, Doug, I would like to request that you attempt to determine where the killer's phone was pinging, and at what time, the night of Darlene's murder."

He raised his eyes to the officer's with significant meaning. "*Both* of his phones," he added with deliberate emphasis, and the investigator looked at him strangely.

Martin paused to glance over at his attorney to make sure he was still recording, and received a nod of confirmation.

He hesitated, before removing the box's lid.

"Izzy found this on Darlene's bed, just after she was killed. She folded a piece of paper into a pocket, as you will see, and placed the item inside. It has not been disturbed, Doug, nor has it yet been dusted for prints. I leave that for you.

"From Izzy's account of where, and how this item was discovered, you should find two sets of significant prints. One set will belong to my late wife. The other will belong to the owner of this item and, by a preponderance of the evidence, I believe that man to be my late wife's killer.

"There is one last document in the packet. I won't remove it now because it is rather detailed, and will take you some time to review."

Martin's face registered a flash of emotion, and he straightened his stance, clearing his throat, before continuing.

"That document is a notarized affidavit that Izzy signed in the presence of myself, and the man you saw enter the house with me, as we returned from the hunting lodge. The notary was present here in Izzy's room to witness our signatures.

"I'm sure that most affidavits are difficult to have introduced at trial, but Alan seems to feel that hearsay exceptions may apply, particularly in light of Izzy's passing."

His attorney nodded, and continued to record what was being said.

Martin drew in a deep breath, and resumed.

"Izzy stated in the affidavit that she saw who was in the house with my late wife the night of her death, and at the time it occurred, as well as the fact that he had been here before. She provided his name."

He met Inspector Michaels' eyes, and slowly lifted the lid from the box, then waited for him to gingerly remove the folded paper, and carefully inspect the item inside.

The officer stood motionless. The muscles around his jaws were clenched, and when he finally raised his eyes to Martin's, they were filled with shocked disbelief.

Chapter Twenty-One

Aunt Celeste sat curled up on one end of the sofa, staring blankly out toward the patio, deep in thought. She'd been up since before daylight, and had been sitting there for a couple of hours, not even bothering to start a pot of coffee.

A sigh escaped her now, as she could tell that Audra was up and moving around in her room. She needed to talk to her, but she wasn't looking forward to it.

She hadn't meant to spy on Audra and Martin, when they were together on the porch, before Martin left after the funeral, but she did see them through the sheers in the living room. They were teasing each other, and Aunt Celeste had smiled at their antics, but continued on her way to change from her dress into something she could relax in.

She had returned to the living room to pick up the heels she remembered kicking off, when they'd returned from the service, and as she was standing back up, she saw their kiss.

Aunt Celeste had hurriedly left the living room, and took her shoes to her bedroom closet. She heard the front door open and close, and when she stepped back into the hallway, she saw Audra slowly entering her own room, with a dreamlike smile on her face.

Even though Audra never admitted it, her aunt had already realized that she had fallen in love with the handsome, and intriguing master of Hawthorn Manor, and knowing Martin as Aunt Celeste did, she didn't doubt that it was mutual.

Under different circumstances, she would have been more than happy about it, but she couldn't deny that with things as they were, she was troubled.

She got up, and moved into the kitchen to get the coffee started, and silently prayed for God to show her how to approach Audra, and that her niece would listen to her.

She hadn't wanted to try talking to her yesterday, while Audra was experiencing so many emotions, but she didn't want things to continue to escalate between Audra and Martin, without at least letting her know her concerns.

She was still propped against the counter next to the coffee pot, watching it percolate, when Audra came in with her customary yawn and stretch, and a sleepy grin for her aunt.

She stopped and looked at the busy percolator with disappointment. "It's still brewing? What happened? Did you oversleep, Aunt C?"

"I've been up for hours, honey, I just forgot to start it."

Audra frowned at her in confusion. "How do you forget to start coffee? That's like forgetting to breathe."

Aunt Celeste laughed, and motioned her over to the couch in the little seating area just off the kitchen, where Dexter could already be seen through the sliding doors, chewing on whatever it was he'd found in the grass. He'd gotten an early start on his busy day.

She sat down, and patted the couch next to her. "Come sit, sweetie, and let Aunt Celeste tell you how to run your life."

Audra tilted her head, and looked at her suspiciously, then shrugged, and came over to flop down beside her, resting her head against her aunt's shoulder.

"I have no coffee," she lamented, in a dull tone.

"I know, baby, and I'm sorry," Aunt Celeste said, with a little smile. "I'm working on it."

Audra sighed dramatically, before lifting her beautiful face up to inspect her aunt carefully. "Is this gonna be a big talk, or a little chat, Aunt C?"

"I'm afraid it's rather large," she confessed, causing even more confusion to rest in Audra's sleepy eyes.

Audra continued to study her quietly, then sat up a little straighter so that she could see her better.

"Is something wrong?"

Aunt Celeste hesitated. "It has the potential to be wrong."

Audra frowned, clearly perplexed.

"Honey, I know you remember when we were sitting in the coffee shop, the day Dee Sanders was so upset with you. After she left, I told you that you had fallen in love with Martin."

Audra cautiously nodded. "I remember."

Aunt Celeste rested her gentle brown eyes on her niece's sweet face. "And you have."

She pressed her lips together, and continued to regard her silently, not admitting anything.

"You and I have always been able to talk, Audra, and I'd like to think that the reason for that is because you know that, no matter what I say to you, everything I say is with love. You do know that, don't you, sweetie?"

She nodded slowly, still regarding her aunt with a bit of misgiving. "Is that what this is about?"

"It is," Aunt Celeste admitted. "Will you let me tell you what my concerns are?"

Audra let out a sigh, and looked out at Dexter with sad eyes. "I probably know what they are."

"Then you tell me," Aunt Celeste suggested.

"You think Martin's too moody, and unpredictable, and you're afraid that he'll end up being mean to me."

Aunt Celeste looked shocked. "What?"

Audra looked even more confused, and giggled. "I have no coffee! Why am I trying to talk sense, with no coffee? So, you're not concerned about that?"

"I most certainly am not!" Aunt Celeste was just as baffled as her niece, by this time. "Honey, I've always known that Martin Satterfield is a man of integrity, and that he's decent and kind. That's one reason I was so quick to defend him early on, when you were so sure he was the devil."

Audra grinned. "He told me that he's not the devil. Actually, what he said was *'I realize that I'm an odious and hateful creature, and I expect that will never change, but I'm not the devil, Miss Campbell,'* and then turned, and walked out of the room."

Aunt Celeste had to compress her lips, to keep from laughing at her niece's very effective impression.

"Well, he's definitely not," she said, "so no, honey, I'm not concerned that Martin would ever be mean to you."

"Then, what is it you're concerned about, Aunt C?" Audra asked, leaning back on her shoulder again, and loosely braiding a section of her hair.

"I'm concerned that the two of you are going to not only fall in love, but want to build a life together, and, honey..." Aunt Celeste tapped her chin to make her look up. "Martin is not a Christian."

Audra's face fell. She continued to braid, and unbraid her hair, without even realizing she was doing it.

"I think he's interested in being one, though," she said, very softly.

"But that's not being one," her aunt reminded her.

"Sweetie, I know I'm not your mom or your dad, but I'm all you have left. I don't think I'm saying anything to you that either of them wouldn't approve of, or say to you, themselves."

She saw a single tear roll down Audra's face, and breathed a sigh of regret for having put it there.

"Baby, I didn't mean to upset you," she said, blinking back her own tears. "I'm so sorry. But, I didn't want you to come to me long after the fact, and demand to know why I didn't warn you, when I could have."

"No, it's not... I mean, you have to say it, I guess, because it's the truth. I know that, Aunt C."

She continued to look thoughtfully out toward the patio, the sunlight reflecting in her eyes. "But what if he becomes one? I think he would."

"He has to do that for himself, not as a means to convince you to marry him, honey. It can't be a bargaining chip."

A fond smile rested on Audra's face for a brief moment, as the mention of a bargaining chip reminded her of the hostile way that she and Martin had slid their contract back and forth, negotiating their way to an agreement.

"He probably won't ask me, anyway," Audra said after a long moment. "He hasn't said anything about love, so I guess I'm not on his radar, as far as something like that."

"I smell the coffee," Aunt Celeste said, nudging Audra to let her get up. "We both need it, so let's balance the rest of anything we say with some caffeine."

Audra willingly joined her at the counter, and gratefully received the cup her aunt brought over.

Aunt Celeste pulled a stool out, and settled down to look over at Audra, with a doting smile. "You know I love you, right, honey?"

"I'm lovable, yes," she said facetiously, with a grin.

"You are. I know that, and Martin knows that."

Aunt Celeste sipped her coffee slowly, and sat thinking for a moment; before she reached over, and gave Audra's one braided strand a little tug.

"I know he hasn't said anything about love, Audra, but that may just be because of how things ended with his late wife. Maybe he's afraid to love again, plus it hasn't been that long since she died."

"Martin never told Darlene that he loved her," Audra said hesitantly, knowing how her aunt would react, "because he didn't love her. And she didn't love him, either."

She put her cup down, and questioned her niece with her eyes, waiting for the rest.

"Aunt C..." Audra struggled with what she wanted to say, but if she and her aunt were going to have this conversation, she felt she should know.

"Darlene sort of swooped in, right after Martin got back from Europe to arrange for his parents' funerals, and to be with Izzy. He didn't know her, at all. But she got him in her sights, and took advantage of the state he was in.

"She convinced him that she could be a big help to him, if she were to come to Hawthorn as his wife, and help him manage the estate, and preside over all the social functions that Martin's mother had always taken care of.

"He said that, even though he'd never been in love, he knew enough to realize that he certainly didn't love her, and that she didn't love him either, and that it was simply a business arrangement, and nothing else."

Aunt Celeste sat silently, trying to imagine what could possibly have made a man as in control, and decisive as Martin Satterfield, yield to such an outlandish suggestion.

Audra seemed to be reading her thoughts.

"He said he hadn't been prepared for the shock, and the emotional aftermath of his parents, and their driver, dying so suddenly and violently, and that he was just trying to function, and wasn't thinking clearly.

"He said that having to bury both of his parents, and then help the driver's family lay him to rest, was mentally and emotionally draining. Also, when he realized how frail Izzy had become, he began to feel that he'd soon lose her too, and it just made him think that if someone else was at least there, at Hawthorn, he wouldn't end up alone. I was surprised to hear him say that, but I guess I can understand it. I can't imagine not having you, especially with Mom and Dad gone, now."

Her aunt leaned over, and gave her a little kiss on the cheek, then returned to her sad reflections, blinking back tears as she realized that Martin's dread of being left alone was so great, that it was enough to cause him to agree with Darlene Parks' preposterous offer.

"Martin said that he had already decided that he wasn't the kind of man who would have the capacity for romantic love, and that agreeing to her suggestion was nothing more than a convenient arrangement. He said that as long as she knew that, and was fine with it, he saw no harm in it, since he did feel he needed help with managing the estate.

"I'm telling you the rest in confidence, Aunt C," Audra continued, "and if Martin knew that I had, he might not be too happy with me."

She reached over, and touched her aunt's arm to draw her out of her thoughts. "The reason she took over the east wing was so that she could continue to entertain her male friends."

Aunt Celeste was horrified. "And Martin knew this?"

"Not at first. They didn't really interact, and his quarters were in the west wing. But it started to become obvious, and Martin said poor Izzy got caught in the middle.

"Darlene was mean to her, and threatened to put her out of the house, with nowhere to go, if she ever told Martin, but he didn't need for Izzy to tell him. Like I said, it started to become obvious."

"Why was she worried about Martin finding out, if he was under no delusions about their marriage?" Aunt Celeste's sad eyes reflected her disappointment for her friend's son.

"Martin didn't care what she did, but she had to agree to discretion, and she wasn't going to be allowed to bring men into his family home, especially men he was likely to encounter around town. Martin is a proud man, Aunt C, you know that."

"I do know that," she admitted softly. "So maybe Darlene thought he might do something extreme, like throw her out of the house, if he found out about her."

"He did become aware of it, but instead of confronting her, he waited, and let her think that he didn't know. It was because of what all of it was doing to Izzy that made him look the other way to keep the peace.

"Martin said Izzy's doctor had told him that she couldn't last much longer. He said he was just trying to keep things quiet and comfortable for her, until the end of her life. He'd decided that as soon as Izzy passed, and could no longer be threatened, that he was immediately putting Darlene out of the house, and doing whatever it took to divorce her."

"It's a wonder she didn't threaten to play the spouse card, and go after the family fortune," Aunt Celeste speculated grimly.

Audra nodded, then decided to come clean. "Aunt C, I already knew about Darlene when I lived here, before."

Aunt Celeste was dumbfounded. "How, in the world, could you have? You didn't even know Martin then."

"Because I saw Darlene and a man, coming out of the motel across the street from Benedetti's, when I was getting take out for us."

She squirmed uncomfortably. "I recognized him, but do you mind if I don't tell you his name? It's a small town, and we have to see him downtown pretty often."

Aunt Celeste lifted her hand halfway from the counter to stop her. "Never mind, baby, I know who it is."

Audra looked at her with wide eyes. "How?"

"Just starting to realize what some of the things I've observed, over the past few years, are beginning to indicate," she said vaguely. "So, no, I don't mind your not telling me," she added.

She drew her brow, as a realization came to her, and looked over at her niece with such a sorrowful expression, that Audra felt her aunt was close to tears.

"What is it, Aunt C?" She touched her arm gently.

"I just hurt for poor Martin," she said in a broken voice. "That man has never been in love before, and now..." She absently patted Audra's arm, as she stopped to think about it.

The look she had seen on Martin's face, as he gazed down at Audra, and held her in his arms, was about as much pure love as Aunt Celeste had ever witnessed. Surely, he knew what was happening to him?

She quietly suspected that Martin would willingly pray any prayer he needed to pray, in order to have Audra as his wife, but Aunt Celeste knew that this kind of prayer wasn't coming to a place of belief in Christ, or accepting Him as savior. It was only a bargaining chip, as she'd said before.

She reached her hand to smooth the back of Audra's hair, and gave her an uncertain smile.

"Please think about the spiritual aspects of all this, baby. That's all I'm asking. Please don't let Martin make a claim that isn't valid, just to win your love."

Audra looked down at her coffee, and nodded. "I know, Aunt C. I won't do that. It wouldn't be fair to either one of us."

She got up to take their cups over to the sink. "I thought I'd be there working today, but Martin called and said he had to be at the police station this morning, and then he and his attorney have another meeting with someone else."

Aunt Celeste put her stool back under the edge of the counter, and straightened up to look at her niece curiously.

"I imagine he still has some loose ends regarding Darlene's murder, but why doesn't he want you to work? Security is there, and you have a key."

Audra stood at the sink staring out the window, wondering the same thing, herself.

"I said all that to him, but he said that he wanted me to stay here with you today."

She turned, and looked back at Aunt Celeste. "He also said that it would be best, if there isn't something we just have to go do in town, for us to stay here."

"That's odd," Aunt Celeste replied. She crossed her arms, and thought about it. "I wonder if this has anything to do with that silly Greg Vance?"

She shook her head, continuing to think about it. "If it does, then no wonder he wants you here with me. I doubt Greg Vance could find a way around Martin's security guards, but if he did, I certainly don't want you alone in that house."

"He'd never get past Blitz," Audra decided, coming back over to stand, and watch Dexter entertaining himself with a couple of squirrels.

She smiled absently at the happy collie, and headed toward her room to get dressed, mumbling over her shoulder about Greg Vance's wanna-be status.

Chapter Twenty-Two

Aunt Celeste peered through the living room sheers, while kneeling backwards on the sofa. She got up, and walked halfway down the hall to call for Audra, then hurried back to her post at the window.

Audra padded into the living room, looking at her aunt with surprise. "What's going on? What are you doing, Aunt C?"

"Come here," she said with a sense of urgency, and Audra dashed over to join her on the sofa.

"Don't open those, honey," Aunt Celeste admonished, as she reached a finger to see what her aunt was looking at. "You can see through the sheers, just look."

Audra leaned over the back of the sofa, and fixed her stare toward the driveway, then took in a sharp breath.

"What is that stupid Greg Vance doing out there?" she demanded angrily, pushing back from the sofa.

"No, ma'am!" Aunt Celeste fairly barked at her. "You are not going outside this house, young lady! I'm not messing around, Audra, you are not to open that door!"

She didn't like it, but she halted her attempt to go out and confront the detective, and just stood there fuming.

"Give me a phone, baby. Any phone, just find me one."

Audra glanced around, and spotted Aunt Celeste's cell phone on the kitchen table, and ran over to retrieve it.

Her aunt took it from her with a harsh, angry look in her eyes. "I've had just about enough of this!"

Aunt Celeste dialed 911, and waited impatiently for the operator to ask her what her emergency was.

"A man has been stalking my niece, and has been aggressive toward her, and now he's sitting out in my driveway, watching the house."

The operator interrupted to determine the street address, and Aunt Celeste hurriedly gave it to her, then continued.

"Listen, I know these calls are recorded, but I don't care. I'm telling you now, that if that man opens his car door, I have a gun, and I will use it!"

The operator rushed to tell Aunt Celeste that she already had police en route, and then began to caution her about her intention to use a firearm.

Aunt Celeste held the phone, looking over at Audra with a slight eye roll, but she knew that the operator was actually doing her job, and trying to help, so she allowed her to continue to persuade her to let the police handle things, and to please not exit her home with a firearm.

"I see a police car coming up the street," Audra said.

"Police are here now, thank you," Aunt Celeste informed the 911 operator abruptly, and hung up the phone.

A cruiser pulled in behind the red car, and as an officer approached it cautiously and signaled something, Greg Vance rolled the window down, and seemed to be casually talking to him, as if he knew him.

"Look at him, all smiley and chatty," Audra grumbled, with a scowl. "I wonder what lie he's making up, about why he's sitting in our driveway."

"If that patrol car leaves, and they allow him to just sit there, then I don't care what the 911 operator said," Aunt Celeste muttered.

Audra stared over at her aunt, as a realization occurred to her. "But he probably has a gun, himself, Aunt C."

"He won't expect *me* to have one, though," she returned, glaring through the sheers.

The officer's partner had begun to step up to the car, but stopped to look closer at its occupant, then lifted his radio and turned back toward his patrol car, apparently notifying dispatch.

"He'd better not be telling dispatch that it's just another cop, and that everything is fine!" Aunt Celeste fumed.

"Do you think he's calling for backup?" Audra's eyes were bright with excitement.

Within minutes, the sound of loud sirens filled the air, and police units arrived from every direction.

"Whoa!" Audra exclaimed. "How many cops do you need, for one guy in your driveway?"

Aunt Celeste drew back the sheers, and shared her niece's expression of bewilderment.

"Is all this because of what I said about having a gun?" she demanded indignantly. "Martin *told* me to say that!"

"Well, he was right about it being the quickest way to get them to show up, but I didn't expect the entire police force to come rolling in," Audra breathed, in awe. "Look, there comes another one."

She looked over at Aunt Celeste with a sly grin. "Can you imagine poor Miss Hepplewhite, right now?"

She giggled, and Aunt Celeste had to smile. "I forgot all about Miss Hepplewhite," she admitted. "Maybe I shouldn't have mentioned the gun, after all."

Audra and her aunt continued to stare out the window together, completely at a loss for such an exaggerated response.

Audra began lifting herself up and down excitedly on the balls of her feet, without actually jumping, and pointed. "They're dragging him out of the car!"

"Good!" Aunt Celeste snarled. "Now cuff him!"

Audra gasped, and put her hands over her mouth. "They heard you!"

One would have thought so, from the way a couple of officers slammed Greg Vance up against his little red car, and slapped restraints on his wrists.

One of the men, who was in a gray suit, rather than a uniform, but who was obviously armed and in charge, reached into Greg Vance's pocket, and took his badge. He flipped open the flat wallet to look inside, and the angry look on his face, as he muttered something to him, was almost more than Audra could stand, and she kept inching closer to the door.

"Get back here!" Aunt Celeste barked, and she obeyed, but not without a rebellious stomping of one foot, and the inevitable crossing of her arms.

"They'll have someone come to the door and talk to us, since we're the ones who called, Audra," she offered as a concession. "Come here, you're missing this. They're putting him in the back of their car."

Audra hopped back onto the sofa, and a smirk of satisfaction rested on her face.

"Into the cage you go, Office Wanna-be! That's what you get, for trying to impersonate our favorite TV cop," she added resentfully.

Suddenly, both Audra and Aunt Celeste gasped together, their eyes wide with surprise.

"Martin just drove up!" Audra shouted in her excitement.

Aunt Celeste grabbed her by the waistband of her jeans.

"You just hold up there, girly! Martin doesn't need any distractions right now, and you are his *biggest* distraction!"

Audra appeared to be in a huff, but she knew that Aunt Celeste was right, and that he would appreciate her staying inside the house.

"He's in a suit," Audra gushed, with approval. "He must have been in that meeting he was talking about, then."

She looked at her aunt with a grin. "Did I ever tell you how Martin was dressed, the first day I went to Hawthorn?"

Aunt Celeste shook her head. "Was it a suit?"

"It was this really unusual white linen shirt, under a sort of thin over shirt, if that's even a thing. Kind of medieval."

Aunt Celeste nodded. "I've seen him in similar clothes, before, very old-world European. He looked dashing."

Audra reminded herself that he wore a suit the day of her father's funeral. She decided that he made anything look good.

Martin was a pacing, gesturing depiction of restlessness, pointing certain men toward something he wanted them to check, looking around when he heard his name called out, or standing with his head bowed, listening to something the man in gray, who had taken Vance's badge, was telling him.

His face was dark with anger, and he occasionally rested his hands on his hips, or raked his hand through his dark hair, and clamped his lips tightly together, in what appeared to be an attempt on his part to dial himself back down.

"This may not the time for a comment like this, but good grief, that is one handsome man!" Aunt Celeste declared.

Audra silently agreed, as she rested her hand on her throat, and concentrated all her attention on the master of Hawthorn Manor, who clearly had something to do with the overwhelming police presence that had arrived in this once quiet, but now shocked neighborhood.

"When Martin Satterfield says 'I'll take care of it,' he doesn't mess around," Aunt Celeste murmured quietly, and Audra glanced over at her with a proud smile, then returned her gaze to him, realizing that he seemed to have intimate knowledge of everything that was transpiring outside.

Aunt Celeste touched Audra, and nodded ahead. Audra saw Miss Hepplewhite and her binoculars, and shrieked with laughter, as the elderly woman recognized the red car, and brandished a glare that should have killed the man, who dared to throw a cigarette butt on Miss Campbell's driveway.

A few of the police cruisers that were parked round the first unit moved enough to allow that car to pull away, with Greg Vance secured in the back seat, looking deflated and crushed.

The officer in the gray suit came back over to Martin, and rested a hand on his shoulder. Martin lowered his head to hear what he was saying, and when the he was done, he clapped Martin on the back a couple of times, and grinned about something, seeming to be in a much better mood now, than when he'd first arrived.

He stopped, as he was heading back to his car, and turned to say else something to Martin with a laugh, and Martin grinned and shook his head, then gave the man a light wave as he got into his unmarked car, and drove away.

After what felt like an eternity to the impatient, breathless, and anxious Audra, he finally turned away from speaking to another officer, and glanced over toward the house, seeing them in the window, and holding up a finger with a little wink.

Audra smiled, and nodded to him. "That means give him a minute," she interpreted for her aunt.

"Does he flash that one minute finger at you a lot, then?" Aunt Celeste asked, looking over at her niece with a teasing grin.

"He does," she admitted. "Especially when I come into the library already talking, and he's on the phone. Which happens a lot," she confessed with a rueful little grimace.

The two continued to monitor the movement of various officers, and idly speculate about what was being said to Martin, when Aunt Celeste nodded toward the street.

"Someone called for a tow truck, so it looks like they're impounding his car."

"It's probably full of little notepads, and donut crumbs," Audra said sourly, and her aunt laughed heartily, and flashed her a fond look.

"Silly girl," she chided, as she glanced back out to watch the car being loaded.

"Good riddance!" she hissed, as the tow truck removed the trespasser's vehicle.

Martin strolled over to stand next to an officer, seeming much more relaxed, with his hands on his hips, and occasionally glancing over at the policeman with a little laugh at something he said. The officer seemed to be making an observation about their process that he personally found funny, and was very animated in his account. It was clear that he was enjoying being a cop today.

He finally gave Martin a clasp on his shoulder, and tossed out a few more lighthearted words to him, on his way back to his cruiser.

One by one, individual units began to pull away, to return to headquarters, or continue to depart to other calls, and Martin was finally freed up to come check on Aunt Celeste and Audra, but not before stepping across the street to a wildly beckoning, and flabbergasted Myra Hepplewhite.

She was looking up at Martin with astonishment, and he laid a hand on her shoulder, smiling down at her, obviously reassuring her. She began nodding, and patting him on the arm before turning to go back into the safety of her own home, satisfied that the man in the little red car wouldn't be throwing any more cigarette butts on Miss Campbell's driveway.

Martin turned, and made his way toward Aunt Celeste's house, looking down at the ground with a little smile.

Audra couldn't wait for him. She flew out the door, and surprised the both of them, by flinging herself into his arms.

He wrapped her up in a tight hug, then dropped a kiss on her forehead, and looked down at her, listening to all of her questions with a trace of amusement in his eyes.

Aunt Celeste came to stand in the doorway that Audra had left wide open.

"Let the man come up for air, Audra," she laughed. "Come in, Martin, and I'll see if I can get a pot of coffee going."

He looked up and grinned at her, and let Audra catch his hand to tow him in.

"I've had a lot of coffee, Miss Campbell, but it wasn't exactly palatable. Your coffee sounds nice."

He came to stand by the counter, glancing down as Audra pulled out a stool for him, and giving her a soft wink as he settled down, and began to rub the back of his neck.

"Official reports have it that you threatened to come out shooting, Miss Campbell," he teased.

She turned from starting the coffee, pursing her lips, and aiming a look of humorous aggravation at him.

"You forgot to warn me that the 911 operator would become so distraught, Martin!"

He laughed quietly at her expression.

"Well, they do tend to become alarmed, when they know a homeowner is not afraid to throw down, but it does seem to accelerate things."

"It's like the police literally materialized out of thin air," she claimed, grabbing a paper towel for her hands, and coming over to join them. "It was all I could do to get Miss Thing, here, to stay put, and stop trying to run out there."

Martin looked over at Audra with a raised brow and a look of gentle reproof.

"Be glad that your aunt put a stop to that. I would have been quite upset with you, I don't care *how* interesting you are."

She flashed him a little scowl, but tempered it with her engaging eyes.

Martin's expression became more serious, and he seemed to be thinking about what he wanted to say. The two women exchanged a quick look, and waited.

"I expect, Audra, that you must have wondered at times, why I seemed to exhibit such an elevated amount of anger and disgust toward Greg Vance. You may have even felt that it might have been a little excessive."

"Maybe, but I also know a creep when I see one, so it all balanced out," she said, smiling softly at him.

"I can't argue with your assessment of him, but being a creep wouldn't have been enough of a catalyst for him to raise my blood pressure, every time I saw him," Martin replied, looking down at his hands, absently tapping his fingers.

He flexed a muscle in his jaw, and drew in a breath.

"Greg Vance killed Darlene."

He continued to study his hands, as his words generated alarmed stares.

Audra laid a hand on his, and coaxed him to look at her. "How long have you known?"

"Izzy told me when I arrived at the house, and the forensics team, and Vance were still there."

"Izzy didn't see him do it, did she, Martin?" Audra asked with a worried look.

"No, thank God, and he apparently had no idea she was even there at the time."

Aunt Celeste gasped. "You mean, he killed your late wife, and then showed up at the crime scene, as if he were trying to figure out who did?"

"He was only interested in making everyone believe that Martin did," Audra said tightly, her green eyes beginning to flash.

"It was rather inconvenient for him that I had such an extensive amount of proof as to my whereabouts," Martin commented dryly. "But he seemed determined to try to chip away at it, regardless of how foolish it made him appear."

"Is there enough evidence to make the charge stick?" Aunt Celeste asked, still concerned about whether or not they could safely consider him to no longer be a threat.

"All the evidence I collected merges into what the district attorney feels is an airtight case," he assured her. "The straw in the wind, as they say, is the fact that Izzy found his certification ID card on the bed, after she discovered Darlene's body.

"Speculation is that he and Darlene had been engaging in some sort of coarse, bizarre role-playing game with it."

Martin loosened his tie, and paused to rub his eyes, and Aunt Celeste noted that there was enough coffee brewed to pour him a cup. He took it gratefully, and gave her a tired smile.

"I expect I do need this. I was up all night."

Martin held onto the warm cup gathering his thoughts, choosing to keep one detail to himself that he had shared with no one, including the police, before proceeding.

"Both Vance's fingerprints and Darlene's were on the card, which was the nail in his coffin, along with the fact that he was found to have fathered the child Darlene was carrying."

Aunt Celeste was clearly shocked by that revelation, since Audra hadn't shared with her that the autopsy results had revealed Darlene Satterfield's pregnancy.

Martin looked up at the clock. "In addition, there were photos of the two of them on Darlene's phone, not to mention various texts, and the government issued phone in his car pinged at the house well before the established time of death."

Audra monitored him with gentle eyes. "You need to go get some rest," she observed quietly.

"Getting rid of me?" he laughed, and made her smile.

"You look worn out."

"Do I?" He rested his provocative blue eyes on hers. "You don't think I look like Errol Flynn?" He lifted his brow, and made her laugh.

"I do, actually," she assured him, with a little blush.

"Martin, who was the other man who had on a suit, and looked as if he was in charge?" Aunt Celeste wondered.

"Doug Michaels," he replied, forcing himself to pull his gaze away from Audra's.

"He's the lead homicide investigator, and Vance's senior officer. He's the one I turned all of the evidence over to. I met with him again this morning, and then with the district attorney.

"I was just leaving there, and heading back to Hawthorn, when my security guard, Rob, heard the call go out on his police scanner, and called me because he thought it sounded like Vance's car. Of course, when he told me the address, I turned around, and headed over here."

He glanced down at Audra's hand on his, and caught it with a little squeeze.

"Are you planning on showing up again to finish my east wing, fair Audra, or shall I be forced to hire someone else?"

"Is tomorrow soon enough?"

"Absolutely." He gave her another little wink. "If you use your key, make coffee, instead of camping out on top of my desk, please."

Martin stood, and gave Aunt Celeste a warm smile, and a light embrace. "You can reholster that side arm, Annie Oakley," he teased.

She waved him off with a grin, and took his cup over to the sink, as Audra walked him to the door, and closed it behind them, lingering on the porch.

"This is why you were so upset when he tried to get in the house, and I wouldn't let him in." It was just a quiet realization.

"Yes." Martin toyed with a strand of her hair, and looked down at her solemnly.

"You can't imagine what it did to me to return to Hawthorn, and find that murderer trying to physically intimidate you, in order to get into the house. I was angry enough to have shot him on the spot, so it's fortunate that I wasn't armed, I suppose."

She couldn't tell from his countenance, if he was serious or not. Audra thought about Martin's expression when he stepped onto the veranda, and confronted Greg Vance, and a slight shudder went through her, as she realized exactly who it was that she had been determined to antagonize.

Martin could read her thoughts, and rested his hands lightly around her waist, giving her a faint smile of soft rebuke. "You must learn to listen to me, you little troublemaker."

She grinned, then gazed up at him, still wondering. "Why did he keep coming here, Martin?"

The muscles around his mouth tightened, and he looked over her head at nothing for a moment, before meeting her eyes.

"At first, I wondered if he believed I had given anything to you for safekeeping," Martin admitted. "But I think he was beginning to realize that I was cornering him, and he was trying to send a message for me to back off, by letting me know that he knew how to find you.

"As inadequate an investigator as he proved to be, he still may have been able to detect how much you mean to me."

Martin lifted a hand to stroke her hair back, then breathed out a tired sigh.

"I need to get back to Hawthorn."

Audra saw how drained he was, and reached a finger to stroke his brow. "I hope you're able to get some rest."

"I'm sure I will." Martin studied her for a moment, before giving her a little smile. "I may have decided."

She looked at him in wonder. "Decided what?"

"About the whole falling in love with you thing. But we'll see how it goes."

He dropped a light kiss on her lips, and released her. "Until tomorrow, fair Audra."

He headed out to his car, and caught a glimpse of his sober face in the rear view mirror, as he started the engine.

He knew that he needed to get back to his quiet, sprawling house and sit down with his pipe. He had a lot of thinking to do, and he wasn't looking forward to any of it.

Chapter Twenty-Three

"Again, you used your key," Martin deduced, coming into the library, and stopping to indicate with a gesture that he was fully dressed, rather than being caught unawares in his robe.

"In an attempt to maintain your dignity," he said lightly.

He came over, and took Audra by her shoulders, then turned her around, and playfully steered her out of the room and through the entryway, stopping at the front door. She looked at him oddly, as he positioned her to one side, then smiled, and opened the door.

"Are you throwing me out, just because I used my key?" she demanded incredulously.

He put a finger to her lips, then leaned around the frame, and rang the functioning, very pleasant doorbell.

She laughed, and lightly applauded.

"Very nice, my Lord Satterfield, although it certainly took you long enough." She paused and thought about it. "When did you find time to repair the doorbell, with everything else that was going on?"

"I approached it the way I approach most things that need to be repaired at Hawthorn," he admitted with a grin. "I threw money at it."

"Bravo!" she laughed. "Shall I return to the library in order to receive today's instructions for the east wing, or would you prefer to just stand back and be amazed?"

"Oh, do amaze me," he suggested, closing the door, and smiling down at her. "I have some calls to return, and other things to take care of, but you can find me in the library for most of the day."

She moved in the direction of the stairs, then seemed to become aware of something, and turned to look back at him with a solemn realization. "I'll be finished, today."

He tried to read her expression. "That doesn't make you happy?"

"I guess."

Audra knew, of course, that she couldn't just continue to drag out the renovation, as an excuse to come to Hawthorn Manor, and if she wasn't going to still be working here, her aunt had more than enough work to keep her busy.

She had lain awake most of the night, wondering how genuine Martin's expressions of tenderness toward her had been, or how much of it was simply his debonair way with women.

She hadn't known him very long, even though she felt they'd quickly developed a bond, once they resolved their early conflicts. Still, she knew nothing of how many women he might have looked at, in the same way he looked at her, or had kissed, with the same passion that he'd kissed her with. It was clear that Martin Satterfield was well traveled and accomplished, and was a profoundly attractive man.

She had wondered if his lighthearted comments about falling in love with her, while they created an excitement and a longing inside her, might very well have been nothing more than his cavalier way of teasing her.

Martin was a very physical man, so his gentle caresses and embraces might only have been how he amused himself. He was also gifted with a sophisticated turning of a phrase that she may have been reading too much into. Besides, he had told her that he didn't think he'd ever have the capacity for romantic love. She couldn't say he hadn't warned her.

She pursed her lips, and studied the floor for a moment then gave a little shrug, glancing back up at him as she laid her hand on the end of the banister, the very place where the master of Hawthorn Manor had surprised her, by catching her in his arms, as she slid down it.

"So I'll be done today, then." She couldn't resist asking, "Unless there's anything else?"

Martin raised his brows slightly, and shook his head. "No, I can't think of anything else. I expect after today, you'll be as free as a bird."

So, that was it, then. A sense of pain slowly surfaced in Audra's heart. She began to feel embarrassed for ever allowing herself to think that she was special to him. She was foolish, she told herself, and was as stupid and ridiculous as those swooning girls, with their casseroles.

She had seemed to be hoping for something, but now, as she heard his words, she dropped her eyes with disappointment, and some level of humiliation, then turned to climb slowly to the east wing, leaving Martin gazing up after her.

He knew what she was wanting him to say, and he hated himself for allowing her to turn away, with the hurt in her eyes she had been unable to hide, but his long night of wrestling with his heart led him to believe it was for the best.

He made his way back to the library, and came around his desk to sink down in his chair with a sigh. He reached over to pull a stack of unopened mail toward him, with the intention of getting caught up on some neglected matters, but he couldn't seem to do more than just sit, staring vacantly down at it.

She didn't pose the question, but Martin knew that Audra was asking him if finishing the east wing meant that he had no further desire for her to return to Hawthorn.

For a fleeting moment, he entertained the notion of suggesting that the west wing was beginning to appear dreary, and could probably use her expertise as well, but he abandoned the idea as nothing more than a flimsy excuse, that Audra would certainly see through.

He knew that simply creating pretenses to have her return wasn't what she was hoping for. She wanted him to be honest and, if he cared for her, and desired to continue spending time with her, she wanted him to say it.

Martin rested his hand against his lips, and tried to determine what his reluctance was. In fact, he'd stayed awake all night, knowing that today was her last day of designing, and that she would look up at him with those beautiful eyes, and wonder if it was also her last day to spend with him.

Evidence of strong emotion surprised Martin, and he wiped it from his cheek. Old fears mocked him now, because of all the pain he had felt, as those who had loved him had gone away, and he knew that if he gave his heart to his fair Audra, and she were to leave as well, he would be done. It would be a pain far greater than any he had ever known, and there would be no healing from its wound.

He had begun to believe that letting her go now might be the lesser pain, before he had completely lost himself to her, rather than taking her as his wife, sharing his name, his home, and his life with her, falling asleep with her, waking with her, building a future with her, only to have her leave him, as the others had done. He hadn't cared when Darlene left. She was nothing to him. But, Martin knew that he would never be able to survive the devastation of having his beautiful Audra one day leave him. It would be the end of him.

It was best to let her move on from her job here, to whatever new opportunity presented itself. Besides, she had stopped staging for her aunt's houses, in order to devote all her time to Hawthorn, and Martin imagined that Celeste Campbell would be relieved to have her niece available again.

Martin leaned back in his chair, and closed his eyes, wanting so badly to go upstairs, and tell her how he really felt, but the host of reasons that plagued him all night long, as to why Audra would be better off without him complicating her life, began to assault him. He knew that his faltering was primarily due to his fear of losing her, but he also knew that she deserved a happier life than he could give her.

Of course, he realized that forty wasn't old, but Audra was a great deal younger, only in her twenties, and was so full of life. When she first arrived at Hawthorn, she was clearly on her guard, and very reserved and matter-of-fact about everything, but as they began to spend more time together, she became naturally more vibrant and carefree.

Martin reflected back on her entertaining performance, when he'd encountered her and her aunt at the market, and knew that it accurately represented who she was, at heart.

He was very much intrigued with her little quirks, and observations, and he smiled to himself now, as he remembered her charming antics to convince him that someone named Dee Sanders was interesting.

She had made him smile and laugh much more in the short while he'd known her, than he had in his entire life, before she came along.

Martin had often wondered if he could offer anything positive to a woman like Audra, or if he was too demanding and exact. He had, on more than one occasion, managed to cause her lovely eyes to dim with disappointment, and would regret his actions but of course, was too proud to apologize.

He didn't want to drain the innocent joy from Audra, and replace it with his grim, cynical view of life. Besides, he wasn't the noble, decent man she had begun to believe him to be.

He pushed the stack of mail over, and almost rose from his chair, but stopped himself, then sprang up fitfully, and crossed over to the large window that afforded him the view of the small lake, to the west of the property. He stared at it blankly without seeing it.

A frown dimmed his poignant, blue eyes. He was guarding a secret, and if he didn't trust Audra, of all people, enough to share it with him, how could he ask her to share his life with him?

He forced himself to admit that it wasn't that he didn't trust her to guard the secret with him, but that he feared that it might cause her to look at him differently, and decide that he was deceitful, and not worth loving. Perhaps he wasn't.

He had never entertained the notion of loving anyone, or being loved, until Audra arrested him with just her presence. Martin was caught between what this woman had been doing to his heart, and his realization that asking her to share his dismal life at Hawthorn would only be self-serving and miserly.

He decided that a walk around the property, or out by the lake might help him think more clearly. He paused before going out the front door, and came over to the foot of the stairs to call up to her, and let her know that he was leaving.

She came to the top of the landing and stood quietly, waiting for him to speak.

He struggled, but refused to allow himself to go to her. Instead, he lifted a hand to indicate the entrance.

"I'm going to be outdoors for a bit, Audra. Do you need anything before I go?"

She rested disenchanted eyes on him. "Are you leaving the property?"

"Just out for a walk," he said, with a little smile.

She continued to gaze steadily at him.

"No, Martin. I don't need anything."

When he turned to go, she spoke again.

"Would you mind terribly, if I leave, and come back to finish tomorrow?"

He wavered, looking up at her wordlessly, then gave in to his desire to climb the stairs and come close to her, searching her eyes with his.

"Why, Audra?"

She looked away, but he had already seen that she had been crying. He had done that to her.

He hesitated, before reaching to take her hand.

"Look at me."

She shook her head, then slipped her hand from his, and turned to go back down the hallway.

Martin drew in a breath and followed her, stopping in the doorway of the room to observe her.

She glanced up at him, but had no reaction to his blocking the door. Instead, she picked up a roll of fabric, and began to resume her work.

"You asked if I cared if you leave," he reminded her softly. "But now you appeared to have changed your mind."

"I'm fine," she murmured.

"You are not fine," he contradicted. "You've obviously been crying."

He came into the room, and lifted the bolt of cloth from her arms, and leaned it against a chair, then took her hand again. "Come with me."

"I'm fine, Martin," she insisted, and he caught her other hand, and searched her face carefully.

"Come, go with me," he repeated.

She frowned in confusion. "You were going for a walk."

"Yes. Come walk with me."

Martin had no idea why he was suddenly asking her to go with him, when it had been his intention to put some space between them, so that he could think more clearly, but he persuaded her, and she let him lead her downstairs.

When they reached the bottom steps of the veranda, he tucked her arm around his, and began walking with her through the lawn, and away from the house.

She stopped, and he looked down at her. He could tell that she was seeing something in him.

"You're different."

Her beautiful, childlike eyes that were reading him now, no longer had the light of happiness in them, that Martin had loved seeing over the past few months.

"Am I?" He was hesitant to ask. "How am I different?"

She still had the traces of her earlier tears, and they threatened her again, but she blinked them back, and continued to survey him.

"You're detached," she answered, after a bit. "That's how you were when I first met you, but then over time, you became kinder and warmer. But today, on my last day here, you're detached, and oddly polite. Is this how we're leaving it?"

"Are we leaving it?" He let his gaze rest on the grass at his feet, and waited.

"You haven't given me any reason to come back," she said, folding her arms to hug herself, and looking away.

Martin lifted his head, and waited quietly for a long moment, until she finally brought her gaze back to his.

"Is there any chance at all, that you love me, Audra?" he asked anxiously.

"You, first!" Her voice broke, and fresh tears appeared, making her angry. She wiped them away impatiently.

"I've never told a woman that I love her," he sighed, letting his eyes wander aimlessly, suddenly feeling vulnerable, which made him uneasy.

"So, as long as you don't say it, then it isn't true?" Audra fought against becoming bitter with him. "That must be nice."

She walked away from him, moving in the direction they had begun, having no idea where the path led, but needing to put some distance between them.

Martin waited to follow her, sensing that they were either at a crossroad or an impasse. The only thing he could feel certain about was that he didn't want to lose her.

Audra stopped, when she realized that the path she'd taken led to the Satterfield family cemetery, and stood looking around, then let her eyes rest on the newest grave.

Martin's beloved Izzy. She knelt and traced the engraved name with her fingertip, and felt overcome with emotion.

She didn't realize that Martin stood behind her, until she heard him speak. "Izzy would have loved you, Audra."

She slowly lifted herself up, and looked back at him as he came to stand beside her, next to Izzy's grave, with unshed tears clouding his eyes.

"You would have been kind to her." He smiled down at that thought, as one rogue tear broke through his defenses.

He hadn't been back to the cemetery since the day of Izzy's funeral, not even returning when her headstone had arrived, and been installed by the monument company.

Martin stared all around him, as he had on the day he laid her to rest, and once again felt threatened by the overwhelming sensation of being left alone.

He knew that if he could only tell Audra the truth of how he felt about her, then perhaps that wouldn't be his fate, but he also knew how selfish that was.

Audra was young and beautiful, and was meant to laugh, and enjoy life. How could he ask such a striking and spirited woman to come sit with him, in the impressive, but silent and lonely Hawthorn Manor, and simply grow old with him?

His conflict was visible in his eyes, and she watched him as he wrestled with what it was he wanted to say.

"You can make jokes about falling in love with me, but you can't actually say you do," Audra observed sadly. "So, I guess that means you don't."

She turned away, and began to make her way back to the house, deciding to finish her work, and just go.

"I do love you."

Martin barely breathed the words, but it was enough to cause her to stop, and turn to look back at him.

His eyes were tightly closed, and his head bowed.

Audra slowly approached him, desperately praying that she'd really heard him say it. She reached her hands to his drawn, handsome face, and silently persuaded him to look at her.

"I do love you, Audra," he admitted, his eyes filled with painful uncertainty.

She moved closer, and lifted her arms to wrap them around his neck, then laid her head on his shoulder, crying softly, having all but given up on this moment ever coming.

"I love *you*, Martin," she whispered, feeling him tremble, as she said the words he'd been longing for.

Martin lifted her face to search for the love she professed, and he found it in her eyes, and in her kiss.

When they returned to the house, Audra began to make her way to the east wing, but Martin stopped her, and drew her to him, then captured her beautiful face in his hands, and looked at her with something in his eyes that Audra had never found in them, before.

His normally sober face had a softness to it, and as his eyes rested on hers, she knew with complete certainty that Martin really was in love with her. It was impossible for him to hide it, and the intensity of it would have been unsettling, if it weren't so touching.

She lifted herself up on her toes to lay a soft kiss on his lips, then traced his brow with her fingertips.

"When will you marry me, Audra?" he demanded, in a low whisper, and she could see that he was fairly holding his breath, as he waited, with an undercurrent of self-consciousness.

Audra felt a stirring of conviction, as she remembered the talk she'd had with Aunt Celeste, who was concerned that Martin was not a Christian.

As she tenderly regarded him, she could see an unusual pleading in the eyes of a man who was normally confident, deliberate, and determined. There was a blend of wavering hope, and apprehension in his manner that Audra yielded to.

She hadn't meant to brush aside her aunt's counsel, but she found herself submissive to his quiet urgency, and softly breathed, "Whenever you say."

The muscles in Martin's shoulders, and around his mouth instantly relaxed with his relief, but as he gently ran his fingers through her long hair, and let his eyes adore her, his brow furrowed, and a heaviness rushed in to settle on him.

"This isn't right," he said, in a somber whisper.

Audra immediately frowned up at him, startled by his words. "What isn't right, Martin? You and I aren't right?"

He drew in a deep breath, and looked at her with undisguised remorse.

"I've been keeping something from you. I was afraid that if I told you, then you would want nothing more to do with me, much less marry me."

Chapter Twenty-Four

Audra stared up at Martin, in disbelief.

"Surely, the fact that you've just admitted that you're keeping something from me, means that you intend to tell me."

"I have to. And then, I suppose, you'll take your leave of me, since you will surely lose all respect for me."

Audra's eyes reflected the love that she had for him, and she smiled gently.

"There's nothing you could say to me that would ever make that necessary, Martin, especially since you and I established, very early on in our relationship, that you didn't kill your late wife."

He smiled faintly at that. "Are you saying that anything less than my being a murderer, would qualify as a reason for me to keep hope alive that we have a future together?"

"I *am* saying that," she freely admitted.

Martin smiled again, and touched her cheek with a soft stroke. "Come sit with me."

He led her into the den, and invited her to settle down beside him on the leather couch.

He held her hand, and she rested her head against his shoulder, and waited while he sorted out how to begin.

"I held onto what Izzy gave me, until I was sure of what other evidence it would lead me to. I finally turned it over to the police, and rather than charge me with obstruction of justice, thankfully, they overlooked my actions, since I was able to provide them with the sufficient proof they needed to be able to close the case."

Audra nodded, but couldn't mask her confusion as to why anything at all to do with Greg Vance's arrest, would be the conversation Martin felt he needed to have with her.

"I am, of course, not an investigator, so it is not for me to say which of the pieces of evidence that I gave them would be the death knell for Vance, but there was that one item that made his denials pointless."

"That ID card that you told us about?" Audra asked, still wondering where Martin could possibly be going with all this.

He nodded, and seemed to hesitate with the rest of what he wanted to say. Finally he expelled a breath, and decided to just be done with it.

"Izzy confessed something to me that she had done, and I kept it from the police."

Audra looked alarmed. "What could Izzy have possibly done, Martin? She was an elderly, fragile lady."

"She tampered with evidence," he said, tightening his facial muscles, and looking down at Audra's face to determine how she was receiving this disclosure.

She seemed to be groping with the likelihood of it. "How could she have? She found the card, and gave it to you."

"She had deliberately done something to the card before I arrived here, and received it from her." He watched her efforts to try to follow what he was saying.

"Izzy found the card on Darlene's bed. She knew, of course, that it was Greg Vance's card, and that his fingerprints would be on it. She felt certain that Darlene's would be on it as well, but she made sure."

Audra drew her brows and stared up at him, confounded. "What do you mean, she made sure?"

Martin was visibly struggling with answering her question, but he steeled himself, and continued. "Izzy placed the card in Darlene's dead hand, and pressed her fingers to it."

Audra let out a small gasp. "Oh, Martin!"

His face was bleak, when Audra's reaction was what he had been expecting.

"She didn't tell me about it, the night she gave it to me. She admitted it later, just before she passed. It was clear that Izzy could tell that her death was imminent.

"She was like you, as far as being a woman of faith. It would have been better for me, of course, if Izzy had never told me what she did, but I suppose that since Izzy believed in eternity, she felt compelled to confess, and ask for forgiveness."

He raised his arm to lay it behind Audra, across the back of the sofa, and she pulled her feet up, as she unconsciously tucked herself closer into him. He gratefully noted her desire to still remain near to him, and rested tender eyes on hers.

"There was no point in scolding her, Audra. What was done, was done. I did tell her that perhaps it might be best to just get rid of it, so that Izzy could feel some relief. The guilt was weighing heavily on her. I didn't want her to spend her last days filled with remorse. She did seem to rest easier, after I suggested this. But, of course, I kept the card, and after she passed, I eventually turned it over to the authorities."

He lapsed into silence, staring vacantly at the floor before sighing, and putting words to his thoughts.

"It could have just ended with Izzy's passing. I knew that the evidence had been tampered with, and that I probably should destroy it. Instead, I not only kept it, but presented it to Doug Michaels, as if it were a smoking gun."

He shook his head, still looking down at nothing. "I suppose in some way, that makes me as despicable as Vance."

"Oh, hardly!" Audra argued fervently. "He's a murderer, and you just wanted him to face justice. It's not like *you* did it, and were trying to pin it on him, Martin!"

He glanced over at her with a loving smile. "And will you always be my champion, as you are now?"

Audra nodded and lifted her face, inviting his kiss. He sat thinking about the weight of the burden he was asking her to share with him, and continued reluctantly.

"When I arrived here, the morning after Darlene's death, all Izzy told me was that it was Vance in the house with Darlene, and that she had found his card. That's what prompted me to collect Vance's cheap cigarette butts after he left, and store them, in the event of any possible DNA tests, even though I didn't know about the pregnancy, at that point.

"I never pressed her for the details of what happened that night, because it took so little for her to become distressed, and when that happened, she would begin to experience arrhythmia, and her chest would hurt, so beyond what I later learned from the autopsy results, I could only speculate as to how things transpired.

"It progressively developed into more of an ordeal for Izzy to talk, since breathing was becoming difficult, but before she died, she finally insisted on telling me about the night Darlene was killed. That's also when she admitted what she'd done to Vance's ID card.

"She had looked out from the butler's pantry after hearing voices, and saw Darlene letting Vance in through the kitchen entrance, and then heading up the back stairs with him.

She remained downstairs at first, carefully staying out of Darlene's way, since she knew she would face her hysterical threats and worse, if Darlene had even a suspicion that Izzy saw them. But when Izzy began to sense that things were headed toward a bad end, she stepped up to the middle landing."

Martin glanced down when Audra reached across him to claim his hand, and absently began stroking it. He marveled at the fact that, at least so far, she hadn't rebuked him, or shown any sign that she was disappointed in him.

"Izzy could hear them, since they made no effort to be quiet. She could tell from the crude and bawdy things that were being said, that they were playing some sort of lewd game, and that much was being made of the fact that Vance was a cop.

"Darlene was demanding to see his badge, and he must have handed her his ID wallet. Izzy said that Darlene made a disparaging comment about his card's photo, and it sounded as if she'd tossed it somewhere, because Vance told her to remind him to find where it landed later, so that he wouldn't have to tell his senior officer that he'd lost it.

"Then she said their conversation was hard to hear for a few minutes, but that Vance suddenly began shouting at Darlene, saying that there was no way she was going to trap him with a kid. Izzy said Darlene gave him a loud ultimatum that involved telling Vance's wife about the two of them.

"Izzy heard Vance speaking to her in an aggressive way, telling her that he didn't take threats from anyone, let alone a woman, and that she wasn't going to be telling his wife anything. She said that it sounded as if he were talking through clenched teeth, and after a few minutes, there was no more sound."

Audra gripped Martin's hand tightly, and looked up at him in shock.

"Oh, Martin! Izzy heard the whole thing! Oh, that poor, sweet woman!"

He nodded, a look of remorse on his face, and it was a moment before he attempted to finish.

"Izzy hurried back down off the landing, and hid in the pantry. I'm sure she was terrified that if Vance discovered her, he'd kill her as well. I can only imagine what all of this was doing to her already diseased heart," he observed, despondently.

"Izzy believed that Vance killed Darlene in the bed. She said she then heard some scuffling sounds in the stairwell, and that must have been Vance bringing Darlene's body down to the foot of the stairs.

"She said she had to hold her hands over her mouth to keep from screaming, when it sounded to her as if he'd slammed Darlene's head against the corner of the post. Izzy stayed hidden in the pantry, even after she knew that Vance had hurried out the kitchen door, afraid that he might remember about the card, and come back.

"She said that when she finally came out of the pantry, Darlene's body was at the bottom of the stairs, posed to look as if she'd fallen, and that there was a small amount of blood where her head made contact with the post.

"Izzy stepped around her, and went up to the room, and searched until she found the card on the bed. That's when she used the hem of her apron to take it by the edges, and came back downstairs to put it in Darlene's hand to ensure that her prints would be on it."

Martin leveled his expressive eyes at Audra. "Izzy wanted to make sure that he was punished for what he'd done, even though she had no affection or loyalty for Darlene.

"But although Izzy knew where I was when Darlene was killed, I suppose she did what she did, in case I found myself in a position to have to defend myself, should I be accused of her death, in spite of my alibi.

"She called the police, and was devastated, to say the least, when one of them turned out to be Vance. He was obsessed with questioning Izzy, I'm sure in order to determine if she knew that he had been here with Darlene.

"He kept grilling her, trying to wear her down. Izzy told me that Doug Michaels intervened, and instructed Vance to leave her alone, and to not question her any further.

"He advised Vance that he, and no one else, would conduct any further interviews with her."

Martin silently reflected on Izzy telling him that Inspector Michaels had personally taken her upstairs to her room, and had urged her to get some rest, promising her that there would be no more questions that night.

Of course, he had returned home early the next morning, and any hopes Greg Vance might have had of badgering Izzy further, once his senior officer left, were dashed by his arrival.

Audra sat mutely processing all of this, thinking of the position Martin now found himself in.

She could understand why he'd not told any of this to Doug Michaels, but at the same time, she felt that all the other evidence Martin had gathered should be enough to convict Greg Vance, even without the ID card. She quietly asked him if this wasn't true.

"Even if that were the case, Audra, if this got out, you can be sure that the defense attorney would immediately move for a mistrial or worse yet, if Vance were convicted, it could be used to overturn his conviction."

They both sat in silence for a long while, each lost in their own speculations about what Izzy had done.

"I thought of asking Izzy to sign another affidavit, not only giving her account of the events of Darlene's murder, but detailing exactly where, on the card, she had placed Darlene's fingers, in case other prints appeared elsewhere on it," Martin admitted quietly. "But she was so sick, and so feeble. I just couldn't put her through anymore. Besides, the waters were already muddied, by that point."

"Did anyone else hear her telling you what happened, Martin?" Audra wondered.

"Dr. Wilhite was on the premises, but I never saw him appear to be standing around, listening," Martin said.

"That's too bad," Audra commented softly. She raised her eyes to his. "Martin, what are you going to do with this?"

"I'm struggling, Audra, I admit it. Greg Vance is Darlene's killer, regardless of what Izzy did with the card.

"I'm not sure I can bring myself to admit to anything now, that would even make it possible for him to go free. Right now, Audra, he's caught dead to rights."

She nodded, then ventured a timid suggestion. "Would you be willing to talk to Pastor Reynolds about it, Martin?"

He seemed confused by her suggestion. "In the manner of a confession? He's not a priest."

"No, he's not a priest, he's a minister, but he would honor the same confidentiality clause, and be able to advise you from an unbiased viewpoint. Pastor Reynolds has a great amount of respect for you, Martin, and he genuinely likes you."

"He and Izzy were actually good friends," Martin said, remembering what the kind pastor had told him about Izzy, at her funeral, and smiling sadly. "Apparently, Izzy was a fan of his tie collection."

He looked down at his fair Audra's sweet face, and there seemed to be much more peace in his eyes now.

"If you believe that I should talk to him, Audra, then I will. I would do anything for you."

She smiled at that, then braved another request.

"Martin... when you're talking to Pastor Reynolds, would you please consider asking him about Christianity? Remember, we had a talk about it, at that inn you took me to?"

"I do remember. That was one of the happiest days of my life, so I remember everything about it."

He laid a soft kiss on her lips and studied her, apparently deep in thought. "Again, I would do anything for you, Audra, even adhering to your faith."

"Oh, but it can't be for me, Martin," she protested quickly. "It has to be for you. Otherwise, it's only to please me, but it wouldn't have any real meaning for you."

"But this is something you want us to share."

"It is," she admitted. "But in order for it to be valid, and have meaning, it has to be for the right reasons."

"Will the good Pastor Reynolds be able to inform me of what those reasons should be?"

Audra nodded, a look of serious entreaty in her eyes.

Martin made no effort to conceal what he felt for her and, after he gave her another lingering kiss, he told her in hushed, heartfelt whispers how much her love and her trust meant to him, then promised her that he would ask Pastor Reynolds to meet with him.

Chapter Twenty-Five

Aunt Celeste looked up, as Audra came into the kitchen with her customary sleepy antics, and lifted a coffee cup, as if she needed to talk her niece into it.

"Please and thank you," Audra said with a grin, and surprised her aunt by stopping to give her a kiss on her cheek.

"To what do I owe this honor?" Aunt Celeste laughed, filling both their cups and taking them over to the counter.

Audra shrugged, as she pulled out a stool. "You just looked as if you deserved a kiss on the cheek."

"I do!" her aunt agreed. "I'm amazing."

Audra smiled up at her. "You really are, Aunt C."

Aunt Celeste settled down next to her, and gave her an inquisitive look. "Okay, baby. What's up?"

"Nothing," Audra denied, laughing. "Can't a girl give her aunt a kiss on the cheek, every once in a while?"

Aunt Celeste remained skeptical.

"I finished the east wing, Aunt C," Audra told her, capturing her warm cup between her hands.

"How do you feel about that?" her aunt asked, still unsure of her niece's demeanor. She didn't seem depressed, but Aunt Celeste had certainly expected her to be, once she had completed her job at Hawthorn.

"I hate to brag on myself," she began with an impish grin, "but it's nothing short of spectacular."

Aunt Celeste laughed. "I'm sure it is, honey, and I hope you'll show it to me, but that's not what I meant."

"I know." Audra studied her coffee cup with a faint smile that seemed to be slowly fading.

Aunt Celeste waited for Audra to gather her thoughts, wondering if it was just her still being sleepy that made her slow to get started, or if she was trying to figure out how to tell her something. She knew her niece very well, and decided that her last guess was the correct one.

"Do you want me to keep asking questions until I ask the right one, honey, or do you want to put me out of my misery, and just tell me what's going on?"

"Martin's in love with me," Audra replied softly, her face lighting up, as she heard herself say it.

"Tell me something I don't know," Aunt Celeste returned dryly, sipping her coffee.

Audra's pretty eyes were wide with surprise. "Did you know that, really?"

"You have got to be kidding me," her aunt returned blandly. "The man wears it like a billboard!"

She watched her niece's face flush with pleasure, and couldn't resist leaning over to give her a little hug.

"He wants me to marry him," Audra blurted out. She looked over at Aunt Celeste with a teasing smile. "I bet I just told you something you didn't know, Aunt C."

Aunt Celeste covered her reaction well, and drew in her breath. "I'm not surprised that he wants you to marry him, Audra, I'm just surprised that he asked you now, right in the middle of everything that's going on."

Audra sat, idly turning her cup around in her hands, thinking about it. "He probably hadn't planned on it. In fact, I'm sure he didn't intend to. But we sort of had a rough patch yesterday, after he seemed to be fine with me finishing the east wing, and just leaving."

"You were angry with him?" her aunt asked quietly.

"More hurt than angry, but I was, with myself. I ended up sobbing, like an idiot. Not in front of him," she hurried to add.

"But he knew I'd been crying. Then, he wanted me to take a walk with him, and we ended up at the family cemetery. I don't know, Aunt C, everything came to a head finally, and we sort had a standoff, then he admitted that he loves me."

Audra stopped, and stared hard at the counter, as a realization began to dawn on her. "Maybe I forced him."

"What do you mean, honey? Are you feeling that he just said what you wanted to hear, to keep from hurting you?"

"No," Audra said slowly. "He meant it. But when he said it, it was like it was painful for him. I had begun walking away from him, to go back to the house, and he said it quickly, almost in a panic, maybe to stop me from leaving.

"I turned around, and he had his head down, and his eyes closed. It was almost like he didn't want to open them, because he thought that if he looked up, I would have just gone, and left him standing there, alone."

Aunt Celeste sat soberly considering this. "Well, honey, maybe he did think that, and I can't say that I blame him."

She folded her arms on the counter and looked over at Audra's worried face.

"Although none of them could help it, everyone he loved, and who loved him, has left him. Think about it," she continued. "Maybe Martin was afraid to love you, and have you leave him as well, which may explain why he seemed to be willing to just accept that it was your last day to be at Hawthorn."

The thought of this immediately brought a sharp sense of grief to Audra. "I would never leave Martin!" she whispered, mainly to herself.

"None of those people, represented by all those graves, meant to leave him either, Audra, but they did.

"I know it's hard to imagine someone as strong and confident and, let's face it, as powerful as Martin Satterfield, having that one thing that terrifies him. The fact that Martin is not a Christian, and doesn't believe in eternity, makes him a target for the fear of abandonment. Especially, if he believes that those who loved him are simply no more, as if they'd never existed at all, and that he will end up that way, himself, with no one to even care, when he dies."

Aunt Celeste saw how her words affected Audra, but decided to leave them just as she'd said them.

"Were you able to convince Martin that you love him, or was he left still hoping?"

Audra shook her head, and replied softly.

"I told him. He does know."

Aunt Celeste looked vacantly down at her coffee, and thought about the rest of what her niece had told her.

"When did he ask you to marry him?"

Audra rested her chin in her hands. "He didn't actually ask me to marry him. He just asked me when I would."

Her aunt waited a moment, before speaking.

"He just assumed that you would, then," she observed.

"Well, wouldn't that be the next logical thing to happen, Aunt C?" Audra was confused. "Why wouldn't he just assume that I would?"

Aunt Celeste looked away, with disappointment on her face. "So, you haven't addressed the issue of his not being a Christian, then? Or is Martin pressuring you to marry him, regardless?"

"He's not pressuring me!" Audra appeared to resent her aunt's question, and got up to take her cup over to the sink. "He wouldn't have to pressure me!"

Aunt Celeste closed her eyes, and leaned her forehead against her hand. "Are you saying that he wouldn't have to pressure you, because he knows you would marry him, whether he became a Christian or not?"

Audra bowed her head at the sink and began shaking, and Aunt Celeste could hear her crying in earnest. She came over to pull her close, and try to comfort her.

"I'm sorry, baby. I didn't mean to make you cry."

Audra took the paper towel her aunt offered her, and wiped her face, then looked at her aunt in anguish.

"What if he decides that he doesn't want to become a Christian, Aunt C? What will I do? I love him!"

Aunt Celeste gently brushed Audra's hair from her wet face, and watched her with worried eyes.

"If I could decide for you, sweetie, I would. But you're the only one who can do that. I would encourage you to think about what your mom and dad's counsel would be though, and to really spend some time praying about it.

"Maybe you could talk to Pastor, if you need to speak to someone who's not so involved."

"He's meeting with Pastor Reynolds today," her niece said, looking at her aunt with the face of a wistful child.

"He is?" Aunt Celeste was more than a little surprised, but felt encouraged. "Is he doing this in order to decide if he wants to become a believer?"

"He's meeting with him about something else, but he promised me that he would ask him about it," Audra said, crumpling the paper towel into a tight wad.

Aunt Celeste breathed out a sigh, and gave Audra a reassuring hug.

"Well then, honey, let's don't worry, until there's a reason to worry. Maybe things will work out the way we're hoping they will. We just need to pray that Martin will be able to really hear and understand whatever Pastor says to him."

Martin sat waiting by Doug Michaels' desk, while he stepped out to speak to another officer, who had a question for him. He felt a small current of both adrenaline and dread coursing through him, and tried to steady himself by taking in a deep, cleansing breath.

He had just left Pastor Reynolds' office, after a one hour meeting turned into two, and he had been immensely gratified by the minister's not judging him, as well as his willingness to understand the reasons that Martin had done what he had, with the evidence Izzy had given him.

He had been prompt to assure Martin that he wasn't entirely sure that he wouldn't have made the same decision, if he were placed in such a position.

He didn't gloss over Martin's actions, or deny that they were wrong, but he did admit that the account of Darlene Satterfield's murder that Izzy provided, clouded the issue and rendered it more gray, than black and white.

It was clear to Pastor Reynolds that Darlene's hands would have touched the card in order for her to examine it closely enough to remark on the photo, and that her prints would have been on its surface, regardless of Izzy's actions.

He wasn't excusing anyone, but he was quick to point out his belief that Isabelle Draper did what she had done in the heat of the moment, not stopping to think, but hurrying, fearing Vance's return, to ensure that there was evidence of his having killed Darlene.

Rather than counsel Martin to admit all of this to the police, he first approached the subject of how all of this was affecting him on a personal level, and Martin admitted that he was distressed.

Pastor Reynolds spoke earnestly to Martin about his need for God to be able to help him, not just with his current dilemma, but all the things he could be expected to face in the years to come.

He explained that God was always ready to be involved in the lives of His children, but that in order for Him to intervene, there first had to be a relationship established, because He would not override a person's free will, but had to be invited into a person's life.

There was a lengthy exchange between them, in which the pastor presented the gospel, and Martin asked very intelligent questions. He seemed to want to trust what the minister was telling him, but he was having a problem accepting that it could be as simple, as he was being asked to consider it to be.

Martin had no trouble believing that both his parents and Izzy had the sort of relationship with God that Pastor Reynolds was describing, and he was fully convinced that Audra and her aunt were genuine in their faith, but he also supposed that all of these people were basically good, which was not a claim he felt he could make about himself.

He felt that the situation he now found himself in, only underscored his critical evaluation of himself.

Pastor Reynolds wrote down some passages for Martin to read and reflect on, and even though Martin had actually read through the Bible as a fascinating piece of literature, he agreed to read what the minister gave him, and Pastor Reynolds had no doubt that he would.

Regardless of Martin Satterfield's attempts to convince the minister that he was not a good man, the pastor had no such doubts regarding his integrity, and knew that his word was to be counted on.

His counsel, regarding the evidence that Martin had turned over to Doug Michaels, was that the lead investigator should have all the facts, regardless of how unpleasant Martin's encounter with him might turn out to be.

Martin wasn't looking forward to doing his duty, but after he left his meeting with Pastor Reynolds, he forced himself to drive over to police headquarters, and essentially bite the bullet.

He glanced up now, as the investigator returned to his desk, and settled down in his chair, regarding Martin with a grin.

"Have you come to take me up on my offer, Martin?"

Martin smiled, knowing that Doug Michaels was referring to an offhand, humorous suggestion he'd made at Celeste Campbell's house, that he should consider a future as an investigator.

"I expect I'm the last person you'd want for that," Martin replied, with a look of remorse already appearing in his eyes.

Doug Michaels furrowed his brow, and peered at him curiously. "Why is that?"

"Because one of the items of evidence I gave you had been tampered with, and I knew it, but gave it to you anyway," he replied, in his blunt, honest way.

Inspector Michaels leaned back in his chair, lifting his arms to rest his head in his hands, and regarded Martin with in a stoic, calm manner. "ID card," he said simply.

Martin just looked at him quietly, surprised that he already seemed to know, but freely admitted it. "Yes."

He searched Doug Michaels' face for any sign of anger or disappointment, but saw nothing, but a completely inscrutable demeanor.

"Doug, if you knew, why haven't I been charged with a felony?" Martin wondered, still trying to read him.

He studied Martin Satterfield closely. "You said you knew in advance."

"Yes."

"But you, yourself, didn't tamper with the evidence."

"No, I didn't. I'm afraid that Izzy confessed, just before she passed, that she had done it."

Doug surprised Martin by suddenly grinning to himself.

"Well, that explains it."

Martin looked at him in complete bewilderment, and the senior officer decided to enlighten him.

"Izzy, as sweet an old lady as she was, apparently hadn't watched enough cop shows in her spare time. When I examined the card, I couldn't, for the life of me, figure out what was going on with the front, right side. There were plenty of legible prints everywhere else, front and back, belonging to both Vance, and your late wife.

"It took me a while to realize what it was I was seeing. I had expected to see prints of the distal phalanx, but of course, that wouldn't have surprised me." Doug Michaels indicated the end of his own finger to demonstrate.

"Izzy was either in a mad rush, or just didn't know much about fingerprints. She had pressed the front, right part of the card against Darlene Satterfield's middle phalanx, and proximal phalanx." He touched the middle, and lower sections of his own finger.

"It was easy to determine that those impressions were likely made later, not just because they overlaid other prints beneath, which were visible between the spaces of the fingers, but because the two fingers Izzy had laid on the card were very firmly pressed down, and were perfectly straightened, which would be unusual for casual contact."

"I'm sorry, Doug," Martin said quietly, looking down at his hands with regret. "I'm afraid that because of Izzy's actions, coupled with my own, a strong piece of evidence will have to be omitted."

"Not necessarily."

Martin wasn't sure the detective had heard him. "I'm sure the defense attorney will call for a mistrial, or the worst possible scenario being that, if Vance is convicted, this could end up being used to overturn his conviction."

"Darlene's prints were all over the card," Investigator Michaels replied casually, with a little shrug. "I see no reason to not include it, but I'll let the DA know about the front, right part of the card. He'll either keep it or toss it, but there won't be a mistrial, either way."

Martin had been able to follow what his friend was saying up until his last words, but failed to see how a mistrial could possibly be avoided, if the card were included as evidence.

Doug Michaels recognized that this was what his friend was still struggling with.

"Martin..." He leaned forward, and rested his arms on his desk. "There was more than enough evidence, thanks to the rest of what you provided, for the DA to run with it. Not only that, but you know that we impounded Vance's SUV."

He nodded and waited, still unable to believe that so far, Doug Michaels hadn't laid down the law to him.

"Forensics found a miniscule bit of blood on the driver's floor carpet. DNA ties it to the victim."

Doug Michaels swiveled slightly in his office chair, and continued. "The only way Vance could have come in contact with it, and tracked it to his car would have been during the murder.

"He never would show up at the house when the call went out, and I kept waiting around for him, because I needed to get to another call.

"He took so long arriving, that I had to finally call another detective to cover for me at the other call. By the time he did drag in, the body had already been removed, and the coroner had gone.

"In fact, in hindsight, he seemed particularly reluctant to go anywhere near the back stairs, and stayed in the central area of the house near the front stairs. That's where he had Izzy cornered, asking her questions.

"I had a couple of rookies clean up the blood, and remove the tape, as soon as forensics gave the okay, because I didn't want Izzy going back in there and seeing it, and then, when I heard Vance in the front of the house getting a little loud, I went in, and escorted Izzy up to her room. All that to say, he never got anywhere near the back stairs, after arriving on the scene."

"Vance must have gotten it on his foot when he slammed Darlene's head against the post," Martin mused softly to himself.

Doug lifted his brows with a look of surprise.

"Say that again?"

"Shortly before she died, Izzy told me the details of what actually happened," Martin admitted. "She heard all of it, from the time Vance arrived, and Darlene led him upstairs, until her body was posed at the foot of the stairs, and he left.

"I know it's hearsay, but if any of it would be helpful to you or to the prosecutor, as a means of constructing his line of questioning, I'd be more than willing to type up Izzy's account and email it to you."

Doug reached for a card, and jotted an email address on the back of it before handing it over to him.

"Do that, Martin, and I'll commute your sentence to time served."

He flashed him a grin, and Martin responded with one of his own, his relief and gratitude clearly evident.

Chapter Twenty-Six

Martin hadn't heard from Audra, all day. He missed her, but he assumed that she must be staging a home or working on her portfolio, since she was still taking some online courses.

He pushed back from his desk, having typed up Izzy's account of the night of Darlene's murder, as clearly and as unembellished as he could. He sent it to Doug Michaels' email address, then set his computer to sleep.

Now he stood and stretched, then wandered into his den to search for his pipe, and to study more of the passages that Pastor Reynolds had asked him to read. He had suggested to Martin that if he approached them, not as something to read, but as something to discover, and excavate, it might give him a different perspective.

Martin was unaware that Pastor Reynolds had devoted a great deal of time throughout the day, praying that as he read them, God would cause the words to reveal their meaning to him, and add understanding.

He lowered himself into his easy chair, and laid the Bible on his lap, first taking the time to prepare and light his pipe.

Pastor Reynolds had suggested the four gospels, particularly the book of John, but he had also mentioned a couple of chapters in the book of Romans, and Martin had remembered being impressed with the writing style of that particular book several years ago, when he'd read it. He made himself comfortable and turned to it.

He took his time, and unlike when he'd read it before, strictly for its prose and beautiful form, he found himself frowning in confusion in places, and then lifting his brows as the meaning became clear.

The more he read, the more he began to see himself, particularly in chapter seven, but it was chapter eight that arrested his attention, and caused him to experience a faint stirring of hope, that it might actually be true that he didn't have to master some level of moral achievement, to somehow qualify for what was clearly being described as a free gift of grace, and that his only effort was accepting it. This must be what Audra had meant, when they talked at the inn.

Pastor Reynolds had placed his list of scriptures on top of a small book, and had laid them both in Martin's hands as he was leaving. Martin's curiosity had been sparked, when he saw that the book's author was C.S. Lewis, because he recognized him to be an intellect, and a rational thinker.

Martin looked around his chair, and located the book. He briefly skimmed over the synopsis, and the blurb on the back, before examining the title, and giving it some thought.

The words "Mere Christianity" seemed a curious choice to Martin, but Pastor Reynolds had told him a bit about its compilation, and that it presented the fundamental essentials of the faith. This intrigued Martin, and he relaxed, and gave it his attention.

He read far into the night, his pipe having grown cold long ago, and the clock striking hours that he hadn't bothered to note. It was heading well into morning when he closed the book, and sat holding it in his hands, his thoughts racing, and his pulse quickening.

Understanding had come to Martin Satterfield. As he made his way up to his west wing quarters and prepared for bed, he knelt for the first time since he was a small boy, and prayed to receive this gift of grace.

He slept a deep, and dreamless sleep, his body resting, and his spirit at peace. There were no dark, despairing thoughts to plague him, and rob him of his quietude, no night haunts of cruel mockery, no relentless accusations, or reminders of his failures. Perhaps more wonderful than all of this, was the absence of the fear of living out his days all alone.

Martin's spirit seemed to infuse his mind with the awareness that all had become new, and that even without his beautiful Audra, he would never be left or forsaken.

He knew, as he opened his eyes, that he had slept much later than he normally did. The sun was already beginning to climb in the sky, and the room was growing warmer with its radiant light.

He lay looking up at the ceiling, and a quiet smile rested around his mouth, as he realized that it hadn't been just a wonderful dream after all, but that he was changed. He thought about the words of Jesus he'd read the night before, "You must be born again."

That was it, he realized. That was the best way to describe what he was feeling. A new birth. His smile found its way to his eyes, and he roused himself out of bed, reaching for his robe, and heading down to start his coffee, and perhaps continue reading a bit more, before settling down to deal with the more mundane issues of the day.

He paused halfway down the stairs, and breathed in deeply, realizing that he smelled coffee. His face reflected his wonder, and then a gentle smile eased his countenance.

As he stepped into the library, he saw her once again, camping out on the front corner of his desk, her hair all down over her face, and her sneakers steadily moving back and forth.

He crossed his arms, and studied her, unable to quell the simple joy that her presence brought him.

"Is the doorbell broken again?"

She smiled to herself, before tossing her hair back, and raising her face to look at him. "I forgot."

"Did you?"

He approached her with a playful smirk of amusement, and came to lean against his desk, looking over at her with eyes of love, that he no longer tried to hide.

She sat examining him, and tilted her head to consider what it was she was seeing. He was at peace.

"You're different," she said quietly.

"The last time you said that, it was not a good thing," he reminded her, with a little laugh.

"This time, it is," she replied, unable to keep herself from searching his face carefully.

"How am I different?" Martin asked lightly, resting his eyes on hers, and reaching to lift a strand of her soft hair back from her face.

Audra thought about it. "It's like..."

She stopped to make the effort to really understand what she was sensing, then tried again.

"It's like that first moment, after a fierce, angry, destructive storm, that has been raging all night long, is finally over, and everything gets really quiet... and then you realize you're okay."

Martin was taken aback by her words, but they resonated inside him, and he realized that his entire life had been a storm.

He had ranted and raved, he had paced, and demanded, and threatened, to no avail. But now, he had come to the end of himself, and his storm was over. And he was okay.

He smiled down at the floor, considering her words, and she silently watched him process them.

She leaned over to whisper in his ear.

"Mr. Satterfield, I find you very interesting."

She made him laugh, and he reached around her to pull her closer, and rest his gaze on her beautiful face.

"I never actually asked you to marry me, did I, Audra? I more or less just told you."

She waited, unsure of where this was leading. He wasn't making any additional comments, but his silence wasn't giving her a sense of uneasiness. She knew he was simply pondering.

Finally, he drew in a deep breath, and flashed her a grin.

"Some little fairy has made coffee for me."

"Me, me, it's me!" she insisted, raising her hand, and making him laugh again.

She hopped down onto her feet, and tugged his hand to lead him to her efforts at making breakfast for him.

Martin slowed down her progress, by insisting that he be allowed to return to his quarters to get dressed.

She gave him a little pout, but released his hand, and headed off to wait for him.

When he came back downstairs, and made his way to the kitchen, Audra was placing a little stack of warm muffins onto a plate. He slipped up behind her, and pulled her against himself, looking over her shoulder with a pleased smile.

"How very domestic, Miss Campbell," he teased lightly. "It would appear that you are preparing yourself to take control of this kitchen."

She turned her face to look up at him, with a grin. "This is the part where I admit that I bought these at a bakery."

Martin laughed, and turned her in his arms to see her pretty eyes. "That won't do at all. I must insist that you acquire at least some culinary skills."

She twisted her lips into a grimace. "I never learned. I can only scramble eggs, and make pancakes from a box."

"Can't you at least make a casserole?" he asked, causing her to break into peals of laughter.

"No, sorry. I guess I'm disqualified, then. Should I send for Dee Sanders, or Torey Jordan?"

"Let's not be hasty. I'll teach you," he promised, smiling at her genuine look of surprise.

"Martin Satterfield, do you mean to tell me that the whole time those poor girls were knocking themselves out, to bless you with their casseroles, you could have just made yourself one?"

"I'm afraid so."

He gave her chin a light stroke, then moved over to pour the aromatic coffee that she obviously did know how to brew.

"You've mastered this part," he approved.

He brought both their coffees to the table, and pulled out a chair for her.

Audra put a muffin on his plate, and he looked at it with a thoughtful expression, then reached for her hand.

She looked at him oddly, but laid her hand in his, then drew in a sharp breath of joyful realization, when she heard the master of Hawthorn Manor offer a simple prayer of thanks for their meal.

When he looked up, she was staring at him with her hands over her mouth, and tears crowding her eyes.

Just as Martin began to wonder about her, she jumped up and came around the table to lift his arms out of her way, and climb onto his lap, holding him tightly, and burying her face against his neck. She was crying softly, but he could sense her glad relief.

Martin closed his eyes and smiled, pressing her close, and sharing this feeling with her.

When she raised up to look at him, he had reached into his pocket, and was holding an exquisite diamond with his eyes full of hope and promise.

"*Now*, will you marry me, Audra?" he whispered.

She stared down at what was surely a treasured heirloom, and he confirmed it.

"It was my mother's. You don't have to wear it forever," he added, knowing that she would probably want to choose her own style of ring. "But would you wear it until we find your forever ring?"

Audra lifted her beautiful eyes to his, and raised her hand to stroke his handsome face. "I *will* marry you, Martin. And, I will never leave you. And, I will love you, forever."

"And I will love *you*, forever." His eyes displayed his joy and peace, and he laughed softly. "We need a new contract."

He gently placed the ring on her slender finger, then slipped his hands into her hair, and gave her a kiss that sealed all their promises.

Yet another happy smile lit up his eyes, when his fair Audra asked him if the ring on her finger could be the one to stay there forever.

Chapter Twenty-Seven

The master of Hawthorn Manor stood leaning against the crowning limbs of an ancient, old tree, and gazed contentedly around him, at the fields and meadows of the Satterfield estate.

He had brought his pipe with him on his morning walk, and lowered himself to rest on one low bough of the gnarled live oak, that he'd played under as a young boy, to lay his tobacco in it, and give it a gentle tamp before lighting it.

Now, he drew on it peacefully, and made silent notes of a needed repair to an old split rail fence, in order to speak to the groundskeepers about it. He smiled, as the demanding bleat of a new lamb reached his ears.

Martin Satterfield had begun frequenting the outlying areas of the property much more often, during the passing year than he ever had before, simply because he had begun to care about its condition.

For so long after he'd returned from his time abroad, he had shown no interest in the daily maintenance, and tending of its orchards or livestock, and had simply allowed those who worked for him to deal with it.

Now, he took it all in with an appreciative smile, and silently thanked God for the haven of rest it provided.

Martin normally waited until later in the morning to walk the property, so that his beautiful wife could accompany him, but he'd stirred early with a desire to see the sun's first blush, and she was sleeping so sweetly that he'd been reluctant to wake her.

Instead, he'd laid a kiss on her cheek, and left a note telling her where he'd gone, and reminding her of how much he loved her.

His smile reached his eyes and his heart, as he thought of his fair Audra, who loved him in a way he'd never known, and who challenged him, made him laugh, and comforted him.

He had long given up any dream of what the fairytales described as "happily ever after" and had lived in dread of a possible "hereafter" but, along with his increasing faith, came hope, and hope brought expectation.

The scorn and mockery, humiliating, public infidelity with its violent aftermath, and the fear of abandonment, as those he had loved and lost who had stepped into the mysterious afterlife that he had once feared, now scrolled into the distant past, and no longer haunted him.

A shaft of bright sunlight broke out from behind a drifting cloud, and its golden warmth encouraged him to step out from under the crown of the old tree, and move into its path.

Martin strolled back in the direction of his home, passing through the cemetery, where the remains of his parents and his sweet Izzy now rested, until the time of their resurrection, when their transformed bodies would be raised imperishable, and joined with their souls, for an eternity that Martin now confidently believed in. He rarely walked through the Satterfield family cemetery now, without a peaceful smile.

His path took him back to the welcoming veranda of Hawthorn Manor, and he opened the door quietly, not wishing to disturb his wife if she were still asleep, although it was not her habit to lie in bed so late.

Martin climbed the stairs to their bedroom, and realized that she had roused from her slumber, then turned to go look for her in the kitchen, knowing that she never woke up without thinking instantly of coffee.

He found her where he knew he would, nesting on a chair with her feet up on the seat, and her long, silky hair tumbling around her, as she cradled her warm coffee cup in her hand, and looked up at him with a little grin.

"I see your beauty sleep has served you well," her husband commented lightly, leaning down for a kiss.

She made a wry grimace, but thanked him with her eyes.

Martin poured himself a second cup of coffee, and came over to sit with her, resting his gaze on her with gentle affection.

"There are new lambs," he informed her, watching her face light up with excitement. "Perhaps, we can visit the pasture to see them later, if you like."

"I do like," she replied, stifling a yawn.

"You're unusually sleepy this morning," Martin observed. "Did you not sleep well, last night?"

"I don't even remember, so I must have," Audra reflected. She put her cup down, before tilting her head in the funny manner she had, whenever she placed her husband under her scrutiny.

"I've either wronged you in some fashion, or I'm about to be asked a favor," he decided with a quiet laugh.

She laughed with him, and moved her feet from her chair onto his lap.

"Is this the favor?" he asked, catching her feet in his hands, and rubbing them lightly. "They're cold, as one might expect, since you appear to be running around barefoot."

"I'm not going to waste a favor on something like feet," Audra replied.

He waited, wondering what his sleepy bride had on her mind, and looked up at her with a challenging grin.

"Out with it, Lady Satterfield."

She shrugged. "I just want to go into town, and I didn't know if you wanted me to drive myself, or if you wanted to come with."

Martin drew his brows, and studied her. "What is our mission, fair Audra?"

"I need to go to the fabric shop."

He continued to look confused. "Are you staging for Aunt Celeste? You don't normally go to the extremes of buying fabric, for something like that."

"No, it's for here. I'm starting a new renovation."

"Are you?" he returned evenly, wondering if she intended to force him to unravel her knitting, thread by thread. "How many more questions am I allowed?"

"Why don't you just skip to the last one?" she asked, using his frequent suggestion to her, against him.

Martin sat silently regarding her for a moment, before lifting her feet and lowering them to the floor, then gesturing for her to come to him.

Audra moved over to sit on his lap and rested her arms around his neck, her eyes teasing his.

"Are we renovating the west wing?" he asked, brushing her hair from her brow, and waiting.

She thought about the scope of his question.

"Not completely."

"Not completely."

He sighed and touched her chin, in gentle reproof.

"In the words of King Solomon, let us hear the conclusion of the whole matter, sweet girl."

Audra grinned at him. "He didn't say sweet girl."

"I threw that part in," he laughed. "How long must I be, in coaxing this mystery out of you?"

"*Part* of the west wing," she informed him.

"Our bedroom?" He seemed surprised by that.

"No, the sitting room just off the bedroom."

As far as Martin was concerned, a sitting room was just that, a room for sitting. He couldn't understand why that warranted the purchasing of fabric, although he knew that regardless of her reason, he would ultimately agree.

"Whatever for, sweetheart?"

"I'm repurposing it," she stated, matter-of-factly.

"I suppose we don't actually sit much in it," he admitted. "What shall its new purpose be, then? A place to store all your impressive fabric?"

She giggled and made him smile, then leaned over to put her lips next to his ear, and whisper a secret as she laid his hand on her belly, forever blessing the rest of his days, and bringing a joy never before imagined, nor dared to be hoped for, to the master of Hawthorn Manor.

Also by

Rhonda Hanson

The Father Series

Father's Choice
Father's Wings
Father's Song

A linked novel to the Father Series

Father's Friend

A seven-year recurring bedtime story

The Adventures Of Pahwoo And Her Friends

Grace Under Pressure Publishing
P.O. Box 337
Bell Buckle, Tennessee 37020

graceunderpressure.com